Dodie Smith

# The
# HUNDRED
# AND ONE
# DALMATIANS

# &

# The
# STARLIGHT
# BARKING

WITH ILLUSTRATIONS BY *Alex T. Smith*

# The
# HUNDRED
## AND ONE
# DALMATIANS

*The Hundred and One Dalmations* first published in
Great Britain 1956 by William Heinemann Ltd
*The Starlight Barking* first published in Great Britain 1967
by William Heinemann Ltd

This edition published 2018 by Farshore

An imprint of HarperCollins*Publishers*
1 London Bridge Street, London SE1 9GF

farshore.co.uk

HarperCollins*Publishers*
1st Floor, Watermarque Building,
Ringsend Road, Dublin 4, Ireland

ISBN 978 1 4052 8875 0
Printed and bound in the UK using 100% renewable electricity
at CPI Group (UK) Ltd
5

A CIP catalogue record for this title is available from the British Library

**MIX**
**Paper from**
**responsible sources**
**FSC™ C007454**

# Contents

# The Happy Couples

NOT LONG AGO, there lived in London a young married couple of Dalmatian dogs named Pongo and Missis Pongo. (Missis had added Pongo's name to her own on their marriage, but was still called Missis by most people.) They were lucky enough to own a young married couple of humans named Mr and Mrs Dearly, who were gentle, obedient and unusually intelligent – almost canine at times. They understood quite a number of barks: the barks for 'Out, please!', 'In, please!', 'Hurry up with my dinner!' and 'What about a walk?' And even when they could not understand, they could often guess – if looked at soulfully or scratched by an eager paw. Like many other much-loved humans, they believed that they owned their dogs, instead of realising that their dogs owned them. Pongo and Missis found this touching and

1

amusing, and let their pets think it was true.

Mr Dearly, who had an office in the City, was particularly good at arithmetic. Many people called him a wizard of finance – which is not the same thing as a wizard of magic, though sometimes fairly similar. At the time when this story starts he was rather unusually rich for a rather unusual reason. He had done the Government a great service (something to do with getting rid of the National Debt) and, as a reward, had been let off his Income Tax for life. Also the Government had lent him a small house on the Outer Circle of Regent's Park – just the right house for a man with a wife and dogs.

Before their marriages, Mr Dearly and Pongo had lived in a bachelor flat, where they were looked after by Mr Dearly's old nurse, Nanny Butler. Mrs Dearly and Missis had also lived in a bachelor flat (there are no such things as spinster flats) where they were looked after by Mrs Dearly's old nurse, Nanny Cook. The dogs and their pets met at the same time and shared a wonderfully happy double engagement, but they were all a little worried about what was to happen to Nanny Cook and Nanny Butler. It would be all right when the Dearlys started a family, particularly if it could be twins, with one twin for each Nanny, but, until then, what were the Nannies going to do? For though they could cook breakfast and provide meals on trays (meals called 'A nice egg by the fire') neither of them was capable of running a smart little house in Regent's Park, where the Dearlys hoped to invite their friends to dinner.

And then something happened. Nanny Cook and Nanny Butler met and, after a few minutes of deep suspicion, took a great liking to each other. And they had a good laugh about their names.

'What a pity we're not a real cook and butler,' said Nanny Cook.

'Yes, that's what's needed now,' said Nanny Butler.

And then they both together had the Great Idea: Nanny Cook would train to be a real cook and Nanny Butler would train to be a real butler. They would start the very next day and be fully trained by the wedding.

'But you'll have to be a parlour maid, really,' said Nanny Cook.

'Certainly not,' said Nanny Butler. 'I haven't the figure for it. I shall be a real butler – and I shall valet Mr Dearly, which will need no training as I've done it since the day he was born.'

And so when the Dearlys and the Pongos got back from their joint honeymoon, there were Nanny Cook and Nanny Butler, fully trained, ready to welcome them into the little house facing Regent's Park.

It came as something of a shock that Nanny Butler was wearing trousers.

'Wouldn't a black dress, with a nice, frilly apron be better?' suggested Mrs Dearly – rather nervously, because Nanny Butler had never been her Nanny.

'You can't be a butler without trousers,' said Nanny Butler, firmly. 'But I'll get a frilly apron tomorrow. It will add a note of originality.' It did.

The Nannies said they no longer expected to be called Nanny, and were now prepared to be called by their surnames, in the correct way. But though you can call a cook 'Cook', the one thing you cannot call a butler is 'Butler', so in the end both Nannies were just called 'Nanny, darling', as they always had been.

After the dogs and the Dearlys had been back from their honeymoons for several happy weeks, something even happier happened. Mrs Dearly took Pongo and Missis across the park to St John's Wood, where they called on their good friend, the Splendid Veterinary Surgeon. She came back with the wonderful news that the Pongos were shortly to become parents. Puppies were due in a month.

The Nannies gave Missis a big lunch to keep her strength up, and Pongo a big lunch in case he should feel neglected (as the fathers of expected puppies sometimes do), and then both dogs had a long afternoon nap on the best sofa. By the time Mr Dearly came home from business they were wide awake and asking for a walk.

'Let us all go for a walk, to celebrate,' said Mr Dearly, after hearing the good news. Nanny Cook said the dinner was well ahead and Nanny

Butler said she could do with a bit of exercise, so off they all set along the Outer Circle.

The Dearlys led the way, Mrs Dearly very pretty in the green going-away suit from her trousseau and Mr Dearly in his old tweed jacket which was known as his dog-walker. (Mr Dearly wasn't exactly handsome but he had the kind of face you don't get tired of.) Then came the Pongos, looking noble; they could both have become Champions if Mr Dearly had not felt that dog-shows would bore them – and him. They had splendid heads, fine shoulders, strong legs and straight tails. The spots on their bodies were jet black and mostly the size of a two-shilling piece; they had smaller spots on their heads, legs and tails. Their noses and eye-rims were black. Missis had a most winning expression. Pongo, though a dog born to command, had a twinkle in his eye. They walked side by side with great dignity, only putting the Dearlys on the leash to lead them over crossings. Nanny Cook (plump) in her white overall, and Nanny Butler (plumper) in a well-cut tail coat and trousers, plus dainty apron, completed the procession.

It was a beautiful September evening, windless, very peaceful. The park and the old, cream-painted houses facing it basked in the golden light of sunset. There were many sounds but no noises. The cries of playing children and the whirr of London's traffic seemed quieter than usual, as if softened by the evening's gentleness. Birds were singing their last song of the day, and further along the Circle, at the house where a great composer lived, someone was playing the piano.

'I shall always remember this happy walk,' said Mr Dearly.

At that moment, the peace was shattered by an extremely strident motor horn. A large car was coming towards them. It drew up at a big house just ahead of them and a tall woman came out on to the front-door steps. She was wearing a tight-fitting emerald satin dress, several ropes of rubies and an absolutely simple white mink cloak, which reached to the high heels of her ruby-red shoes. She had dark skin, black eyes with a tinge of red in them, and a very pointed nose. Her hair was parted severely down the middle and one half of it was black and the other white – rather unusual.

'Why, that's Cruella de Vil,' said Mrs Dearly. 'We were at school together. She was expelled for drinking ink.'

'Isn't she a bit showy?' said Mr Dearly, and would have turned back. But the tall woman had seen Mrs Dearly and come down the steps to meet her. So Mrs Dearly had to introduce Mr Dearly.

'Come in and meet my husband,' said the tall woman.

'But you were going out,' said Mrs Dearly, looking at the chauffeur who was waiting at the open door of the large car. It was painted black and white, in stripes – rather noticeable.

'No hurry at all. I insist on your coming.'

The Nannies said they would get back and see about dinner, and take the dogs with them, but the tall woman said the dogs must come in, too. 'They are so beautiful. I want my husband to see them,' she said.

'What is your married name, Cruella?' asked

Mrs Dearly, as they walked through a green marble hall into a red marble drawing-room.

'My name is still de Vil,' said Cruella. 'I am the last of my family so I made my husband change his name to mine.'

Just then the absolutely simple white mink cloak slipped from her shoulders to the floor. Mr Dearly picked it up.

'What a beautiful cloak,' he said. 'But you'll find it too warm for this evening.'

'I never find anything too warm,' said Cruella. 'I wear furs all the year round. I sleep between ermine sheets.'

'How nice,' said Mrs Dearly, politely. 'Do they wash well?'

Cruella did not seem to hear this. She went on: 'I worship furs, I live for furs! That's why I married a furrier.'

Then Mr de Vil came in. He was a small, worried-looking man who didn't seem to be anything besides a furrier. Cruella introduced him and then said: 'Where are those two delightful dogs?'

Pongo and Missis were sitting under the grand piano feeling hungry. The red marble walls had made them think of slabs of raw meat.

'They're expecting puppies,' said Mrs Dearly, happily.

'Oh, are they? Good!' said Cruella. 'Come here, dogs!'

Pongo and Missis came forward politely.

'Wouldn't they make enchanting fur coats?' said Cruella to her husband. 'For spring wear, over a black suit. We've never thought of making coats out of dogs' skins.'

Pongo gave a sharp, menacing bark.

'It was only a joke, dear Pongo,' said Mrs Dearly, patting him. Then she said to Cruella: 'I sometimes think they understand every word we say.'

But she did not really think it. And it was true.

That is, it was true of Pongo. Missis did not understand quite so many human words as he did. But she understood Cruella's joke and thought it a very bad one. As for Pongo, he was furious. What a thing to say in front of his wife

when she was expecting her first puppies! He was glad to see Missis was not upset.

'You must dine with us – next Saturday,' said Cruella to Mrs Dearly.

And as Mrs Dearly could not think of a good excuse (she was very truthful) she accepted. Then she said they must not keep the de Vils any longer.

As they went through the hall, a most beautiful white Persian cat dashed past them and ran upstairs. Mrs Dearly admired it.

'I don't like her much,' said Cruella. 'I'd drown her if she wasn't so valuable.'

The cat turned on the stairs and made an angry, spitting noise. It might have been at Pongo and Missis – but, then again, it might not.

'I want you to hear my new motor horn,' said Cruella, as they all went down the front-door steps. 'It's the loudest horn in England.'

She pushed past the chauffeur and sounded the horn herself, making it last a long time. Pongo and Missis were nearly deafened.

'Lovely, lovely dogs,' Cruella said to them, as she got into the striped black-and-white car.

'You'd go so well with my car – and my black-and-white hair.'

Then the chauffeur spread a sable rug over the de Vils' knees and drove the striped car away.

'That car looks like a moving Zebra Crossing,' said Mr Dearly. 'Was your friend's hair black and white when she was at school?'

'She was no friend of mine; I was scared of her,' said Mrs Dearly. 'Yes, her hair was just the same. She had one white plait and one black.'

Mr Dearly thought how lucky he was to be married to Mrs Dearly and not to Cruella de Vil. He felt sorry for her husband. Pongo and Missis felt sorry for her white cat.

The golden sunset had gone now and the blue twilight had come. The park was nearly empty and a park-keeper was calling, 'All out, all out!' in a far-away voice. There was a faint scent of hay from the sun-scorched lawns, and a weedy, watery smell from the lake. All the houses on the Outer Circle that had been turned into Government Offices were now closed for the night. No light shone in their windows. But the

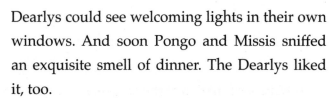 

Dearlys could see welcoming lights in their own windows. And soon Pongo and Missis sniffed an exquisite smell of dinner. The Dearlys liked it, too.

They all paused to look down through the iron railings at the kitchen. Although it was in the basement, this was not at all a dark kitchen. It had a door and two large windows opening on to one of the narrow paved yards which are so often found in front of old London houses. The correct name for these little basement yards is 'the area'. A narrow flight of steps led up from the area to the street.

The Dearlys and the dogs thought how very nice their brightly lit kitchen looked. It had white walls, red linoleum, and a dresser on which was blue-spotted china. There was a new-fashioned electric stove for the cooking, and an old-fashioned kitchen fire to keep the Nannies happy. Nanny Cook was basting something in the oven, while Nanny Butler stacked plates on the lift which would take them up through the dining-room floor as if delivering the Demon King in a pantomime. Near the fire were two cushioned dog-baskets. And already two superb dinners, in shining bowls, were waiting for Pongo and Missis.

'I hope we haven't tired Missis,' said Mr Dearly, as he opened the front door with his latch-key.

Missis would have liked to say she had never felt better in her life. As she could not speak, she tried to show how well she felt, and rushed down to the kitchen lashing her tail. So did Pongo, looking forward to his dinner and a long, fire-lit snooze beside his dear Missis.

'I wish we had tails to wag,' said Mr Dearly.

# The Puppies Arrive

CRUELLA DE VIL'S dinner party took place in a room with black marble walls, on a white marble table. The food was rather unusual.

The soup was dark purple. And what did it taste of? Pepper!

The fish was bright green. And what did it taste of? Pepper!

The meat was pale blue. And what did that taste of? Pepper!

Everything tasted of pepper, even the ice-cream – which was black.

There were no other guests. After dinner, Mr and Mrs Dearly sat panting in the red marble drawing-room, where an enormous fire was now burning. Mr de Vil panted quite a bit, too. Cruella, who was wearing a ruby satin dress with ropes of emeralds, got as close to the fire as she could.

'Make it blaze for me,' she said to Mr de Vil.

Mr de Vil made such a blaze that the Dearlys thought the chimney would catch fire.

'Lovely, lovely!' said Cruella, clapping her hands with delight. 'Ah, but the flames never last long enough!' The minute they died down a little, she shivered and huddled herself in her absolutely simple white mink cloak.

Mr and Mrs Dearly left as early as they felt was polite, and walked along the Outer Circle trying to get cool.

'What a strange name "de Vil" is,' said Mr Dearly. 'If you put the two words together, they make "devil". Perhaps Cruella's a lady-devil! Perhaps that's why she likes things so hot!'

Mrs Dearly smiled, for she knew he was only joking. Then she said: 'Oh, dear! As we've dined with them, we must ask them to dine with us. And there are some other people we ought to ask. We'd better get it over before Missis has her puppies. Good gracious, what's that?'

Something soft was rubbing against her ankles.

'It's Cruella's cat,' said Mr Dearly. 'Go home, cat. You'll get lost.'

But the cat followed them all the way to their house.

'Perhaps she's hungry,' said Mrs Dearly.

'Very probably, unless she likes pepper,' said Mr Dearly. He was still gulping the night air to cool his throat.

'You stroke her while I get her some food,' said Mrs Dearly. And she went down the area steps and into the kitchen on tiptoe, so as not to wake Pongo and Missis who were asleep in their baskets. Soon she came up with some milk and half a tin of sardines. The white cat accepted both, then began to walk down the area steps.

'Does she want to live with us?' said Mrs Dearly.

It seemed as if the white cat did. But just then Pongo woke up and barked loudly. The white cat turned and walked away into the night.

'Just as well,' said Mr Dearly. 'Cruella would have the law on us if we took her valuable cat.'

Then they went down into the kitchen to receive the full force of Pongo's welcome. Missis, though sleepy, was fairly formidable, too. There was a whirling mass of humans and dogs on the kitchen hearthrug – until Mrs Dearly remembered, far too late, that Mr Dearly's dress suit would be covered with white hairs.

It must have been about three weeks later that Missis began to behave in a very peculiar manner. She explored every inch of the house, paying particular attention to cupboards and boxes. And the place that interested her most was a large cupboard just outside the Dearlys' bedroom. The Nannies kept various buckets and brooms in this cupboard and there wasn't a spare inch of space. Every time Missis managed to get in, she knocked something over with a clatter and then looked very ill-treated.

'Bless me, she wants to have her puppies there,' said Nanny Cook.

'Not in that dark, stuffy cupboard, Missis, love,' said Nanny Butler. 'You need light and air.'

But when Mrs Dearly consulted the Splendid Veterinary Surgeon, he said what Missis needed most was a small, enclosed place where she would feel safe, and if she fancied the broom cupboard, the broom cupboard she'd better have. And she'd better have it at once and get used to it – even though the puppies were not expected for some days.

So out came the brooms and buckets and in went Missis, to her great satisfaction. Pongo was a little hurt that he was not allowed to go with her, but Missis explained to him that mother dogs like to be by themselves when puppies are expected, so he licked his wife's ear tenderly, and said he quite understood.

'I hope the dinner party won't upset Missis,' said Mr Dearly, when he came home and found Missis settled in the cupboard. 'I shall be glad when it's over.'

It was to be that very night. As there were quite a lot of guests the food had to be normal, but Mrs Dearly kindly put tall pepper grinders in front of the de Vils. Cruella ground so much pepper that most of the guests were sneezing, but Mr de Vil used no pepper at all. And he ate much more than in his own house.

Cruella was busy peppering her fruit salad when Nanny Butler came in and whispered to Mrs Dearly. Mrs Dearly looked startled, asked the guests to excuse her, and hurried out. A few minutes later, Nanny Butler came in again and whispered to Mr Dearly. He looked startled, excused himself and hurried out. Those guests who were not sneezing made polite conversation. Then Nanny Butler came in again.

'Ladies and gentlemen,' she said, dramatically, 'puppies are arriving earlier than expected. Mr and Mrs Dearly ask you to remember that Missis has never before been a mother. She needs absolute quiet.'

There was an instant silence, broken only by a stifled sneeze. Then the guests rose, drank a whispered toast to the young mother and tiptoed from the house.

All except Cruella de Vil. When she reached the hall she went straight to Nanny Butler, who was seeing the guests out, and demanded: 'Where are those puppies?'

Nanny Butler had no intention of telling,

but Cruella heard the Dearlys' voices and ran upstairs. This time she was wearing a black satin dress with ropes of pearls, but the same absolutely simple white mink cloak. She had kept it round her all through dinner, although the room was very warm (and the pepper very hot).

'I must, I must see the darling puppies,' she cried.

The cupboard door was a little open. The Dearlys were inside, soothing Missis. Three puppies had been born before Nanny Butler, on bringing Missis a nourishing chicken dinner, had discovered what was happening.

Cruella flung open the door and stared down at the three puppies.

'But they're mongrels – all white, no spots at all!' she cried. 'You must drown them at once.'

'Dalmatians are always born white,' said Mr Dearly, glaring at Cruella. 'The spots come later.'

'And we wouldn't drown them even if they were mongrels,' said Mrs Dearly, indignantly.

'It'd be quite easy,' said Cruella. 'I've drowned dozens and dozens of my cat's kittens. She always chooses some wretched alley-cat for their father so they're never worth keeping.'

'Surely you leave her one kitten?' said Mrs Dearly.

'If I'd done that, I'd be overrun with cats,' said Cruella. 'Are you sure those horrid little white rats are pure Dalmatian puppies?'

'Quite sure,' snapped Mr Dearly. 'Now please go away. You're upsetting Missis.'

And indeed Missis was upset. Even with the Dearlys there to protect her and her puppies, she was a little afraid of this tall woman with black-and-white hair who stared so hard. And that poor cat who had lost all those kittens! Never, never, would Missis forget that! (And one day she was to be glad that she remembered it.)

'How long will it be before the puppies are old enough to leave their mother?' asked Cruella. 'In case I want to buy some.'

'Seven or eight weeks,' said Mr Dearly. 'But there won't be any for sale.' Then he shut the cupboard door in Cruella's face and Nanny Butler firmly showed her out of the house.

Nanny Cook was busy telephoning the Splendid Vet but he was out on another case. His wife said she would tell him as soon as he came home and there was no need to worry – it sounded as if Missis was getting on very well.

She certainly was. There was now a fourth puppy. Missis washed it and then Mr Dearly dried it, while Mrs Dearly gave Missis a drink of warm milk. Then the pup was put with the other three, in a basket placed where Missis could see it. Soon she had a fifth puppy. Then a sixth – and a seventh.

The night wore on. Eight puppies, nine puppies! Surely that would be all? Dalmatians do not often have more in their first family. Ten puppies! Eleven puppies!

Then the twelfth arrived and it did not look like its brothers and sisters. The flesh showing through its white hair was not a healthy pink but a sickly yellow. And instead of kicking its little legs, it lay quite still. The Nannies, who were sitting just outside the cupboard, told Mr and Mrs Dearly that it had been born dead.

'But, with so many, its mother will never miss it,' said Nanny Cook, comfortingly.

Mr Dearly held the tiny creature in the palm of his hand and looked at it sorrowfully.

'It isn't fair it should have no life at all,' said Mrs Dearly, with tears in her eyes.

Something he had once read came back to Mr Dearly. He began to massage the puppy; then he tousled it gently in a towel. And suddenly there was a faint hint of pink around its nose –

and then its whole little body was flushed with pink, beneath its snowy hair. Its legs moved! Its mouth opened! It was alive!

Mr Dearly quickly put it close to Missis so that she could give it some milk at once, and it stayed there, feeding, until the next puppy arrived – for arrive it did. That made thirteen!

Shortly before dawn, the front door-bell rang. It was the Splendid Vet, who had been up all night saving the life of a dog that had been run over. By then, all the puppies had been born and Missis was giving breakfast to eight of them – all she could manage at one time.

'Excellent!' said the Splendid Vet. 'A really magnificent family. And how is the father bearing up?'

The Dearlys felt guilty. They had not given Pongo a thought since the puppies had begun to arrive. He had been shut up in the kitchen. All night long he had paced backwards and forwards and only once had he heard any news – when Nanny Cook had come down to make coffee and sandwiches. She had told him that

Missis was doing well – but only as a joke, for she had no idea he would understand.

'Poor Pongo, we must have him up,' said Mrs Dearly. But the Splendid Vet said mother dogs did not usually like to have father dogs around when puppies had just been born. At that moment there was a clatter of toenails on the polished floor of the hall – and upstairs, four at a time, came Pongo. Nanny Cook had just gone down to make some tea for the Splendid Vet, and the anxious father had streaked past her the minute she opened the kitchen door.

'Careful, Pongo!' said the Splendid Vet. 'She may not want you.'

But Missis was weakly thumping her tail. 'Go down and have your breakfast and a good sleep,' she said – but nobody except Pongo heard a sound. His eyes and his wildly wagging tail told her all he was feeling, his love for her and those eight fine pups enjoying their first breakfast. And those others, in the basket, waiting their turn – how many were there?

'It's a pity dogs can't count,' said Mrs Dearly.

But Pongo could count, perfectly. He went downstairs with his head high and a new light in his fine, dark eyes. For he knew himself to be the proud father of fifteen.

# Perdita

'AND NOW,' said the Splendid Vet to the Dearlys, 'you must get a foster mother.'

He explained that though Missis would do her best to feed fifteen puppies, doing so would make her terribly thin and tired. And the strong puppies would get more milk than the weak ones. The puppy Mr Dearly had brought to life was very small and would need special care.

The largest pup of all had a black patch all over its ear and one side of its face. This is a bad fault in a Dalmatian – which should be born pure white, as Mr Dearly had told Cruella de Vil. Some people would have drowned this patched pup, because it would never be valuable. But the Dearlys felt particularly fond of it because it had started life with a bit of bad luck. (And they liked being able to recognise it. Until the spots started to come through, some weeks later, the big puppy with the patch and the small, delicate puppy were the only ones who could be told apart from the others.)

The Splendid Vet said the foster mother would have to be some poor dog who had lost her own puppies but still had milk to give. He thought he could get such a dog. But as he wasn't sure, the Dearlys had better telephone all the Lost Dogs' Homes. And until the foster mother was found, they could help Missis by feeding the pups with a doll's feeding bottle or an old-fashioned fountain-pen filler.

Then the Splendid Vet went home for an hour's sleep before starting his day's work.

Nanny Cook got breakfast and Nanny Butler took Pongo for a run. And Missis was persuaded to leave her family for a few minutes' walk. When she came back, Mrs Dearly had tidied the cupboard. Missis gave the second lot of pups a meal and then she and her family of fifteen had a glorious sleep. And Pongo, down in the kitchen, had a glorious sleep, too, knowing that all was well.

As soon as the shops opened, Mrs Dearly went out and bought a doll's feeding bottle and a fountain-pen filler. And then Mr Dearly and the Nannies took turns at feeding puppies. Mrs Dearly fancied this job herself but was busy telephoning, trying to find a foster mother. The Nannies were too fat to be comfortable in the cupboard, so soon Mr Dearly got the feeding job all to himself and became very good at it and just a bit bossy. Of course he couldn't go to business, which was awkward as he had an important business deal on.

Luckily there was a telephone in the Dearlys' bedroom and it had a long cord to it. So Mr Dearly was able to telephone while he was feeding the pups. There he was, in a dark cupboard with Missis, fifteen puppies and the telephone. He nearly upset his important business deal by holding a pup to his ear and giving the telephone a drink of milk.

No sooner had Mr Dearly put the telephone down than the Splendid Vet rang up to say he had not been able to find a foster mother. Neither had Mrs Dearly, anywhere in London. She now started to ring up Lost Dogs' Homes outside London. It was late afternoon before she heard of a mother dog with some milk to give, nearly thirty miles from London. And this dog had only just been brought in and would have to be kept some days in case she was claimed.

Mr Dearly put his head out of the cupboard. After being up all night and feeding pups all day he was beginning to feel pretty tired, but he was determined to go on helping Missis until the foster mother arrived. 'Why not go and see if you can borrow that dog?' he said. 'Say we'll give it back if its owner turns up.'

So Mrs Dearly got the car from the old stable at the back of the house and drove off hopefully. But when she got to the Dogs' Home she found that the mother dog had already been claimed. She was glad for the dog's sake, but terribly disappointed. She thought of poor Missis getting exhausted by too many puppies, and of Mr Dearly, who might easily refuse to come out of the cupboard for a good night's sleep, and she began to think she never would find a foster mother.

It was now almost dark, a gloomy, wet October evening. It had been raining all afternoon, but Mrs Dearly hadn't minded when she was feeling hopeful. Now, as she started back for London, the weather made her feel more and more depressed. And the rain got so heavy that the windscreen wiper could hardly keep pace with it.

She was driving across a lonely stretch of common when she saw what looked like a bundle lying in the road ahead of her. She slowed down and as she drew closer she saw that it was not a bundle but a dog. Instantly, she thought it must have been run over. Dreading what she might find, she stopped the car and got out.

At first she thought the dog was dead, but as she bent down it struggled to its feet showing no signs of injury. It was so plastered with mud that she could not see what kind of dog it was. What she could see, by the light from the car's headlights, was the poor creature's pitiful

thinness. She spoke to it gently. Its drooping tail gave a feeble flick, then dropped again.

'I can't leave it here,' thought Mrs Dearly. 'Even if it hasn't been run over, it must be near starvation. Oh, dear!' With seventeen dogs at home already she had no wish to take back a stray, but she knew she would never bring herself just to hand this poor thing in at a police station.

She patted it and tried to get it to follow her. It was willing to, but its legs were so wobbly that she picked it up and carried it. It felt like a sack of bones. And, as she noticed this, she also noticed something else. Hurriedly, she laid the dog on the seat of the car, on a rug, and turned on the light. Then she saw that this was a mother dog and that in spite of its starving condition it still had some milk to give.

She sprang into the car and drove as fast as she safely could. Quite soon she was in the London suburbs. She knew it would still take her some time to get home, because of the traffic, so she stopped at a little restaurant. Here the owner let her buy some milk and some cold meat and lent her his own dog's dishes. The starving dog ate and drank ravenously, then at once settled to sleep. The nice owner of the restaurant took back his dishes and wished Mrs Dearly luck as she drove away.

She got home just as the Splendid Vet was arriving to see Missis and the puppies. He carried the stray dog in and down to the warm kitchen. After a careful examination he said he thought her thinness was due more to having had puppies than to long starvation and that, if she was fed well, the milk intended for her own puppies might continue. He guessed they had been taken away from her and she had got lost looking for them.

'She ought to have a bath,' said Nanny Cook, 'or she'll give our puppies fleas.'

The Splendid Vet said a bath was a good idea, so the dog was carried into a little room which had been fitted up as a laundry. Nanny Cook got on with the bath as fast as she could because she was afraid Mr Dearly might want to do the job himself. Mrs Dearly had gone upstairs to tell him what was happening.

The stray seemed delighted with the warm water. She had just been covered with soap when Pongo came back from a walk with Nanny Butler and ran through the open door of the laundry.

'He won't hurt a lady,' said the Splendid Vet.

'I should hope not, when she's going to help nurse his puppies,' said Nanny Cook.

Pongo stood on his hind legs and kissed the wet dog on the nose, telling her how glad he was to see her and how grateful his wife would be. (But no human heard him.) The stray said: 'Well, I'll do my best, but I can't promise anything.' (No human heard that, either.)

Just then Mr Dearly came hurrying in, to see the new arrival.

'What kind of a dog is she?' he asked.

At that moment, Nanny Cook began to rinse off the soap – and everyone gave a gasp. This dog was a Dalmatian, too! But her spots, instead of being black, were brown – which in Dalmatians is called not 'brown' but 'liver'.

'Eighteen Dalmatians under one roof,' said Mr Dearly, gloatingly. 'Couldn't be better.'

(But it could, as he was one day to learn.)

Wet, the poor liver-spotted dog looked thinner than ever.

'We'll call her Perdita,' said Mrs Dearly, and explained to the Nannies that this was after a character in Shakespeare. 'She was lost. And the Latin word for lost is "perditus".' Then she patted Pongo, who was looking particularly intelligent, and said anyone would think he understood. And indeed he did. For though he had very little Latin beyond 'Cave canem', he had, as a young dog, devoured Shakespeare (in a tasty leather binding).

Perdita was dried in front of the kitchen fire and given another meal. The Splendid Vet said she ought to start mothering puppies as soon as possible to encourage her to provide more milk, so after she was quite dry and had taken a nap, two puppies were removed from the cupboard while Missis went out for a little air. The Splendid Vet said she would not know they had gone – which is possible, as she could not count as well as Pongo could. But she knew all about those puppies going because Pongo had told her and she had sent polite messages to Perdita. Missis felt a bit unhappy about giving any puppies up but she knew it was for their good.

Before leaving, the Splendid Vet warned the Dearlys that if Perdita could not feed the puppies they must not be returned to Missis, for her sense of smell would tell her that they had been with some other dog and she might turn against them. And this does happen with some dogs. It would never have happened with Missis, but it will already have been seen that she and Pongo were rather unusual dogs. And so was Perdita. And so, if people only realised it, are many dogs. In fact, usual dogs are really more unusual than unusual dogs.

Anyway, Perdita was able to feed the two puppies. Pongo went upstairs and told Missis so (though to the Dearlys it only sounded like the thumping of his tail). Then he said goodnight and went back to the kitchen, where his basket was ready for him. Perdita had the basket Missis usually slept in. She had fed and washed the two puppies and was now having a light supper. (The Splendid Vet had said she must eat all she possibly could, to get her strength back.) Pongo had a snack himself, to encourage her. Then the Nannies went to bed and the kitchen was left in darkness except for the glow from the fire. And, when the two puppies were asleep, Perdita told Pongo her story.

She had been born in a large country house, not far from the common where Mrs Dearly had found her. Although very pretty, she had been less valuable than her brothers and sisters; her spots were rather small and her tail inclined to curl (it had straightened as she grew older). As no one rich or important wanted to be her pet, she was given to a farmer, who, though not cruel to her, never gave her the love all Dalmatians need. And he let her run wild, which is not good for any kind of dog.

A time came when she felt a great desire to marry. But no marriage was arranged for her and, as the farm was over a mile from any village,

no dog had come courting her. So, one day, she set out to find a husband for herself.

Her way to the village lay across the common, where she saw a large, handsome car, which had been driven on to the grass. A group of people were having a picnic – and with them was a superb liver-spotted Dalmatian. Now, liver-spotted Dalmatians are unusual. Perdita had been the only one in her family, and always thought herself a freak. She instantly knew that the dog on the common was no freak but a most valuable animal, for he wore a magnificent collar and was being offered a piece of chicken by a richly dressed lady. At that moment, he saw Perdita.

It was love at first sight. Without even bothering to eat the chicken, he came bounding to her and they were away into a wood together before anyone could stop them. Here they made swift arrangements for their marriage, promising to love each other always. Then the happy husband told his wife she must, of course, come and live with him, and led her back to the common. But, as they reached it, along came the farmer Perdita lived with, in his rattling old car. He dragged her into it – and the picnic party bundled her husband into their car. Both dogs struggled and howled but it was useless. The cars drove off in opposite directions.

Nine weeks after her marriage, Perdita had eight puppies. The farmer did not give her extra food, or help to feed the puppies himself so she got thinner and thinner; by the time her family was a month old, she was just skin and bone. Then the farmer put down some food for the puppies to eat and they quickly learnt how to, but they still went on taking all the milk Perdita could give them, so she never had a chance to regain her weight. She was such a very young mother, barely full-grown herself, but she loved her babies dearly and did all she could for them. And as she got thinner they got fatter.

The spots on Dalmatians begin to come through after two weeks. By the time Perdita's family were six weeks old it was obvious that they were going to be beautifully marked and very valuable – Perdita heard the farmer say so, to a stranger who came to the farm one morning. She was still helping to feed them; they would eat all the farmer offered and then come to her for milk. Then she and they would all have a happy sleep in the old box she had been given for a bed.

One afternoon, she woke to find not one puppy in bed with her. She searched the farm-house, she searched the farmyard. No puppies anywhere. She ran on to the road, fearing they might have been run over. On and on she went, pausing every few minutes to bark. No answering puppy-bark came to her. Soon it began to rain. She thought of the puppies all getting wet, and barked more and more desperately. A car nearly ran over her; she only saved herself by jumping into a muddy ditch, where the mud even got into her eyes and ears. By the time she reached the common where she had met her husband, she was shivering and weak on her legs. The thought of her lost husband added to her misery at the loss of the puppies. She had eaten nothing since the previous afternoon – the farmer only gave her one meal a day. At last, faint with hunger and utterly broken-spirited, she collapsed. And there, not long after, Mrs Dearly found her.

That was Perdita's whole story; except that she never told Pongo that the farmer had named her 'Spotty' – because she liked 'Perdita' so much better.

Pongo sympathised with all his heart and did his best to comfort her. He said he did not think the puppies were lost. It was more likely that they had been sold – perhaps to the stranger who came to see them. And this might be the best thing that could have happened to them – for if they were valuable they were sure to be well taken care of. There would never have been enough food at the farm for them when they got really big. Perdita knew all this was true. And the two tiny puppies in the basket with her were wonderfully comforting – so were the kind things Pongo said about being grateful to her for feeding them. Soon she felt much happier and slid into a warm, well-fed sleep.

Pongo lay awake for a long time, wishing Missis and all the puppies could have been with him in the firelit kitchen. He strolled over and looked at the two puppies asleep with Perdita, and felt proud and protective – and extremely sorry for Perdita. Really, she was a very pretty girl – if not a patch on his Missis.

Then he went back to his basket, had a last wash, and settled down. The fire sank lower; soon the kitchen was lit only by a faint light from a street lamp on the Outer Circle. Pongo slept. Perdita slept. And the two puppies, who had come successfully through their first day in the world, slept as peacefully as if they had been with their own mother.

Up in the cupboard, Missis had just served supper for eight and was a trifle tired. Mr Dearly had just served supper for five and was so exhausted by his day of puppy-feeding that he had to crawl out of the cupboard on his hands and knees. Mrs Dearly got him to bed and fed him with hot milk from a Thermos. They slept with their door open, in case Missis needed anything,

but she was very peaceful – though just before she fell asleep she did wonder a little about the strange female down in the kitchen with Pongo. She didn't worry, exactly; she just wondered.

On the top floor, Nanny Cook slept dreaming of Dalmatian puppies dressed as babies, and Nanny Butler slept dreaming of babies dressed as Dalmatian puppies.

What with four humans, three dogs and fifteen puppies, it really was a very sleep-full house.

# Cruella de Vil
# Pays Two Calls

THE NEXT DAY, five more puppies were brought down to Perdita and she fed them splendidly. So Mr Dearly went to his business. He hurried back early to do some pup-feeding and found that Mrs Dearly was feeding the upstairs puppies and the Nannies were taking it in turns to feed the kitchen puppies. He was a little jealous but soon got over it – for he knew that what really mattered was that pups should get plenty of milk without exhausting Missis and poor, thin Perdita too much.

Perdita now had her bed in the dresser cupboard where there would not be too much light for the puppies' eyes. These began to open in eight days. And a week after that the puppies' spots began to show.

What a day it was when Mr Dearly sighted the first spot! After that, spots came thick and fast, though they would not all be through for some months. In a very few days it was possible to recognise every pup by its spots. There were seven girls and eight boys. The prettiest of all the girls was the tiny pup whose life Mr Dearly had saved at birth, but she was very small and delicate. When pigs have families, the smallest, weakest piglet is often called the cadpig. Mr Dearly always called the tiny puppy 'Cadpig', which can be a nice little name when spoken with love.

Patch, the pup born with a black ear, was still the biggest and strongest puppy. He always seemed to be next to the Cadpig, as if these two already knew they were going to be special friends. There was a fat, funny, boy-puppy called Roly Poly, who was always getting into mischief. And the most striking pup of all was one who had a perfect horse-shoe of spots on his back – and had therefore been named 'Lucky'. He was terrifically energetic and showed from the beginning that he was going to be the ring-leader of all his brothers and sisters.

A few days after the first spots came through, something very upsetting happened: Perdita's milk supply failed. She was miserable about it because she loved the seven pups she had been feeding as much as if they were her own. And she was very, very frightened. Now that she was no longer useful, why should the Dearlys keep her in this warm, comfortable house where – for the first time in her life – she had been given enough to eat? But it was not the food and warmth that mattered most to her. It was the love. She had been treated as one of the family. The thought of leaving it all was more than she could bear.

And what happened to dogs nobody wanted? All sorts of fears awoke in her heart.

The morning she found she had no milk to offer at all, she crept unhappily out of the dresser cupboard and saw Mrs Dearly having a mid-morning cup of tea with the Nannies. Mrs Dearly held out a biscuit. Perdita did not take it. She just laid her head against Mrs Dearly's knee and gave a little moan.

Mrs Dearly stroked her and said: 'Poor Perdita! I wish we could explain to her that we are helping to feed her seven puppies, so she doesn't need to worry. Darling Perdita, you are washing them beautifully and keeping them warm at night. We couldn't possibly do without you.'

She had no hope of being understood; she just thought her soothing tone would be comforting. But Perdita was picking up more and more human words every day and understood perfectly. She was wild with relief. For the first time, she showed really high spirits, jumping up and kissing Mrs Dearly, then dashing back to wash the puppies all over again.

Not many days after this, all pups began learning to lap milk for themselves and could soon eat milk puddings and bread soaked in gravy. They were now much too big to go on living in cupboards. Missis and her eight were moved down to the laundry, while Perdita's seven had the run of the kitchen – where they got terribly under the Nannies' feet.

'What a pity they can't be in the laundry with

their brothers and sisters,' said Nanny Cook, one morning.

'Missis might hurt them – she wouldn't know them for her own now,' said Nanny Butler. 'And she and Perdita would fight.'

Pongo heard this and decided something must be done. For he knew that, whatever usual dogs would do, Missis would know her own puppies and she and Perdita would not fight. So he had a word with Missis, under the laundry door, and that afternoon, when the Nannies were upstairs, he took a flying leap at the door and managed to burst it open. Out hurtled Missis and eight puppies and when the Nannies came downstairs they found Pongo, Missis and Perdita all playing happily with fifteen puppies – who were now so mixed up that it took the Nannies all their time to decide which pups had been brought up by which mother.

After that, all pups lived in the laundry. The door was kept open and a piece of wood was put across it high enough to keep all puppies in – but low enough to be jumped by

Missis and Perdita when they wanted to come into the kitchen.

By now it was December but the days were fine and surprisingly warm so the puppies were able to play in the area several times a day. They were quite safe there for the gate at the top of the steps which led to the street now had a strong spring to keep it closed. One morning, when the three dogs and the fifteen puppies were taking the air, Pongo saw a tall woman looking down over the area railings.

He recognised her at once. It was Cruella de Vil.

As usual, she was wearing her absolutely simple white mink cloak, but she now had a brown mink coat under it. Her hat was made of fur, her boots were lined with fur, and she wore big fur gloves.

'What will she wear when it's really cold?' thought Nanny Butler, coming out into the area.

Cruella opened the gate and walked down the steps, saying how pretty the puppies were. Lucky, always the ring-leader, came running towards her and nibbled at the fur round the tops of her boots. She picked him up and placed him against her cloak, as if he were something to be worn.

'Such a pretty horse-shoe,' she said, looking at the spots on his back. 'But they all have pretty markings. Are they old enough to leave their mother yet?'

'Very nearly,' said Nanny Butler. 'But they won't have to. Mr and Mrs Dearly are going to keep them all.' (Sometimes the Nannies wondered just how this was going to be managed.)

'How nice!' said Cruella, and began going up the steps still holding Lucky against her cloak. Pongo, Missis and Perdita all barked sharply and Lucky reached up and nipped Cruella's ear. She gave a scream and dropped him. Nanny Butler was quick enough to catch him in her apron.

'That woman!' said Nanny Cook, who had just come out into the area. 'She's enough to frighten the spots off a pup. What's the matter, Lucky?'

For Lucky had dashed into the laundry and was gulping down water. Cruella's ear had tasted of pepper.

Every day now, the puppies grew stronger and more independent. They now fed themselves entirely, eating shredded meat as well as soaked bread and milk puddings. Missis and Perdita were quite happy to leave them now for an hour or more at a time, so the three grown-up dogs took Mrs Dearly and Nanny Butler for a good walk in the park every morning, while Nanny Cook got the lunch and kept an eye on the puppies. One morning, when she had just let them out into the area, the front door-bell rang.

It was Cruella de Vil and when she heard Mrs Dearly was out she said she would come in and wait. She asked many questions about the Dearlys and the puppies and went on talking so long that at last Nanny Cook said she really must go down and let the puppies in, as a cold wind was blowing. Cruella then said she would walk in the park and hope to meet Mrs Dearly. 'Perhaps I can see her from here,' she said, strolling to the window.

Nanny Cook also went to the window, intending to point out the nearest way into the park. As she did so, she noticed a small black van standing in front of the house. At that very moment, it drove off at a great pace.

Cruella suddenly seemed in a hurry. She almost ran out of the house and down the front-door steps.

'Can't think how she can move so fast, huddled in all those furs,' thought Nanny Cook, closing the front door. 'And those poor pups, in only their own thin little skins, catching their death of cold!'

She hurried down to the kitchen and opened the door to the area.

Not a pup was in sight.

'They're playing me a trick. They're hiding,' Nanny Cook told herself. But she knew there was nowhere for fifteen puppies to hide. All the same, she looked behind every tub of shrubs – where not even a mouse could have hidden. The gate at the top of the steps was firmly closed – and no pup could possibly have opened it. Still, she ran up to the street and searched wildly.

'They've been stolen, I know they have!' she moaned, bursting into tears. 'They must have been in that black van I saw driving away.'

Cruella de Vil seemed to have changed her mind about going into the park. She was already halfway back to her own house, walking very fast indeed.

# Hark, Hark, the Dogs do Bark!

THROUGH HER TEARS, Nanny Cook stared towards the park. She could now see Mrs Dearly, Nanny Butler and the three dogs, who had just turned for home. It seemed a strange and terrible thing that they could be strolling along so happily, when every step brought them nearer to such dreadful news.

As they came across the Outer Circle, Nanny Cook ran to meet them – crying so much that Mrs Dearly found it hard to understand what had happened. The dogs heard the words 'puppies', saw Nanny Cook's tears, and rushed down to the area. Then they went dashing over the whole house, searching, searching. Every few minutes, Missis and Perdita howled, and Pongo barked furiously.

While the dogs searched and the Nannies cried on each other's shoulder, Mrs Dearly telephoned

Mr Dearly. He came home at once, bringing with him one of the Top Men from Scotland Yard. The Top Man found a bit of sacking on the area railings and said the puppies must have been dropped into sacks and driven away in the black van. He promised to Comb the Underworld, but warned the Dearlys that stolen dogs were seldom recovered unless a reward was offered. A reward seemed an unreasonable thing to offer a thief, but Mr Dearly was willing to offer it.

He rushed to Fleet Street and had large advertisements put on the front pages of the evening papers (this was rather expensive) and arranged for even larger advertisements to be on the front pages of the next day's morning papers (this was even more expensive). Beyond this, there seemed nothing he or Mrs Dearly could do except try to comfort each other and comfort the Nannies and the dogs. Soon the Nannies stopped crying and joined in the comforting, and prepared beautiful meals which nobody felt like eating. And, at last, night fell on the stricken household.

Worn out, the three dogs lay in their baskets in front of the kitchen fire.

'Think of my baby Cadpig in a sack,' said Missis, with a sob.

'Her big brother Patch will take care of her,' said Pongo, soothingly – though he felt most unsoothed himself.

'Lucky is so brave he will bite the thieves,' wailed Perdita. 'And then they will kill him.'

'No, they won't,' said Pongo. 'The pups were stolen because they are valuable. No one will kill them. They are only valuable while they are alive.'

But even as he said this a terrible suspicion was forming in his mind. And it grew and grew as the night wore on. Long after Missis and Perdita, utterly exhausted, had fallen asleep, he lay awake staring at the fire, chewing the wicker of his basket as a man might have smoked a pipe.

Anyone who did not know Pongo well would have thought him handsome, amusing and charming, but not particularly clever. Even the Dearlys did not quite realise the depths of his mind. He was often still so puppyish. He would run after balls and sticks, climb into laps far too small to hold him, roll over on his back to have his stomach scratched. How was anyone to guess that this playful creature owned one of the keenest brains in Dogdom?

It was at work now. All through the long December night he put two and two together and made four. Once or twice he almost made five.

He had no intention of alarming Missis and Perdita with his suspicions. Poor Pongo! He not only suffered on his own account, as a father; he also suffered on the account of two mothers. (For he had come to feel the puppies had two mothers, though he never felt he had two wives – he looked on Perdita as a much-loved young sister.) He would say nothing about his worst fears until he was quite sure. Meanwhile, there was an important task ahead of him. He was still planning it when the Nannies came down to start another day.

As a rule, this was a splendid time – with the fire freshly made, plenty of food around and the puppies at their most playful. This morning

– well, as Nanny Butler said, it just didn't bear thinking about. But she thought about it, and so did everybody else in that pupless house.

No good news came during the day, but the Dearlys were surprised and relieved to find that the dogs ate well. (Pongo had been firm: 'You girls have got to keep your strength up.') And there was an even greater surprise in the afternoon. Pongo and Missis showed very plainly that they wanted to take the Dearlys for a walk. Perdita did not. She was determined to stay at home in case any pup returned and was in need of a wash.

Cold weather had come at last – Christmas was only a week away.

'Missis must wear her coat,' said Mrs Dearly.

It was a beautiful blue coat with a white binding; Missis was very proud of it. Coats had been bought for Pongo and Perdita, too. But Pongo had made it clear he disliked wearing his.

So the coat was put on Missis, and both dogs were dressed in their handsome chain collars. And then they put the Dearlys on their leashes and led them into the park.

From the first, it was quite clear the dogs knew just where they wanted to go. Very firmly, they led the way right across the park, across the road, and to the open space which is called Primrose Hill. This did not surprise the Dearlys as it had always been a favourite walk. What did surprise them was the way Pongo and Missis behaved when they got to the top of the hill. They stood side by side and they barked.

They barked to the north, they barked to the south, they barked to the east and west. And each time they changed their positions, they began the barking with three very strange, short, sharp barks.

'Anyone would think they were signalling,' said Mr Dearly.

But he did not really mean it. And they were signalling.

Many people must have noticed how dogs like to bark in the early evening. Indeed, twilight has sometimes been called 'Dogs' Barking Time'. Busy town dogs bark less than country dogs, but all dogs know all about the Twilight Barking.

# LONDON

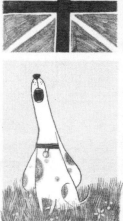

**SOHO**

**PICCADILLY**

**·· OXFORD ST. ·**

**MARBLE ARCH**

It is their way of keeping in touch with distant friends, passing on important news, enjoying a good gossip. But none of the dogs who answered Pongo and Missis expected to enjoy a gossip, for the three short, sharp barks meant: 'Help! Help! Help!'

No dog sends that signal unless the need is desperate. And no dog who hears it ever fails to respond.

Within a few minutes, the news of the stolen puppies was travelling across England, and every dog who heard at once turned detective. Dogs living in London's Underworld (hard-bitten characters; also hard-biting) set out to explore sinister alleys where dog thieves lurk. Dogs in Pet Shops hastened to make quite sure all puppies offered for sale were not Dalmatians in disguise. And dogs who could do nothing else swiftly handed on the news, spreading it through London and on through the suburbs, and on, on to the open country: 'Help! Help! Help! Fifteen Dalmatian puppies stolen. Send news to Pongo and Missis Pongo, of

Regent's Park, London. End of Message.'

Pongo and Missis hoped all this would be happening. But all they really knew was that they had made contact with the dogs near enough to answer them, and that those dogs would be standing by, at twilight the next evening, to relay any news that had come along.

One Great Dane, over towards Hampstead, was particularly encouraging.

'I have a chain of friends all over England,' he said, in his great, booming bark. 'And I will be on duty day and night. Courage, courage, O Dogs of Regent's Park!'

It was almost dark now. And the Dearlys were suggesting – very gently – that they should be taken home. So, after a few last words with the Great Dane, Pongo and Missis led the way down Primrose Hill. The dogs who had answered them were silent now, but the Twilight Barking was spreading in an ever-widening circle. And tonight it would not end with twilight. It would go on and on as the moon rose high over England.

The next day, a great many people who had read Mr Dearly's advertisements rang up to sympathise. (Cruella de Vil did, and seemed most upset when she was told the puppies had been stolen while she was talking to Nanny Cook.) But no one had anything helpful to say. And Scotland Yard was Frankly Baffled. So it was another sad, sad day for the Dearlys, the Nannies and the dogs.

Just before dusk, Pongo and Missis again showed that they wished to take the Dearlys for a walk. So off they started and again the dogs led the way to the top of Primrose Hill. And again they stood side by side and gave three sharp barks. But this time, though no human ear could have detected it, they were slightly different barks. And they meant, not 'Help! Help! Help!' but 'Ready! Ready! Ready!'

The dogs who had collected news from all over London replied first. Reports had come in from the West End and the East End and South of the Thames. And all these reports were the same:

'Calling Pongo and Missis Pongo of Regent's

Park. No news of your puppies. Deepest regrets. End of Message.'

Poor Missis! She had hoped so much that her pups were still in London. Pongo's secret suspicion had led him to pin his hopes to news from the country. And soon it was pouring in – some of it relayed across London. But it was always the same:

'Calling Pongo and Missis Pongo of Regent's Park. No news of your puppies. Deepest regrets. End of Message.'

Again and again Pongo and Missis barked the 'Ready!' signal, each time with fresh hope. Again and again came bitter disappointment. At last only the Great Dane over towards Hampstead remained to be heard from. They signalled to him – their last hope!

Back came his booming bark:

'Calling Pongo and Missis Pongo of Regent's Park. No news of your puppies. Deepest regrets. End of –'

The Great Dane stopped in mid-bark. A second later he barked again: 'Wait! Wait! Wait!'

Dead still, their hearts thumping, Pongo and Missis waited. They waited so long that Mr Dearly put his hand on Pongo's head and said: 'What about coming home, boy?' For the first time in his life, Pongo jerked his head from Mr Dearly's hand, then went on standing stock still. And at last the Great Dane spoke again, booming triumphantly through the gathering dusk.

'Calling Pongo and Missis Pongo. News! News at last! Stand by to receive details.'

A most wonderful thing had happened. Just as the Great Dane had been about to sign off, a Pomeranian with a piercing yap had got a message through to him. She had heard it from a Poodle who had heard it from a Boxer who had heard it from a Pekinese. Dogs of almost every known breed had helped to carry the news – and a great many dogs of unknown breed (none the worse for that and all of them bright as buttons). In all, four hundred and eighty dogs had relayed the message, which had travelled over sixty miles as the dog barks. Each dog had given the 'Urgent' signal, which had silenced all gossiping dogs. Not that many dogs were merely gossiping that night; almost all the Twilight Barking had been about the missing puppies.

This was the strange story that now came through to Pongo and Missis: some hours earlier, an elderly English Sheepdog, living on a farm in a remote Suffolk village, had gone for an afternoon amble. He knew all about the missing puppies and had just been discussing them with the tabby cat at the farm. She was a great friend of his.

Some little way from the village, on a lonely heath, was an old house completely surrounded by an unusually high wall. Two brothers, named Saul and Jasper Baddun lived there, but were merely caretakers for the real owner. The place had an evil reputation – no local dog would have dreamed of putting its nose inside the tall iron gates. In any case, these gates were always kept locked.

It so happened that the Sheepdog's walk took him past this house. He quickened his pace, having no wish to meet either of the Badduns.

And at that moment, something came sailing out over the high wall.

It was a bone, the Sheepdog saw with pleasure; but not a bone with meat on it, he noted with disgust. It was an old, dry bone, and on it were some peculiar scratches. The scratches formed letters. And the letters were SOS.

Someone was asking for help! Someone behind the tall wall and the high, chained gates! The Sheepdog barked a low, cautious bark. He was answered by a high, shrill bark. Then he heard a yelp, as if some dog had been cuffed. The Sheepdog barked again, saying: 'I'll do all I can.' Then he picked up the bone in his teeth and raced back to the farm.

Once home, he showed the bone to the tabby cat and asked her help. Then, together, they hurried to the lonely house. At the back, they found a tree whose branches reached over the wall. The cat climbed the tree, went along its branches, and then leapt to a tree the other side of the wall.

'Take care of yourself,' barked the Sheepdog.

'Remember those Baddun brothers are villains.'

The cat clawed her way down, backwards, to the ground, then hurried through the overgrown shrubbery. Soon she came to an old brick wall which enclosed a stable yard. From behind the wall came whimperings and snufflings. She leapt to the top of the wall and looked down.

The next second, one of the Baddun brothers saw her and threw a stone at her. She dodged it, jumped from the wall and ran for her life. In two minutes she was safely back with the Sheepdog.

'They're there!' she said, triumphantly. 'The place is seething with Dalmatian puppies!'

The Sheepdog was a formidable Twilight Barker. Tonight, with the most important news in Dogdom to send out, he surpassed himself. And so the message travelled, by way of farm dogs and house dogs, great dogs and small dogs. Sometimes a bark would carry half a mile or more, sometimes it would only need to carry a few yards. One sharp-eared Cairn saved the chain from breaking by picking up a bark from nearly a mile away, and then almost bursting herself getting it on to the dog next door. Across miles and miles of country, across miles and miles of suburbs, across a network of London streets the chain held firm, from the depths of Suffolk to the top of Primrose Hill – where Pongo and Missis, still as statues, stood listening, listening.

'Puppies found in lonely house. SOS on old bone –' Missis could not take it all in. But Pongo missed nothing. There were instructions for reaching the village, suggestions for the journey, offers of hospitality on the way. And the dog chain was standing by to take a message back to the pups – the Sheepdog would bark it over the wall in the dead of night.

At first Missis was too excited to think of anything to say, but Pongo barked clearly: 'Tell them we're coming! Tell them we start tonight! Tell them to be brave!'

Then Missis found her voice: 'Give them all our love! Tell Patch to take care of the Cadpig! Tell Lucky not to be too daring! Tell Roly Poly to keep out of mischief!' She would have sent a message to every one of the fifteen pups if

Pongo had not whispered: 'That's enough, dear. We mustn't make it too complicated. Let the Great Dane start work now.'

So they signed off and there was a sudden silence. And then, though not quite so loudly, they heard the Great Dane again. But this time he was not barking towards them. What they heard was their message, starting on its way to Suffolk.

# To the Rescue!

AS THEY WALKED the Dearlys home, Pongo said to Missis: 'Did you hear who owns the house where the puppies are imprisoned?'

Missis said: 'No, Pongo. I'm afraid I missed many things the Great Dane barked.'

'I will tell you everything later,' said Pongo.

He was faced with a problem. He now knew that his terrible suspicions were justified and it was time Missis learned the truth. But if he told her before dinner she might lose her appetite, and if he told her afterwards she might lose her dinner. So still he said nothing. And he made her eat every crumb of dinner and then join him in asking for more – which the Nannies gave with delight.

'It may be a long time before we get another meal,' he explained.

While the Nannies fed the Dearlys, the dogs

made their plans. Perdita at once offered to come to Suffolk with them.

'But you are still much too delicate for the journey, dear Perdita,' said Missis. 'Besides, what could you do?'

'I could wash the puppies,' said Perdita.

Both Pongo and Missis then said they knew Perdita was a beautiful puppy-washer but her job must be to comfort the Dearlys. And she felt that herself.

'If only we could make them understand why we are leaving them!' said Missis, sadly.

'If we could do that, we shouldn't have to leave them,' said Pongo. 'They would drive us to Suffolk in the car. And send the police.'

'Oh, let us have one more try to speak their language,' said Missis.

The Dearlys were sitting by the fire in the big white drawing-room. They welcomed the two dogs and offered them the sofa. But Pongo and Missis had no wish for a comfortable nap. They stood together, looking imploringly at the Dearlys.

Then Pongo barked gently: 'Wuff, wuff, wuffolk!'

Mr Dearly patted him but understood nothing.

Then Missis tried: 'Wuff, wuff, wuffolk!'

'Are you telling us the puppies are in Suffolk?' said Mrs Dearly.

The dogs wagged their tails wildly. But Mrs Dearly was only joking. It was hopeless and the dogs knew it always would be.

Dogs can never speak the language of humans and humans can never speak the language of dogs. But many dogs can understand almost every word humans say, while humans seldom learn to recognise more than half a dozen barks, if that. And barks are only a small part of the dog language. A wagging tail can mean so many things. Humans know that it means a dog is pleased, but not what a dog is saying about his pleasedness. (Really, it is very clever of humans to understand a wagging tail at all, as they have no tails of their own.) Then there are the snufflings and sniffings, the pricking of ears – all meaning different things. And many, many words are expressed by a dog's eyes.

It was with their eyes that Pongo and Missis spoke most that evening, for they knew the Dearlys could at least understand one eye-word. That word was 'love' and the dogs said it again and again, leaning their heads against the Dearlys' knees. And the Dearlys said 'Dear Pongo', 'Dear Missis', again and again.

'They're asking us to find their puppies, I know they are,' said Mrs Dearly, never guessing that, as well as declaring their love, the dogs were saying: 'We are going to find the puppies. Please forgive us for leaving you. Please have faith in our safe return.'

At eleven o'clock the dogs gave Mrs Dearly's hand one last kiss and took Mr Dearly out for his last run. Perdita joined them for this. She had spent the evening with the Nannies, feeling that Pongo and Missis might wish to be alone with their pets. Then all three dogs went to their baskets in the warm kitchen and the house settled for the night.

But it did not settle for long. Shortly before midnight, Pongo and Missis got up, ate some biscuits they had hidden, and took long drinks of water. Then they said a loving goodbye to Perdita, who was in tears, nosed open a window at the back of the house, and got out into the mews. (They knew they could not open the gate at the top of the area steps.) Carefully, they nosed the window shut, so that Perdita would not get a chill, and then went round to the area railings to give her one last smile. (Dogs smile in various ways; Pongo and Missis smiled by wrinkling their noses.) She was there at the kitchen window, bravely trying to wag her tail.

Beyond Perdita, Missis could see the three cushioned baskets in the rosy glow from the fire. She thought of the many peaceful nights she had spent in hers, in the happy days when a dog could fall asleep looking forward to breakfast. Poor Missis! Of course she loved Pongo, the puppies, the Dearlys and the Nannies – and dear, kind Perdita – best of everything in the world. But she also loved her creature comforts. Never had her home seemed so dear to her as now when she was leaving it for a dangerous, unknown world.

And it was such a cold world. The night was fine, the stars were brilliant, but the wind was keen. If only she could have brought her beautiful blue coat, now hanging on a peg in the warm kitchen!

Pongo saw her shiver. It is a hard thing for a loving husband to see his wife shiver.

'Are you cold, Missis?' he asked, anxiously.

'No, Pongo,' said Missis, still shivering.

'I am,' said Pongo, untruthfully. 'But I shall soon warm up.'

He tail-wagged goodbye to Perdita, then started off briskly along the Outer Circle, looking very spirited. Missis kept pace with him; but after its last wag to Perdita her tail went down.

After a few minutes, Pongo said: 'Are you warmer now, Missis?'

'Yes, Pongo,' said Missis, still shivering. And still her tail was down.

Pongo knew that if he could not cheer her up she would never be able to face the hardships that lay ahead. And he thought he could do with some cheering up himself. So he began a little speech, intended to give them both courage.

'I sometimes think,' he said, 'that you and I have become a bit pampered. Well, pampering does good dogs no harm, provided they don't come to depend on it. If they do, they become old before their time. We should never lose our liking for adventure, never forget our wild ancestry.' (They were then passing the Zoo.) 'Oh, I know we are worried about the puppies but the more we worry, the less we shall be able to help them. We must be brave, we must even be gay, we must know we cannot fail. Are you warmer now, Missis?'

'Yes, Pongo,' said Missis. But still she shivered and still her tail drooped.

They were now nearly at the bridge which leads from the Outer Circle towards Camden Town.

'Stop for a moment,' said Pongo. And he turned and looked back along the curve of the Circle. No car was in sight, no light was in any window. The lamp-posts were like sentinels guarding the sleeping park.

'Think of the day when we come back with fifteen puppies running behind us,' said Pongo.

'Oh, Pongo, are you sure?'

'Absolutely sure,' said Pongo. 'Are you a little warmer now, dear Missis?'

'Yes, Pongo,' said Missis. 'And this time it is true.'

'Then onwards to Suffolk!' said Pongo.

And as they ran towards the bridge Missis carried her tail as high as his.

'Not too high, Missis dear,' said Pongo. 'Let our hearts be gay, but not our tails.' For when a

Dalmatian's tail is curled high over the back it is called a 'gay' tail and is a bad fault.

Missis was still laughing at this little joke when her heart gave a wild flutter. Coming towards them was a policeman.

Instantly, Pongo led the way into a back street, and they were soon safely out of the policeman's sight. But seeing him had reminded Missis of something.

'Oh, Pongo!' she wailed. 'We are illegal. We are out without our collars.'

'And a good thing, too,' said Pongo, 'for a dog can be grabbed by the collar. But I do wish we could have brought your coat.' He had noticed that she was shivering again – though this time it was because she had been scared by the policeman.

'I don't,' said Missis, bravely. 'For if I wore a coat, how should I know how cold the puppies were? They have no coats. Oh, Pongo, how can they make the journey from Suffolk in such wintry weather? Suppose it snows?'

'They may not have to make the journey yet,' said Pongo.

Missis stared in astonishment. 'But we must get them back quickly or the dog thieves will sell them.'

'Nothing will happen to them yet,' said Pongo. And now he knew it was time to tell his wife the truth. 'Let's rest a moment,' he said, and led Missis into the shelter of a doorway. Then he went on gently: 'Dear Missis, our puppies were not stolen by ordinary dog thieves. Try not to be too frightened. Remember we are going to rescue them. Our puppies were stolen by Cruella de Vil's orders – so that she can have their skins made into a fur coat. Oh, Missis, be brave!'

Missis had collapsed. She lay on the doorstep, panting, her eyes full of horror.

'But it will be all right, dear Missis! They will be safe for months yet. They are much too small to be – to be used for a fur coat yet.'

Missis shuddered. Then she struggled to her feet.

'I will go back!' she cried. 'I will go back and tear Cruella de Vil to pieces.'

'That would do no good at all,' said Pongo,

firmly. 'We must rescue the puppies first and think of our revenge later. On to Suffolk!'

'On to Suffolk, then!' said Missis, staggering along on shaky legs. 'But we shall come back, Cruella de Vil!'

Soon Missis began to feel better, for Pongo made her see that puppies whose skins were wanted for a fur coat would be well fed and well taken care of, and kept together. Ordinary dog thieves might have sold them already, and to different people. She asked many questions and he told of his early suspicions – how he had suddenly recalled the evening they had first seen Cruella and sat under the piano in the red drawing-room.

'She said we would make enchanting fur coats, Missis.'

'For spring wear, over a black suit,' said Missis, remembering. 'And she did take a lot of interest in the puppies.'

'And she kept Nanny Cook talking while they were stolen,' said Pongo. 'But I wasn't quite sure until this evening, at the Twilight Barking.

You didn't hear as much as I did, Missis. Our puppies are at Hell Hall, the ancestral home of the de Vils.'

And he knew, though he kept this from Missis, that the SOS on the old bone meant 'Save Our Skins'.

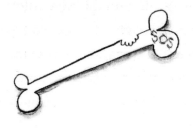

# At the Old Inn

PONGO HAD no difficulty in taking the right road out of London, for he and Mr Dearly had done much motoring in their bachelor days and often driven to Suffolk. Mile after mile the two dogs ran through the deserted streets, as the December night grew colder. At last London was left behind and, just before dawn, they reached a village in Epping Forest where they hoped to spend the day.

They had decided they must always travel by night and rest during daylight. For they felt sure Mr Dearly would advertise their loss and the police would be on the look out for them. There was far less chance of their being seen and caught by night.

They had barely entered the sleeping village when they heard a quiet bark. The next moment, a burly Golden Retriever was greeting them.

'Pongo and Missis Pongo, I presume? All arrangements were made for you by Late Twilight Barking. Please follow me.'

He led them to an old, gabled inn and then under an archway to a cobbled yard.

'Please drink here, at my own bowl,' he said. 'Food awaits you in your sleeping quarters but water could not be arranged.'

(For no dog can carry a full water-bowl.)

Pongo and Missis had only had one drink since they left home, at an old drinking trough for horses, which had a lower trough for dogs. They now gulped thirstily and gratefully.

'My pride as an innkeeper tempts me to offer you one of our best bedrooms,' said the Golden Retriever. 'They combine old world charm with all modern conveniences – and no charge for breakfast in bed. But it wouldn't be wise.'

'No, indeed,' said Pongo. 'We might be discovered.'

'Exactly. We are putting you in the safest place any of us could think of. Naturally every dog in the village came to the meeting after the

Late Barking – when we heard this village was to have the honour of receiving you. Step this way.'

At the far end of the yard were some old stables, and in the last stable of all was a broken-down stage coach.

'Just the right place for Dalmatians,' said Pongo, smiling, 'for our ancestors were trained to run behind coaches and carriages. Some people still call us Coach Dogs or Carriage Dogs.'

'And your run from London has shown you are worthy of your ancestors,' said the Golden Retriever. 'When I was a pup we sometimes took this old coach out for the school picnic, but no one has bothered with it for years now. You should be quite safe, and some dogs will always be on guard. In case of sudden alarm, you can go out by the back door of the stable and escape across the fields.'

There was a deep bed of straw on the floor of the coach and neatly laid out on the seat were two magnificent chops, half a dozen iced cakes and a box of peppermint creams.

'From the butcher's dog, the baker's dog and

the dog at the sweet-shop,' said the Retriever. 'I shall arrange your dinner. Will steak be satisfactory?'

Pongo and Missis said it would indeed, and tried to thank him for everything, but he waved their thanks away, saying: 'It's a very great honour. We are planning a small plaque – to be concealed from human eyes, of course – saying: PONGO AND MISSIS SLEPT HERE.'

Then he took them to the cobwebbed window and pointed out a smaller edition of himself, who was patrolling the inn courtyard.

'My youngest lad, already on guard. He's hoping to see you for a moment, when you're rested, and ask for your paw-marks – to start his collection. A small guard of honour will see you out of the village, but I shan't let them waste too much of your time. Goodnight – though it's really good morning. Pleasant dreams.'

As soon as he had gone, Pongo and Missis ate ravenously.

'Though perhaps we should not eat too heavily before sleeping,' said Pongo, so they left a couple of peppermint creams. (Missis, later, ate them in her sleep.) Then they settled down in the straw, close together, and got warmer and warmer.

Missis said: 'Do you feel sure our puppies will be well fed and well taken care of?'

'Quite sure. And they will be safe for a long time, because their spots are nowhere near big enough for a striking fur coat yet. Oh, Missis, how pleasant it is to be on our own like this!'

Missis thumped her tail with joy – and with relief. For there had been moments when she had felt – not jealous, exactly, but just a bit wistful about Pongo's affection for Perdita. She loved Perdita, was grateful to her and sorry for her; still – well, it was nice to have her own husband to herself, thought Missis. But she made herself say:

'Poor Perdita! No husband, no puppies! We must never let her feel we want to be on our own.'

'I do hope she can comfort the Dearlys,' said Pongo.

'She will wash them,' said Missis – and fell asleep.

How gloriously they slept! It was their first really deep sleep since the loss of the puppies. Even the Twilight Barking did not disturb them. It brought good news, which the Retriever told them when he woke them, as soon as it was dark. All was well with the pups, and Lucky sent a message that they were getting more food than they could eat. This gave Pongo and Missis a wonderful appetite for the steaks that were waiting for them.

While they ate, they chatted to the Retriever and his wife and their family, who lived at various houses in the village. And the Retriever told Pongo how to reach the village where the next day was to be spent – this had been arranged by the Twilight Barking. The steaks were finished and a nice piece of cheese was going down well when the Corgi from the Post Office arrived with an evening paper in her mouth. Mr Dearly had put in his largest advertisement yet – with a photograph of Pongo and Missis (taken during the joint honeymoon).

Pongo's heart sank for he felt the route planned for them was no longer safe. It led through many villages, where even by night they might be noticed – unless they waited till all humans had gone to bed, which would waste too much time. He said: 'We must travel across country.'

'But you'll get lost,' said the Retriever's wife.

'Pongo never loses his way,' said Missis, proudly.

'And the moon will be nearly full,' said the Retriever. 'You should manage. But it will be hard to pick up food. I had arranged for it to await you in several villages.'

Pongo said they had eaten so much that they could do without food until the morning, but he hated to think dogs might be waiting up for them during the night.

'I will cancel it by the Nine o'clock Barking,' said the Retriever.

There was a snuffling at the back door of the stable. All the dogs of the village had arrived to see Pongo and Missis off.

'We should start at once,' said Pongo. 'Where's our young friend who wants paw-marks?'

The Retriever's youngest lad stepped forward shyly, carrying an old menu. Pongo and Missis put their pawtographs on the back of it for him, then thanked the Retriever and his family for all they had done.

Outside, two rows of dogs were waiting to cheer. But no human ear could have heard the cheers, for every dog had now seen the photograph in the evening paper and knew an escape must be made in absolute silence.

Pongo and Missis bowed right and left, gratefully sniffing their thanks to all. Then, after a last goodbye to the Retriever, they were off across the moonlit fields.

'On to Suffolk!' said Pongo.

# Cross Country

THEY WERE well rested and well fed and they soon reached a pond where they could drink – the Retriever had told them to be on the look out for it. (It would not have been safe for them to drink from his bowl again; too many humans were now about.) And their spirits were far higher than when they had left the house in Regent's Park. How far away it already seemed, although it was less than twenty-four hours since they had been in their baskets by the kitchen fire. Of course they were still anxious about their puppies, and sorry for the poor Dearlys. But Lucky's message had been cheering, and they hoped to make it all up to the Dearlys one day. And anyway, as Pongo said, worrying would help nobody, while enjoying their freedom to race across the fields would do them a power of good.

He was relieved to see how well Missis ran

and what good condition she was in. So much food had been given to her while she was feeding the puppies that she had never got pitifully thin – as Perdita had, when she had fed her own puppies without being given extra food.

'You are a beautiful dog, Missis,' said Pongo. 'I am very proud of you.'

At this, Missis looked even more beautiful and Pongo felt even prouder of her. After a minute or so, he said: 'Do you think I'm looking pretty fit?'

Missis told him he looked magnificent, and wished she had said so without being asked. He was not a vain dog, but every husband likes to know that his wife admires him.

They ran on, shoulder to shoulder, a perfectly matched couple. The night was windless and therefore seemed warmer than the night before, but Pongo knew there was a heavy frost; and when, after a couple of hours across the fields, they came to another pond, there was a film of ice over it. They broke this easily and drank, but Pongo began to be a little anxious about where they would be by daybreak, for they would need good shelter in such cold weather. As they were now travelling across country, he thought it unlikely they would find the village that had been expecting them, but he felt sure most dogs would by now have heard of them and would be willing to help. 'Only we must be near some village by dawn, or we shall meet no dogs,' he thought.

Soon after that a lane crossed the fields and, as they had just heard a church clock strike midnight, Pongo felt there was now little chance of their meeting any humans on the road. He wanted to find a signpost and make sure they were travelling in the right direction. So they went along the lane for a mile until they came to a sleeping village. There was a signpost on the green, which Pongo read by the light of the moon. (He was very good at reading – as a pup he had played with alphabet blocks.) All was well. Their journey across the fields had saved them many miles and they were now deep in Essex. (The village where they might have stayed was already behind them.) By going north, they would reach Suffolk.

The only depressing thing was that the wonderful steak dinner seemed such a long time ago. And there was no hope of getting food as late as this. They just had to go on and on through the night, getting hungrier and hungrier.

And by the time it began to get light, they were also extremely chilly – partly because they were hungry and tired, and partly because it was getting colder and colder. The ice on the ponds they passed was thicker and thicker – at last they came to a pond where they could not break through to drink.

And now Pongo was really anxious, for they had reached a part of the country where there seemed to be very few villages. Where could they get food and shelter? Where could they hide and sleep during the bitterly cold day ahead of them?

He did not tell Missis of his fears and she would not even admit that she was hungry. But her tail drooped and her pace got slower and slower. He felt terrible: tired, hungry, anxious, and deeply ashamed that he was letting his beautiful wife suffer hardship. Surely there would be a village soon, or a fair-sized farm?

'Should we rest a little, Pongo?' said Missis, at last.

'Not until we've found some dogs to help us, Missis,' said Pongo. Then his heart gave a glad leap. Ahead of them were some thatched cottages! It was full daylight now and he could see smoke twisting up from several chimneys. Surely some dog would be about?

'If anyone tries to catch us, we must take to the fields and run,' said Pongo.

'Yes, Pongo,' said Missis, though she did not now feel she could run very far.

They reached the first cottage. Pongo gave a low bark. No dog answered it.

They went on and soon saw that this was not a real village but just a short row of cottages, some of them empty and almost in ruins. Except for smoke rising from a few chimneys there was no sign of life until they came to the very last cottage. As they reached it, a little boy looked out of a window.

He saw them and quickly opened the cottage door. In his hand was a thick slab of bread and butter. He appeared to be holding it out to them.

'Gently, Pongo,' said Missis, 'or we shall frighten him.'

They went through the open gate and up the cobbled path, wagging their tails and looking with love at the little boy – and the bread and butter. The child smiled at them fearlessly and waved the bread and butter. And then, when they were only three or four yards away, he stooped, picked up a stone and slung it with all his force. He gave a squeal of laughter when he saw the stone strike Pongo, then went in and slammed the door.

At that moment, the dogs heard a man's voice inside the cottage. They turned and ran as fast as they could, along the road and then into a field.

'Are you hurt, Pongo?' cried Missis, as they ran. Then she saw that he was limping. They stopped behind a haystack. Pongo's leg was bleeding – the stone must have had a very sharp edge. But what hurt him most was the bruise on the bone. He was trembling with pain and rage.

Missis was terrified, but she did not let him see this. She licked his wound and said there was nothing a good rest would not cure.

'Rest? Where?' said Pongo.

Missis saw that the haystack was very loosely made. She scrabbled at it fiercely, saying: 'Look, Pongo, you can creep in and get warm. Then sleep for a while. I will find us some food – I will, I will! The first dog I meet will help me.'

By now she had made a large hole in the haystack. Pongo looked at it longingly. But no! He could not let her go alone. He struggled to his feet, wincing with pain, and said: 'I must come with you to find food. And I will bite that child.'

'No, Pongo, no!' cried Missis, horrified. 'Remember he is only a very young human. All very young creatures are ignorantly cruel – often our dear puppies hurt me badly, not knowing they were doing so. To bite a human is the greatest crime a dog can commit. You shall not let that cruel, thoughtless child put such a sin on your conscience. Your pain and anger will pass, but the guilt would remain with you for always.'

Pongo knew she was right and already the desire to bite the child was passing. 'But I won't let you go alone,' he said.

'Then let us both rest a while first,' said crafty Missis. 'Come on, there's room for two.' And she crept into the haystack.

'We should find food first, or we shall be too weak to find it when we wake up,' said Pongo. But he followed her into the haystack.

'Just sleep for a few minutes, Pongo – while I keep guard,' said Missis, coaxingly.

Pongo could fight on no longer. Sleep came to him while he thought he was still arguing.

Missis waited a few minutes, then crept out

and pulled hay round Pongo to hide him. She no longer felt sleepy; she was far too anxious. Even her appetite had gone for the moment. Still, she knew she must find food for them both – and she had no idea how to, for she was almost sure there was no dog anywhere near to help her. But pretending to Pongo that she felt brave had made her really feel a little braver and her tail was no longer down.

She could still see the thatched cottages and she noticed some hens at the back of them. Perhaps the hens would have some stale crusts that she could – well, borrow. She went back.

The first cottage she reached was the one where the little boy lived. And now he was at the back, staring at her! This time, he had an even larger slab of bread and butter, with some jam on it. He ran towards her, holding it out.

'Perhaps he really means it now,' thought Missis. 'Perhaps he's sorry he hurt Pongo.' And she went forward hopefully – though well prepared to dodge stones.

The child waited until she was quite close.

Then again he stooped for a stone. But he was on a patch of grass, with no stones handy. So, instead, he threw the slab of bread and butter. He threw it with rage, not love, but that made it no less valuable. Missis caught it neatly and bolted.

'Bless me,' she thought, 'he's just a small human who likes throwing things. His parents should buy him a ball.'

She took the bread and butter back to the haystack and laid it down by her sleeping husband's nose. So far, she had not even licked it, but now she let herself nibble off one very small corner. It tasted so glorious that her appetite came back with a rush, but she left all the rest for Pongo to find when he woke. Again she pulled the hay round him, and then ran to the road. But she saw a man outside the cottage where the little boy lived so she did not dare to go back to visit the hens. She ran in the opposite direction.

It was now a very beautiful winter morning. Every blade of grass was silvered with hoar frost and glittering in the newly risen sun. But

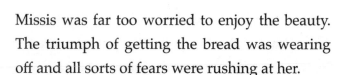
Missis was far too worried to enjoy the beauty. The triumph of getting the bread was wearing off and all sorts of fears were rushing at her.

Suppose Pongo was seriously injured? Suppose he was too lame to go on? Suppose she could find no food close at hand? If she had to go far, she knew she would get lost. She even got lost in Regent's Park, almost every time the Dearlys were off the leash. They often laughed at the way she would stand still, wildly staring around for them. Suppose she never found her way back to Pongo and he searched and searched and never found her? Lost dog! The very words were terrible!

And was she, even now, quite sure of her way back to the haystack?

'It isn't fair,' thought Missis. 'No one as worried as I am ought to feel hungry, too.' For she was ravenous – and thirsty. She tried licking the ice in a ditch but it hurt her tongue without quenching her thirst.

She was beginning to think she must go back and make sure where the haystack was, when she came to an old redbrick archway leading to a long gravel drive. Her spirits rose. Surely this must be the entrance to some big country house, such as she had stayed at several times when she and Mrs Dearly were both bachelors? Such houses had many dogs, large kitchens, plenty of food. Joyfully she ran through the archway.

She could see no house ahead of her because the drive twisted. It was overgrown with weeds, and it went on so long that she began to wonder if it really did lead to a house. Indeed, it was now so wild and neglected that it seemed more like a path through a wood than the approach to a house. And it was so strangely silent; never in her life had Missis felt quite so alone.

More and more frightened, she ran round one more bend – and suddenly she was out in the open, with the house in front of her.

It was very old, built of mellow red brick like the archway, with many little diamond-paned windows and one great window that reached almost to the roof. The windows twinkling in the early morning sunshine looked cheerful and welcoming, but there was no sign of life

anywhere. And there was grass growing in the cracks of the wide stone steps which led to the massive oak door.

'It's empty!' thought Missis, in despair.

But it was not empty. Looking out of an open window was a Spaniel, black except for his muzzle, which was grey with age.

'Good morning,' he said, most courteously. 'Can I be of any help to you, my dear?'

# Hot Buttered Toast

IT WAS wonderful how quickly the Spaniel took in the story Missis poured out to him, for he had not heard any news by way of the Twilight Barking.

'Haven't listened to it for years,' he said. 'Indeed, I doubt if I could get it now. There isn't another dog for miles. Anyway, Sir Charles needs me at twilight – he needs me almost all the time. I'm only off duty now because he's in his bath.'

They were now in a large, stone-floored kitchen, where the Spaniel had led Missis after inviting her to jump in through the window. He went on: 'Breakfast before you tell me any more, young lady,' and led her to a large plate of meat.

'But it's your breakfast,' said Missis, trying not to look as hungry as she felt.

'No, it isn't. It's my supper, if you really want to know. I'd no appetite – and I shan't have any for breakfast, which will be served to me any minute. Tea's my meal. Hurry up, my dear. It will be thrown away if you don't eat it.'

Missis took one delicious gulp. Then she stopped.

'My husband –'

The Spaniel interrupted her. 'We'll see about his breakfast later. Finish it all, my child.'

So Missis ate and ate and then had a long drink from a white pottery bowl. She had never seen a bowl like it.

'That's an eighteenth-century dog's drinking bowl,' said the Spaniel, 'handed down from dog to dog in this family. And now, before you get too sleepy, you'd better bring your husband here.'

'Oh, yes!' said Missis, eagerly. 'Please tell me how to get back to the haystack.'

'Just go to the end of the drive and turn left.'

'I'm not very good at right and left,' said Missis, 'especially left.'

The Spaniel smiled; then looked at her paws. 'This will help you,' he said. 'That paw with the pretty spot – that is your right paw.'

'Then which is my left paw?'

'Why, the other paw, of course.'

'Back or front?' asked Missis.

'Just forget your back paws.'

Missis was puzzled. Could she forget her back paws? And, if she could, would it be safe?

The Spaniel went on: 'Look at your front paws and remember: Right paw, spot. Left paw, no spot.'

Missis stared hard at her paws. 'I will practise,' she said, earnestly. 'But please tell me how to turn left.'

'Turn on the side of the paw which does not have a spot.'

'Whichever way I am going?'

'Certainly,' said the Spaniel. 'The paw with the spot will always be your right paw. You can depend on that.'

'If I turned towards you now, would I be turning left?' asked Missis, after thinking very hard.

'Yes, yes. Splendid!' said the Spaniel.

Missis then turned round and faced the other way. 'But now you are on the side of the paw with the spot,' she said worriedly, 'so my right paw has turned into my left.'

The Spaniel gave it up. 'I will show you the haystack,' he said, and led her out through what once must have been a fine kitchen-garden but was now a mass of weeds. Beyond it were the fields. Missis could just see the thatched cottages and the haystack.

'It's the only haystack,' said the Spaniel. 'All the same, keep your eyes on it all the time you run. I would come with you but my rheumatism prevents me – and Sir Charles will need me to carry his spectacle-case downstairs. We are an old, old couple, my dear. He is ninety and I – according to a foolish human reckoning that one year of a dog's life represents seven years of human life – I am a hundred and five.'

'I should never have guessed it,' said Missis, politely – and truthfully.

'Anyway, I'm still young enough to know a pretty dog when I see one,' said the Spaniel, gallantly. 'Now off you go for your husband. You'll have no difficulty in finding your way back because you will see our chimneys from the haystack.'

'Right or left?' asked Missis, brightly.

'In front of your delightful nose. If I'm not here, just take your husband into the kitchen and I'll join you as soon as I can.'

Missis raced off happily across the frosty fields, never taking her eyes off the haystack and feeling very proud when she reached it without getting lost. Pongo was still heavily asleep, with the bread and butter by his nose.

Poor Pongo! Waking up was awful, what with his sleepiness, the pain in his leg and his horror at learning Missis had been dashing about the countryside alone. But he felt better when she had told him the news, which she did while he ate the bread and butter. And though his leg hurt he found he could run without limping.

'Which way do we go?' he asked, as they came out of the haystack.

Missis looked worried. There were no chimneys ahead of her nose – because she was facing in exactly the opposite direction. But

Pongo saw the chimneys and took her towards them. Just before they reached the kitchen-garden, Missis said: 'Pongo, do dogs have spots on their right paws or on their left paws?'

'That depends on the dog,' said Pongo.

Missis shook her head. 'It's hopeless,' she thought. 'How can I depend on a thing that depends?'

The Spaniel was waiting for them.

'I've settled Sir Charles by the fire,' he said, 'so I've an hour or so to spare. Come to breakfast, my dear fellow.'

He led Pongo to the kitchen, where there was now another plate of food.

'Surely, it's your breakfast, sir?' said Pongo.

'Had mine with Sir Charles. Don't as a rule take breakfast, but meeting your pretty wife gave me an appetite, so I accepted a couple of slices of bacon. Sir Charles was so pleased. Go ahead, my dear chap, I couldn't eat another bite.'

So Pongo ate and ate and drank and drank.

'And now for a long sleep,' said the Spaniel.

He led them up a back staircase and along

many passages till they came to a large, sunny bedroom in which was a four-poster bed. Beside it was a round basket. 'Mine,' said the Spaniel, 'but I never use it. Sir Charles likes me on the bed. Luckily that's made already because John – he's our valet – is already off for his day out. Jump up, both of you.'

Pongo and Missis jumped on to the four-poster and relaxed in bliss.

'No one will come up here until this evening,' said the Spaniel, 'because Sir Charles can't manage the stairs until John gets back. The fire should last some hours yet – we always light it for Sir Charles to have his bath in front of it. No new-fangled plumbing in this house. Sleep well, my children.'

The sunlight, the firelight, the tapestried walls were all so beautiful that it seemed a waste not to stay awake and enjoy them. So they did – for nearly a whole minute. The next thing they knew was that the Spaniel was gently waking them. The sun was already down, the fire dead, the room a little chilly. Pongo and Missis stretched sleepily.

'What you need is tea,' said the Spaniel. 'But first a breath of air. Follow me.'

There was still a faint glow from the sunset as they wandered around the wintry, tangled garden. As Pongo looked back towards the beautiful old redbrick house, the Spaniel told them it was four hundred years old and that nobody now lived there but himself, Sir Charles and the valet, John. Most of the rooms were shut up.

'But we dust them, sometimes,' he said. 'That's a very long walk for me.'

The great window was lit by the flicker of firelight. 'It's in there we sit, mostly,' the Spaniel told them. 'We should be warmer in one of the smaller rooms but Sir Charles likes to be in the Great Hall.' A silvery bell tinkled. 'There! He's ringing for me. Tea's ready. Now, do just as I tell you.'

He led them indoors and then into a large high room at the far end of which was an enormous fire. In front of it sat an old gentleman, but they could not yet see him very well because there was a screen round the back of his chair.

'Please lie down at the back of the screen,' whispered the Spaniel. 'Later, Sir Charles will fall asleep and you can come closer to the fire.'

As Pongo and Missis tiptoed to the back of the screen, they noticed that there was a large table beside Sir Charles on which was his luncheon tray – finished with now, and neatly covered by a table-napkin – and everything necessary for tea. Water was already boiling in a silver kettle over a spirit lamp. Sir Charles filled the teapot and put the tea-cosy on. Then he lifted a silver cover from a plate on which there were a number of slices of bread. By now the Spaniel had joined him and was thumping his tail.

'Hungry, are you?' said Sir Charles. 'Well, we've a good fire for our toast.'

Then he put a slice of bread on a toasting fork. It was no ordinary toasting fork for it was made of iron and nearly four feet long. It was really meant for pushing logs into position. But it was just what Sir Charles needed, and he handled it with great skill, avoiding the flaming logs and toasting the bread where the wood glowed red hot. A slice of toast was ready in no time. Sir Charles buttered it thickly and offered a piece to the Spaniel, who ate it while Sir Charles watched.

Missis was a little surprised that the courteous Spaniel had not offered her the first piece. She was even more surprised when he received a second piece and ate that, too, while Sir Charles watched. She began to feel very hungry – and very anxious. Surely the kind Spaniel had not invited them to tea just to watch him eat? Then a third piece of toast was offered – and this time Sir Charles happened to turn away. Instantly the Spaniel dropped the toast behind the screen. Piece after piece travelled this way to Pongo and Missis, with the Spaniel only eating one now and then – when Sir Charles happened to be looking. Missis felt ashamed of her hungry suspicions.

'Never known you with such a good appetite, my boy,' said the old gentleman, delightedly. And he made slice after slice of toast until all the bread was gone. Then cakes were handed on in the same way. And then Sir Charles offered the Spaniel a silver bowl of tea. This was put down so close to the edge of the screen that Pongo and Missis were able to drink some while Sir Charles was looking the other way. When he saw the bowl empty, he filled it again and again so everyone had enough. Pongo and Missis had always had splendid food, but they had never before had hot buttered toast and sweet milky tea. It was a meal they always remembered.

At last Sir Charles rose stiffly, put another log on the fire, and then settled back in his chair and closed his eyes. Soon he was asleep and the Spaniel beckoned Pongo and Missis to the fire. They sat on the warm hearth and looked up at the old gentleman. His face was deeply lined and all the lines drooped and somehow he had a look of the Spaniel – or the Spaniel had a look of Sir Charles. Both of them were lit by the firelight and beyond them was the great window, now blue with evening.

'We ought to be on our way,' whispered Pongo to Missis. But it was so warm, so quiet, and they were both so full of buttered toast that they drifted into a light and delightful sleep.

Pongo awoke with a start. Surely someone had spoken his name?

The fire was no longer blazing brightly but there was still enough light to see that the old gentleman was awake and leaning forward.

'Well, if that isn't Pongo and his missis,' he murmured, smilingly. 'Well, well! What a pleasure! What a pleasure!'

Missis had opened her eyes now.

The Spaniel whispered: 'Don't move, either of you.'

'Can you see them?' said the old gentleman, putting his hand on the Spaniel's head. 'If you can, don't be frightened. They won't hurt you. You'd have liked them. Let's see, they must have died fifty years before you were born – more than that. They were the first dogs I ever knew. I used to ask my mother to stop the carriage and let them get inside – I couldn't bear to see them running behind. So, in the end, they just became house dogs. How often they sat there in the firelight. Hey, you two! If dogs can come back, why haven't you come back before?'

Then Pongo knew that Sir Charles thought they were ghost dogs. And he remembered that Mr Dearly had named him 'Pongo' because it was a name given to many Dalmatians of those earlier days when they ran behind carriages. Sir Charles had taken him and Missis for Dalmatians he had known in his childhood.

'Probably my fault,' the old gentleman went on. 'I've never been what they call "psychic" nowadays. This house is supposed to be full of ghosts but I've never seen any. I dare say I'm only seeing you because I'm pretty close to the edge now – and quite time, too. I'm more than ready. Well, what a joy to know that dogs go on, too – I've always hoped it. Good news for you, too, my boy.' He fondled the Spaniel's ears. 'Well, Pongo and his pretty wife, after all these years! Can't see you so well, now, but I shall remember!'

The fire was sinking lower and lower. They could no longer see the old gentleman's face, but soon his even breathing told them he was asleep again. The Spaniel rose quietly.

'Come with me now,' he whispered, 'for John will be back soon to get supper. You have given my dear old pet a great pleasure. I am deeply grateful.'

They tiptoed out of the vast, dark hall and made their way to the kitchen, where the Spaniel pressed more food on them.

'Just a few substantial biscuits – my tin is always left open for me when John is away.'

Then they had a last drink of water and the Spaniel gave Pongo directions for reaching Suffolk. It was full of 'rights' and 'lefts' and Missis did not take in one word. The Spaniel noticed her dazed look and said playfully:

'Now which is your right paw?'

'One of the front ones,' said Missis, brightly. At which Pongo and the Spaniel laughed in a very masculine way.

Then they thanked the Spaniel and said goodbye. Missis said she would always remember that day.

'So shall I,' said the Spaniel, smiling at her. 'Ah, Pongo, what a lucky dog you are!'

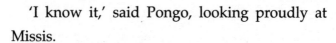 

'I know it,' said Pongo, looking proudly at Missis.

Then they were off.

After they had been running across the fields for some minutes, Missis said anxiously:

'How's your leg, Pongo?'

'Much, much better. Oh, Missis, I am ashamed of myself. I made such a fuss this morning. It was partly rage. Pain hurts more when one is angry. You were such a comfort to me – and so brave.'

'And you were a comfort to me, the night we left London,' said Missis. 'It will be all right as long as we never lose courage both together.'

'I'm glad you did not let me bite that small human.'

'Nothing should ever make a dog bite a human,' said Missis, in a virtuous voice.

Pongo remembered something. 'You said only the night before last that you were going to tear Cruella de Vil to pieces.'

'That is different,' said Missis, grimly. 'I do not consider Cruella de Vil is human.'

Thinking of Cruella made them anxious for

the puppies and they ran on faster, without talking any more for a long time. Then Missis said: 'Pongo, how far away from the puppies are we now?'

'With good luck we should reach them tomorrow morning,' said Pongo.

Just before midnight they came to the market town of Sudbury. Pongo paused as they crossed the bridge over the River Stour.

'Here we enter Suffolk,' he said, triumphantly.

They ran on through the quiet streets of old houses and into the market square. They had hoped they might meet some dog and hear if any news of the puppies had come at the Twilight Barking, but not so much as a cat was stirring. While they were drinking at the fountain, church clocks began to strike midnight.

Missis said gladly: 'Oh, Pongo, it's tomorrow! Now we shall be with our puppies today!'

# What They Saw from the Folly

AS THE NIGHT wore on, they travelled through many pretty villages to a countryside wilder than any they had yet seen. There were more woods and heaths, fewer farms. So wild was it that Pongo would risk no short cuts and stuck cautiously to the roads, which were narrow and twisted. The moon was behind clouds so he could not read what few signposts there were.

'I'm so afraid we may go through our village without knowing it,' he said. 'For as we have not been able to send any news by the Twilight Barking, nobody will be on the look out for us.'

But he was wrong. Suddenly, out of the darkness, came a loud 'Miaow'.

They stopped instantly. Just ahead of them, up a tree, was a tabby cat. She said:

'Pongo and Missis? I suppose you are friendly?'

'Yes, indeed, Madam,' said Pongo. 'Are you, by any chance, the cat who helped to find our puppies?'

'That's me,' said the cat.

'Oh, thank you, thank you!' cried Missis.

The cat jumped down. 'Sorry to seem suspicious of you, but some dogs just can't control themselves when they see a cat – not that I've ever had any trouble. Well, here you are.'

'How very kind of you to keep watch for us, Madam,' said Pongo.

'No hardship, I'm usually out at night. You can call me Tib. My real name's Pussy Willow but that's too long for most people – a pity, really, as it's a name I could fancy.'

'It suits you so well,' said Pongo, in a courtly tone he had picked up from the Spaniel, 'with your slender figure and soft grey paws.' He was taking a chance in saying this for it was too dark for him to see her figure, let alone her paws.

The cat was delighted. 'Well, I have kept my figure – and it was my paws got me the name

Pussy Willow. Now you'll be wanting a bite of food and a good long rest.'

'Please tell us if all is still well with our puppies,' said Missis.

'It was, yesterday afternoon – when I last saw them. Lively as crickets and fat as butter, they were.'

'Could we see them – just a glimpse – before we eat or sleep?' asked Missis.

'We can't climb trees, as Mrs Willow can,' said Pongo.

'You won't need to,' said the cat. 'The Colonel's made other arrangements. But you can't see the puppies before they are let out for exercise and that'll be hours yet. Those Badduns are late risers. Well, come along and meet the Colonel.'

'A human Colonel?' asked Missis, puzzled.

'Bless me, no. The Colonel's our Sheepdog. A perfect master of strategy – you ask the sheep. He calls me his Lieutenant.'

The cat was now leading them along the road. Pongo asked how far it was to the farm.

'Oh, we're not going to the farm now. The

Colonel's spending the night at the Folly. Crazy place, but it's coming in very useful.'

The darkness was thinning. Soon the road ran across a stretch of heath on which, still some way ahead of them, a dark mass stood out against the gradually lightening sky. After a few moments, Pongo saw that the dark mass was a great stone wall.

'There you are,' said the cat. 'Your puppies are behind that.'

'It looks like the wall of a prison,' said Pongo.

'Nasty place,' said the cat. 'The Colonel will tell you its history.'

She led them from the road over the rough grass of the heath. As they drew nearer, Pongo saw that the wall curved – as the wall of a round tower curves. Above it rose the trunks of tall trees, their bare branches black against the sky.

'You'd think there would be a castle, at least, inside that huge wall,' said the cat. 'And they do say there was going to be, only something went wrong. All that's there now – well, you can see for yourself.'

She led the way to the rusty iron gates, and Pongo and Missis peered through the bars. There was now enough light for them to see some distance. Beyond a stretch of grass as wild as the surrounding heath, they saw the glint of water – but, strangely, it seemed to be black water. Then they saw the reason why. Reflected in it was a black house.

It was the most frightening house Pongo and Missis had ever seen. Many of the windows in its large, flat face had been bricked up and those that were left looked like eyes and a nose, with

the front door for a mouth. Only there were too
many eyes, and the nose and the mouth were not
quite in the right places, so that the whole face
looked distorted.

'It's seen us!' gasped Missis – and it really did
seem as if the eyes of the house were staring at
them from its cracked and peeling black face.

'Well, that's Hell Hall for you,' said the cat.

She moved on and they followed her, round
the curving wall. After a few minutes they saw a
tower rising high above the tree-tops. It was built
of rough grey stone, like the wall, and was rather

like a church tower. But there was no church. The tower simply jutted out of the wall. Some of the narrow windows were broken and their stonework was crumbling. The place was not yet a ruin but looked as if it quite soon might be one.

'Well may they call it a Folly!' said the cat.

Missis did not know what the word meant but Pongo had seen a Folly before and was able to explain. The name is often given to expensive, odd buildings built for no sensible reason, buildings that it was a foolishness to build.

The cat miaowed three times and there were three answering barks from inside the tower. A moment later came the sound of a bolt being drawn back.

'The Colonel's the only dog I ever knew who could manage bolts with his teeth,' said the cat, proudly.

Pongo instantly decided he would learn to manage bolts.

'Come in, come in,' said a rumbling voice, 'but let me have a look at you first. There's not much light inside yet.'

An enormous Sheepdog came out. Pongo saw at once that this was none of your dapper military men but a lumbering old soldier man, possibly a slow thinker but widely experienced. His eyes glittered shrewdly and kindly through his masses of grey-and-white woolly hair.

'Glad to see you're large Dalmatians,' he said, approvingly. 'I've nothing against small dogs but the size of all breeds should be kept up. Well, now, what's been happening to you? There was a rare to-do on the Twilight Barking last night, when no one had any news of you.'

He led the way into the Folly, while Pongo told of their day with the Spaniel.

'Sounds a splendid fellow,' said the Colonel. 'Sorry he's not on the Barking. Now, tuck in, you two. I provided breakfast just in case you turned up.'

There was plenty of good, farm-house food and a deep, round tin full of water.

'How did you get it all here?' asked Pongo, astonished.

'I rolled the round tin from the farm – with

the food inside it,' said the Colonel. 'I stuffed the tin with straw so that the food wouldn't fall out. And then I borrowed a small, seaside bucket from my young pet, Tommy – the dear little chap would lend me anything. I can carry that bucket by its handle. Six trips to the pond on the heath got the water here – lucky it thawed yesterday. Drink up! Plenty more where that came from.'

The cat acted as hostess during the meal. Pongo was careful always to address her as 'Mrs Willow'.

'What's this Mrs Willow business?' said the Colonel suddenly.

'Pussy Willow happens to be my given name,' said the cat. 'And I'm certainly a Mrs.'

'You've got too many names,' said the Colonel. 'You're "Puss" because all cats are "Puss". You're "Pussy Willow" because it's your given name. You're "Tib" because most people call you that. I call you "Lieutenant" or "Lieutenant Tib". I thought you liked it.'

'I like "Lieutenant" but not "Lieutenant Tib".'

'Well, you can't be "Mrs Willow" on top of everything else. You can't have six names.'

'I'm entitled to nine names as I've nine lives,' said the cat. 'But I'll settle for "Lieutenant Willow" – with "Puss" for playful moments.'

'Right,' said the Colonel. 'And now we'll show our guests their sleeping quarters.'

'Oh, please,' begged Missis. 'Couldn't we get just a glimpse of the puppies before we sleep?'

The cat shot a quick look at the Colonel and said: 'I've told them the pups won't be out for hours yet.'

'Besides, you'd get too excited to sleep,' said the Colonel. 'You must both have a good rest before you start worrying.'

'Worrying?' said Pongo, sharply. 'Is something wrong?'

'I give you my word there is nothing wrong with your puppies,' said the Colonel.

Pongo and Missis believed him – and yet they both thought there was something odd about his voice, and about the look the cat had given him.

'Now up we go,' the Colonel went on, briskly.

'You're sleeping on the top floor because that's the only floor where the windows aren't broken. Want a ride, Lieutenant Wib – I mean Lieutenant Tillow – oh, good heavens, cat!'

'If there's one thing I object to being called, it's plain "cat",' said the cat.

'Quite right. I don't like being called plain "dog",' said the Colonel. 'I apologise, Lieutenant Willow. Now jump on my back unless you want to walk.'

The cat jumped on the Colonel's back and held on by his long hair. Pongo had never before seen a cat jump on a dog's back with friendly intentions. He was deeply impressed – both by the Colonel's trustfulness and the cat's trustworthiness.

The narrow, twisting stairs went up through five floors of the Folly, most of them full of broken furniture, old trunks and all manner of rubbish. On the top floor was a deep bed of straw, brought up by the Colonel in a sack. But what interested Missis far more was the narrow window – surely it must look towards Hell Hall?

She ran to see. Yes, beyond the tree-tops and

a neglected orchard was the back of the black house – which was as ugly as the front, though it did not have such a frightening expression. At one side was a large stable yard.

'Is that where the puppies will come out?' she asked.

'Yes, yes,' said the Colonel, 'but it won't be for – well, for some time, yet.'

'I shall never sleep until I've seen them,' said Missis.

'Yes, you will, because I shall talk you to sleep,' said the Colonel. 'Your husband has asked me to tell him the history of Hell Hall. Now come and lie down.'

Pongo was as anxious to see the puppies as Missis was but he knew they should sleep first, so he coaxed her to lie down. The Colonel pulled the straw round both of them.

'It's chilly in here – not that I feel it,' he said. Then he sent the cat to start collecting food for the next meal, and began to talk, in his rumbling voice. This was the story he told.

Hell Hall had once been an ordinary farm-

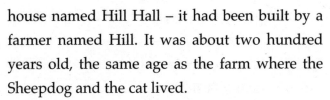 

house named Hill Hall – it had been built by a farmer named Hill. It was about two hundred years old, the same age as the farm where the Sheepdog and the cat lived.

'The two houses are quite a bit alike,' said the Colonel, 'only our place is painted white and well cared for. I remember Hell Hall before it was painted black and it really wasn't bad at all.'

The farmer named Hill had got into debt and sold Hill Hall to an ancestor of Cruella de Vil's, who liked its lonely position on the wild heath. He intended to pull the farm-house down and build himself a fantastic house which was to be a mixture of a castle and a cathedral, and had begun by building the surrounding wall and the Folly. (The Colonel had heard all this while visiting the Vicarage.)

Once the wall, with its heavy iron gates, was finished, strange rumours began to spread. Villagers crossing the heath at night heard screams and wild laughter. Were there prisoners behind the prison-like wall? People began to count their children carefully.

'Some of the stories – well, I shan't tell you just as you're falling asleep,' said the Colonel. 'I didn't hear them at the Vicarage. But I will tell you something – because it won't upset you as it, naturally, upset the villagers. It was said that this de Vil fellow had a long tail. I didn't hear that at the Vicarage, either.'

Missis had taken in very little of this and was now fast asleep, but Pongo was keenly interested.

'By this time,' the Colonel went on, 'people were calling the place Hell Hall, and the de Vil chap plain devil. The end came when the men from several villages arrived one night with lighted torches, prepared to break open the gates and burn the farm-house down. But, as they approached the gates, a terrific thunderstorm began and put the torches out. Then the gates burst open – seemingly of their own accord – and out came de Vil, driving a coach and four. And the story is that lightning was coming not from the skies but from de Vil – blue forked-lightning. All the men ran away screaming, and never came back. And neither did de Vil. The house stood empty for thirty years. Then someone rented it. It's been rented again and again, but no one ever stays.'

'And it still belongs to the de Vil family?' asked Pongo.

'There's only Cruella de Vil left of the family now. Yes, she owns it. She came down here some years ago and had the house painted black. It's red inside, I'm told. But she never lived here. She lets the Baddun brothers have it rent free, as caretakers. I wouldn't let them take care of any kennel of mine.'

Those were the last words Pongo heard, for as the story ended sleep wrapped him round. The Sheepdog stood looking down at the peaceful couple.

'Well, they're in for a shock,' he thought, and then lumbered his way downstairs.

It was less than an hour later when Missis opened her eyes. She had been dreaming of the puppies; she had heard them barking – and they were barking! She sprang out of the straw and dashed to the window. No pup was to be seen but she could hear the barking clearly – it was coming from inside the black house. Then the barking grew louder, the door to the stable yard opened and out came a stream of puppies.

Missis blinked. Surely her puppies could not have grown so much in less than a week? And surely she had not had so many puppies? More and more were hurrying out, the whole yard was filling up with fine, large, healthy Dalmatian puppies, but –

Missis raised her head in a wail of despair. These puppies were not hers at all! The whole thing was a mistake! Her puppies were still lost, perhaps starving, perhaps even dead. Again and again she howled in anguish.

Her first howl had wakened Pongo. He was beside her in a couple of seconds and staring at the yard full of milling, tumbling puppies. And they were still coming out of the house, rather smaller puppies now –

And then they saw him – smaller, even, than they had remembered. Lucky! There was no mistaking that horseshoe of spots on his back.

And after him came Roly Poly, falling over his feet as usual. Then Patch and the tiny Cadpig and all the others. All well, all lashing their tails, all eager to drink at the low troughs of water that stood about in the yard.

'Look, Patch is helping the Cadpig to find a place,' said Missis, delightedly. 'But what does it mean? Where have all those other puppies come from?'

Dazed as he was with sleep, Pongo's keen brain had gone into instant action. He saw it all. Cruella must have begun stealing puppies months before – soon after that evening when she had said she would like a Dalmatian fur coat. The largest pups in the yard looked at least five months old. Then they went down and down in size. Smallest and youngest of all were his own puppies, which must obviously have been the last to be stolen.

He had barely finished explaining this to Missis when the Sheepdog reached the top of the stairs – he had been downstairs getting in fresh water and had heard Missis howl.

'Well, now you know,' he said. 'I was hoping you could have had your sleep out first.'

'But why are you both looking so worried?' asked Missis. 'Our puppies are safe and well.'

'Yes, my dear. You go on watching them,' said Pongo, gently. Then he turned to the Colonel.

'You come downstairs and have a drink, my boy,' said the Colonel.

# In the Enemy's Camp

OH, HOW Pongo needed that drink!

'And now stroll down to the pond with me,' said the Colonel, gripping the handle of a little tin bucket in his teeth. 'You won't feel like trying to sleep any more just at present.'

Pongo felt he would never be able to sleep again.

'I blame myself for letting you in for this shock,' said the Colonel, as they went out into the early morning sunlight. 'Because you can't blame the Lieutenant. She's not a trained observer. When she told me the place was "seething with Dalmatian puppies" I naturally thought she meant your puppies only. After all, fifteen puppies can do quite a bit of seething. It was only yesterday, after I'd made the Folly my headquarters and could see over the wall, that I found out the true facts. Of course I sent the news over yesterday's Twilight Barking but couldn't reach you.'

'How many puppies are there?' asked Pongo.

'Can't tell, exactly, because they never keep still. But I'd say – counting yours – getting on for a hundred.'

'A hundred?'

They had reached the pond. 'Have another drink,' suggested the Colonel.

Pongo gulped down some more water, then stared hopelessly at the Sheepdog.

'Colonel, what am I going to do?'

'Will your lady wife want just to rescue her own puppies?'

'She may at first,' said Pongo. 'But not when she realises it would mean leaving all the others to certain death.'

'Anyway, your pups aren't old enough for the journey,' said the Colonel. 'I suppose you know that?'

Pongo did know it. His plan had been to let his puppies stay at Hell Hall until they were a little bigger, while he and Missis kept watch over them, ready to rescue them if danger threatened. He told the Colonel this.

'And that's exactly what you must do,' said the Colonel.

'But what about the other puppies?'

'I shall spread the news of them throughout England. Other parents may come to the rescue.'

'I doubt it, after all this time,' said Pongo.

'If the worst comes to the worst, would your pets give them a home?'

Pongo couldn't imagine the Dearlys refusing to help any dog. But getting on for a hundred! Still, the drawing-room was very large.

'I don't believe they'd turn them away,' he said. 'But, Colonel, I could never get the whole lot of them to London.'

'Not as they are, of course. Every dog jack of them has to be trained. They must learn to march, to obey orders – I may teach the bigger ones how to forage.'

'I wouldn't mind learning that myself,' said Pongo.

'Splendid! Now how about trying your mouth

at carrying this pail? That's a trick you ought to learn. No, no – hold your head further out. Then the pail won't bang into your chest. Excellent!'

Pongo found he could carry the bucket of water quite easily. His spirits were rising now. With this wonderful old Colonel to help him he would rescue every puppy. He set the bucket down in the Folly.

'You're looking better,' said the Colonel. 'You may be able to sleep now. There's nothing more you and your lady can do until it's dark. Then you shall meet your family. Meanwhile, I'll send in word that you've arrived.'

Something was puzzling Pongo. 'Colonel, why did Cruella steal so many Dalmatians? She can't want more than one Dalmatian fur coat?'

The Sheepdog looked astonished. 'Surely you know her husband's a furrier? I understand she only married him for his furs.'

So that was it! Pongo had forgotten. But if the de Vils planned to sell Dalmatian coats to the public, then Hell Hall was nothing less than a Dalmatian fur farm and no Dalmatian would ever be safe again unless Cruella's career came to an end. 'I must cope with that when I get back to London,' thought Pongo, grimly, as he mounted the stairs.

He found Missis stretched out on the bare boards by the window. She had watched until the puppies had all gone in, then toppled into sleep. He pulled straw around her and lay down very close, to keep her warm. She did not stir. His last waking thoughts were humble ones. He had expected the Sheepdog to be some doddering old country gaffer. How much now depended on this shrewd, kind old soldier!

It was dark when the Colonel woke them.

'All still well with the pups, but no news of any other parents over the Twilight Barking. I sent word of your safe arrival and good wishes to you came pouring in. All Dogdom awaits news from this quiet village. I've said you'll bark a few words yourself when you're fully rested.'

'Willingly,' said Pongo.

'Now down we go to dinner,' said the Colonel. They went down and had an excellent meal of sausages which the cat had collected during the day. She was away at the farm – the Colonel said there would be hurt feelings if she did not join her pets at tea, to drink a saucer of milk. 'And I must go back later, because my young pet, Tommy, likes me there while he has his bath. So let's be moving.'

He rose and pushed open a window. 'The defences of Hell Hall are childish,' he said. 'What's the use of padlocked gates at the front when one can get in at the back, through this Folly?'

Pongo then saw that the Folly had a door and a window opening on to the grounds of Hell Hall as well as the door and window opening on to the heath and was, indeed, a sort of gatehouse. The Colonel had originally entered through the window on the heath side. The door into the grounds was bolted on the Hell Hall side, so the Colonel led Pongo and Missis through the window.

'Now we'll be cautious,' he said. 'That window might blow shut and there's no handle on the

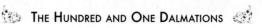 

outside. And it might take some time to unbolt this door.' He drew back the bolt on the door into the Folly, pushed the door open and rolled a heavy stone against it. 'Now, if you should want to get out in a hurry – But I don't think you will. Shouldn't wonder if you couldn't spend the night with your pups.'

Missis gasped with delight and began to ask questions.

'I'll explain as we go,' said the Colonel, starting towards Hell Hall.

A full moon was rising above the black house.

'Colonel, what's that on the roof?' said Pongo. 'Surely it isn't television – here?'

'Oh, yes, it is,' said the Colonel. 'And there's scarcely a cottage in the village hasn't got it since the electricity came. Mostly on the Hire Purchase – though there won't be much Purchase here. I'm told the Badduns haven't paid anything for months.'

He then outlined his plans, and it soon appeared that television played an important part in them. The Baddun brothers were so fond of it that they could not bear any puppy to bark while it was on. And unless the puppies were warm they barked like mad. The warmest room in the house was the kitchen – which was where the television set was – so that was where the pups now lived (unless they were taking exercise in the stable yard). Some pups liked watching the television, some just slept; anyway, none of them barked, so the Badduns could enjoy themselves in peace. All this the Colonel had heard from Lucky, during long, barked conversations.

'That lad of yours is as bright as a button,' said the Colonel. 'He's months ahead of his age.'

Pongo and Missis swelled with pride.

The plan was that Lucky should bring his brothers and sisters out to the stable yard while the Badduns were watching television.

'But it will be too cold for them to stay out long,' said the Colonel, 'and I don't see why you shouldn't go back into the kitchen with them. Lucky tells me there's no light except from the TV screen, so if you crouch down you should be quite safe. Even if the Badduns do see you, they'll just think you're two of the larger pups. But there's hardly any chance you will be seen because Lucky tells me the Badduns stay glued to the TV until it ends and then roll over and go to sleep – they've got mattresses on the kitchen floor. I see no reason why you shouldn't spend the night there. I'll call you at dawn and you can get out before the Badduns wake.'

Pongo and Missis thought this was a wonderful idea.

'Can we sleep there every night?' asked Missis.

The Colonel said he hoped so and that it was at night that the pups would have to be drilled and trained for their march to London.

'Lucky says nothing wakes the Badduns, so I plan to come into the kitchen. I shall hold classes there and drill ten pups at a time in the stable yard. But you two must spend a quiet night there first and report conditions to me.'

By now they were almost at the stable yard.

'Don't tell me any more now, Colonel,' said Pongo. 'I'm too excited to take it in. Are you all right, Missis?'

For Missis was trembling. 'I can't believe I'm really going to see them,' she said.

The Colonel opened the gate to the stable yard. Missis gave a soft moan and hurled herself across the yard. She had seen Lucky. There he stood, at the back door, waiting for them.

And behind him, in the long dark passage leading to the kitchen, were all his brothers and sisters. Who could describe what the mother and father felt during the next few minutes, as they tried to cuddle fifteen wagging, wriggling, licking puppies all at once? Everyone tried to be quiet but there were so many whimpers of bliss, so much happy snuffling, that the Sheepdog got nervous.

'Will they hear in there?' he asked Lucky.

'What, the Badduns?' said Lucky – rather indistinctly, because he had his mother's ear in his mouth. 'No, they've got their precious television on extra loud.'

Still, the Colonel was relieved when the first joy of the meeting was over.

'Quiet, now!' said Pongo.

'Quiet as mice!' said Missis.

But they were pleasantly surprised at how quiet the pups instantly were. The only sound came from some dead leaves stirred by fifteen lashing little tails.

'Now, still!' said Lucky.

All the tails stopped wagging.

'I'm teaching them to obey orders,' said Lucky to the Colonel.

'Good boy, good boy. Let's see, I made you a Corporal this afternoon, didn't I? I now make you a Sergeant. If all goes well, you shall have your Commission next week. Now I'm off to see my little pet, Tommy, have his bath.'

He told Pongo he would be back in a couple of hours. 'Slip out and tell me what you think of things – or send the Sergeant with a message.'

'Won't you come in and see the TV, sir?' said Lucky.

'Not while the Badduns are awake,' said the Colonel. 'Even they couldn't mistake me for a Dalmatian.'

As soon as he had gone, Lucky sent the other

puppies to the kitchen, then took his father and mother in.

'You must stay at the back until your eyes get used to the dark,' he said.

And, indeed, it was dark! The only light came from the television screen and the kitchen fire, which were at opposite ends of the very large kitchen. And as the walls and ceiling were painted dark red they reflected no light. It was extremely warm – much warmer than one fire could have made it. This was because there was

central heating. Cruella de Vil had put it in when she planned to live in the house.

At last Pongo and Missis found they could see fairly well, and it was a strange sight they saw. Only a few feet away from the television, two men lay sprawled on old mattresses, their eyes fixed on the screen. Behind them were ranged row after row of puppies, small pups at the front, large pups at the back. Those who did not care for television were asleep round the kitchen fire. The hot, red room was curiously cosy, though Pongo felt it was a bit like being inside a giant's mouth.

Lucky whispered: 'I thought we could settle Mother with the family and then I could show you around a bit. All the pups want to get a glimpse of you. Father, you are going to rescue them all?'

'I hope so,' said Pongo, earnestly – wondering more and more how he was going to manage it.

'I told them you would, but they've been pretty nervous. I'll just send the word round that they can count on you.' He whispered to a pup at the end of a row and the word travelled like wind over a cornfield. There was barely a sound that a human ear could have heard, except a couple of tail thumps, instantly repressed. All knew they must not give away the fact that Pongo was in their midst, and when he went silently along the rows there was scarcely a movement. But he could feel great waves of love and trust rolling towards him. And suddenly all the pups were real and living for him, not just a problem he had to face. He felt as if he were the father of them all. And he knew that he could never desert them.

He felt a special sympathy for the big pups in the two back rows. Some of them were fully half-grown – young dogs rather than puppies, lollopy creatures with clumsy feet. They made him remember his own, not very far away, youth. He wondered how long their skins would be safe from Cruella – would she have the patience to wait much longer? Did the big pups know that danger drew closer every day? Something in their eyes told him they did. And many of them had been in this horrible place for months, without hope, until Lucky had spread the news that his father and mother were coming. Proud Lucky now, taking his father along the rows of hero-worshipping pups!

Blissfully happy, Missis sat with her children clustered about her. She had eyes only for them but they were determined she should not miss the television. She had never seen it before (Mr and Mrs Dearly did not care for it) and found it difficult to follow. The pups did not follow it completely as they had not yet learned enough human words; but they liked the little moving figures, and watched in the perpetual hope of seeing dogs on the screen.

'Can we have it when we get back home?' said the Cadpig.

'Indeed, you shall, my darling,' said Missis. Somehow, somehow, the Dearlys must be made to buy a set.

Pongo had now silently 'met' all the pups. He told Lucky he would like to have a good look at the Badduns. So Lucky took him a little way up the back staircase, where they could see without being noticed.

No one would have guessed that Saul and Jasper Baddun were brothers. Saul was heavy and dark, with a forehead so low that his bushy eyebrows often got tangled with his matted hair. Jasper was thin and fair, with a chin so sharp and pointed that it had worn holes in all his shirts – not that he had many. Both brothers looked very dirty.

'They never change their awful old clothes,' whispered Lucky, 'and they never wash. I don't think they are real humans, Father. Is there such a thing as a half-human?'

Pongo could well believe it after seeing the Badduns, but he couldn't imagine what their non-human half was. It was no animal he had ever seen.

'Have they ill-treated any of you?' he asked, anxiously.

'No, they're too frightened of being bitten,' said Lucky. 'They're terrible cowards. Some of the big pups did think of attacking them –

but there seemed no way of getting out. And if they'd killed the Badduns there would have been no one to feed us. Oh, Father, how glad I am you've come!'

Pongo licked his son's ear. Pups, like boys, do not like fathers to be too sentimental (mothers are different), but this was a very private moment.

Then they went and sat with Missis and the family. It seemed strange that they could all be so peaceful right in the enemy's camp. Gradually the Pongos' puppies fell asleep – all except Lucky, Patch and the Cadpig. Lucky was not sleepy. Patch was – but stayed awake because the Cadpig was awake. And the Cadpig stayed awake because she was crazy about television.

Many of the big pups, too, were lying down to sleep, stretching luxuriously, feeling – for the first time since they had been imprisoned in Hell Hall – that there was someone they could rely on. Pongo had come! And Missis, too. They had looked at her shyly, quite understanding that she must care for her own children first, but hoping she would have a little time for them later. Some of them could hardly remember their mothers. But the younger pups could remember theirs and they were not sleeping. Slowly, silently, they were inching their way towards Missis.

She had been watching the television, beginning to get the hang of it, with the Cadpig's help. Then some tiny sound, close at hand, brought her attention back to her family. But the sound had not come from her family. There were now nearly thirty puppies, not so very much bigger than her own, just a few feet away, all staring at her hopefully.

'Goodness, they're grubby,' was her first thought. 'Didn't their mothers teach them to wash themselves?'

Then she felt a pang of pity. What mother had any of them now? She smiled at them all – and they wrinkled their little noses in a return smile. Then she looked beyond them, to the larger pups. Some of the half-grown girls reminded her of herself at their age – so slim, so silly. They knew how to wash themselves but there were many things they didn't know, many ways in which they needed a mother's advice. And suddenly all the puppies were her puppies, she was their mother – just as Pongo had felt he was their father. And, indeed, the younger ones creeping closer and closer to her were now so mingled with her own that she could scarcely tell where her little family ended and her larger family began.

Drowsiness spread throughout the warm, red room. Even the Baddun brothers dozed. They did not much like the programme that was on the television and wanted to be fresh for their very favourite programme, which was due later. Even Missis slept a little, knowing that Pongo would keep watch. At last only three pairs of eyes were open. Pongo was wide awake, thinking, thinking. Lucky was wide awake, for he thought of himself as a sentry, who must not sleep on duty. And the Cadpig was wide awake, watching her lovely, lovely television.

Suddenly there was a thunder of thumps on the front door. The sleeping pups awoke in alarm. The Baddun brothers lumbered to their feet and stumbled towards the door. But before

they got there it had
been flung open.

Outside, against the
moonlit sky, stood a
figure in a long white
cloak.

It was Cruella de Vil.

# Sudden Danger

FOR A FEW seconds, she stared into the dimly lit room. Then she shouted:

'Saul! Jasper! Turn off that television! And turn on the light!'

'We can't turn on the light because we've no electric bulbs left,' said Saul Baddun. 'When the telly finishes, we go to bed.'

'And if we turn the telly off there'll be no light at all,' said Jasper Baddun.

'Well, turn the sound off, anyway,' said Cruella, angrily.

Jasper did as he was told, and the little figures moving on the screen were suddenly voiceless. The Cadpig yapped indignantly. Missis, who was crouching low in the midst of her family, instantly hushed her. Pongo, also crouched low, got ready to spring at Cruella if she attacked any pup. But she seemed scarcely to notice any of them. Those near her shrank back as she strode into the room.

'I've got a job for you, my lads,' she said to the Badduns. 'The pups must be killed tonight – every single one of them.'

The Badduns gaped at her. 'But they're not big enough to be made into fur coats yet,' said Saul.

'The largest ones are, and the little ones can be made into gloves. Anyway, they've got to die – before someone finds them. There's been so much in the papers about the Dearlys' dogs. All England's on the hunt for Dalmatians.'

'But how could anyone find them here?' said Jasper Baddun. 'Why can't they just stay on, growing bigger and bigger?'

'It's too risky,' said Cruella. 'Someone might hear them yapping and tell the police. My husband's going to ship the skins abroad – except the ones I keep for my own coat. I shall have it reversible – Persian lamb one side and Dalmatian dog the other – and wear the dog inside until people forget about the Dearlys' pups. When that happens, I'll collect another lot and we'll start our Dalmatian fur farm again. But this lot must be got rid of – quickly.'

'How?' said the Badduns, both together.

'Any way you like. Poison them, drown them, hit them on the head. Have you any chloroform in the larder?'

'Not a drop,' said Saul Baddun. 'And no ether, either.'

'We can't afford luxuries,' growled Jasper Baddun.

'Drown them, then.'

'Dogs can swim,' said Saul Baddun. 'Anyway, the pond's less than a foot deep.'

'Then you must hit them on the head,' said Cruella.

Saul Baddun had gone pale. 'What, hit ninety-seven pups on the head?' he said, shakily. 'We couldn't do it. Have pity, Mrs de Vil. We'd be wore out.'

'Listen,' said Cruella de Vil. 'I don't care how you kill the little beasts. Hang them, suffocate them, drop them off the roof – good gracious, there are dozens of lovely ways. I only wish I'd time to do the job myself.'

'Couldn't you make time, Mrs de Vil?' said Jasper. 'You'd do it so beautifully – it'd be a pleasure to watch you.'

Cruella shook her head. 'I've got to get back to London.' Then a fiendish look came into her eyes. 'Here's an idea for you. Shut them up without food and then they'll kill each other.'

'But they'd make such a horrible noise about it,' said Saul Baddun. 'We'd never be able to hear the telly.'

'Besides, they'd damage each other's skins,' said Cruella. 'That would ruin their value. You must kill them carefully. Then you can start the skinning.'

'But we can't skin them!' wailed Jasper. 'We don't know how.'

'My husband will show you,' said Cruella. 'We'll both drive down tomorrow night. And we shall count the bodies – just remember that, will you? If you've let even one pup escape, I'll turn you out of Hell Hall. Now you'd better get busy. Goodnight.'

Fortunately, few of the pups knew enough Human to understand Cruella's words fully, but they all felt she was evil. And as she made her way to the door she aimed a kick at a small pup who was dangerously close to her. It was more frightened than hurt but it gave a loud wail of anguish. Several of the bigger pups snarled indignantly at Cruella. Lucky, remembering the time he had nibbled her ear, barked out hastily: 'Don't bite her, chaps! She tastes hot!'

So Cruella got to the door unhurt. She flung it open and the moonlight shone on her black-and-white hair and her absolutely simple white mink cloak. Then she looked back at the roomful of puppies.

'Goodbye, you horrid little beasts,' she said. 'I shall like you so much better when you're skins instead of pups. And I shall simply love the ones who are made into my own coat. How I'm looking forward to it!'

They saw her walk out past the pond which reflected the black house, and on to the great iron gates, which she unlocked and locked again, behind her. Then, through the silent winter night, came the sound of a powerful car driving away, followed by one strident blast from the loudest motor-horn in England.

How well Pongo and Missis remembered that terrifying sound! It took them back to the happy evening when they had stood beside the striped black-and-white car on the Outer Circle. How safe and contented they had been then, little guessing what dangers lay ahead!

Jasper Baddun hurriedly shut the front door, saying: 'If we've got to do the pups in, we'd better keep them all in one place.'

Pongo felt stunned. If only he could think! If only the Sheepdog were there to advise him!

Missis whispered: 'If you wish to attack those villains, I will help you, Pongo.'

Lucky said quickly: 'They always carry knives.'

Pongo's brain was beginning to work. 'If we attack them, they may kill us,' he whispered to Missis. 'And then there will be no one to help the pups. Quiet! Let me think.'

The Badduns were talking together in low grunts.

'One thing's certain,' said Jasper. 'We can't do it tonight or we shall miss *What's My Crime?*'

It was their very favourite television programme. Two ladies and two gentlemen, in faultless evening dress, had to guess the crime committed by a lady or gentleman in equally faultless evening dress. Stern moralists said this programme was causing a crime wave and filling the prisons, because people committed crimes in the hope of being chosen as contestants. But crime is usually waving and the prisons are usually full, so probably *What's My Crime?* had not made much difference. Both the Badduns longed to appear as contestants, but they knew they would never be chosen unless they committed a really original crime, and they had never been able to think of one.

'We could kill the pups after *What's My Crime?*, Jasper,' said Saul. 'We ought to do it tonight, while they're sleepy. They'll be more dangerous when they're wide awake.'

'It's a nuisance, that's what it is,' said Jasper. 'And whatever way we do it we shall be exhausted. First the killing and then the skinning!'

'Maybe we'll get the knack of the skinning,' said Saul. 'Then we can skin while we watch the telly.'

'Still, ninety-seven pups!' said Jasper. Then a wild gleam came into his eyes. 'Saul, I bet no one else has ever murdered ninety-seven Dalmatians. It might do the trick for us! It might get us on to *What's My Crime?*

'Now you're talking!' said Saul Baddun. 'You and me, in evening dress with carnations in our buttonholes – and all England watching us. But we must think out some really striking way of doing our crime. Could we skin them alive?'

'They'd never keep still,' said Jasper. 'What about boiling them?'

Pongo whispered to Missis: 'We shall have to attack. It's our only hope.'

'I'll get the biggest pups to help you,' said Lucky, quietly. 'We'll all help. I can bite quite well.'

And then – something happened! The Cadpig, whose eyes were fixed on the silent television screen, gave three short, sharp barks. No human ear would have known that those barks meant *What's My Crime?*, but the Baddun brothers, startled by the noise, looked towards the Cadpig and, in doing so, noticed the television screen. Saul Baddun let out a roar of rage, Jasper Baddun gave a howl of misery. It was on! *What's My Crime?* – but without any sound, of course. They were missing it, their favourite of all programmes, and just when for the first time they had hopes of appearing on it! They hurled themselves at the television set. Saul turned the sound on full blast. Jasper adjusted the picture. Then they flung themselves down on their mattresses, grunting with delight.

'They won't stir for the next half-hour,' whispered Lucky.

At last Pongo's brain sprang into full action! Instantly he whispered to Lucky: 'March the pups out to the stable yard! Your mother and I will mount guard over the Badduns.'

Lucky whispered: 'If we could go out through the larder, we could eat tomorrow's breakfast on our way. That's the door – by the fireplace. It's bolted, but I expect you can unbolt it, can't you, Father?'

Pongo had never even tried to unbolt a door, but he had seen the Sheepdog do it. 'Yes, Lucky,' he said firmly. 'I can unbolt it.'

They tiptoed across the kitchen. Then Pongo stood on his hind legs and took the bolt in his teeth. It would not budge. He rested his teeth and took a good look at the bolt in the light from the fire. He saw the knob was turned down and would have to be raised before the bolt would slide.

'Now we shan't be long,' he said to Lucky, and again took the knob in his teeth. He raised it, tried to slide it. Still it would not slide. He thought: 'Lucky will lose confidence in me,' and he dragged and dragged until he thought his teeth would break. Then he began to fear that if the bolt did shoot back it would make a loud noise. Just then there was a burst of applause from the television – someone had guessed a contestant.

(He had stolen two hundred bath plugs from hotels.) Pongo made a desperate effort. The bolt shot back. The larder door swung open.

'I knew you'd do it, Father,' said Lucky, proudly.

'Just a matter of knowing how,' said Pongo, running his tongue round his teeth to make sure they were all still there.

A cold draught came from the larder. It had been the dairy when Hell Hall was a farm and there were wooden slats instead of windows. The moonlight, shining in through the slats, made bright stripes on the stone floor. Meat for the puppies' breakfast was already set out in long troughs – because the Badduns hated working in the early morning. There were small troughs for the little pups and big ones for the larger pups.

Pongo said to Lucky: 'Wait until I get back to your mother. Then, while she and I stand ready to attack the Badduns, march all the pups in here. Tell them no pup is to eat until the last pup has a place at a trough. I will join you then and give the word to start eating.'

It was remarkable how quickly the pups left the kitchen, under Sergeant Lucky's whispered directions. Row after row marched out, like children leaving a school hall after prayers, except that the big pups left first, as they were nearest the door. Pongo and Missis watched the Badduns anxiously, for the hundreds of little toenails made a clitter-clatter on the kitchen floor and there were a few scuffles, snuffles and snorts – though never even the smallest bark, for the pups guessed their lives depended on their silence. But the Badduns had eyes and ears for nothing but television.

Lucky left his own brothers and sisters to the last – and last of all to leave was the Cadpig. She was an intelligent little puppy and quite understood that she had to escape, but, oh, how she hated leaving the television! She went out backwards, still staring at the screen.

Then Pongo and Missis sped swiftly and silently across the big red kitchen. They looked back from the larder door and saw that the Badduns had not stirred.

'How much longer will *What's My Crime?* last?' whispered Pongo.

'Twenty minutes,' said the Cadpig, promptly and wistfully.

Pongo and Missis closed the larder door. The bolt on the inside was low down and easy to manage. Pongo shot it home at once, while the pups looked on admiringly. Every pup had its place at a trough but not one lick of food had been eaten.

'One, two, three – feed!' commanded Pongo.

In fifty-nine seconds flat every scrap of food had been eaten.

'But what about you and Mother?' said Lucky. 'I think I can find the Badduns' Sunday dinner.'

He found it, on a shelf – two steaks, rather poor grade, but Pongo and Missis swiftly ate them. Then Pongo gave troops the right to forage and led a search through the larder. Everything eatable was eaten, the big pups sharing with the little pups most fairly.

'Anything in that cupboard?' said Pongo, at last.

'Only coke for the central-heating furnace,' said Lucky. 'Well, the Badduns won't find anything to eat tomorrow, will they?'

'Let them eat coke,' said Pongo.

The entire meal had taken nearly five minutes. Pongo now felt he must get his troops out of Hell Hall as fast as possible. There had been no time to think out plans for the future – he was counting on the Colonel's advice. All that could be done now was to lead the pups to the Folly. The outer door of the larder was easily opened, then across the old orchard they went and in at the door which the Colonel had so thoughtfully propped open. Missis gave one backwards glance at black Hell Hall under the full moon. What would the Badduns do when they found not one pup in the kitchen?

There was not room for ninety-seven pups on the ground floor of the Folly, nor would there have been in the crowded upstairs rooms, so Pongo marched everyone out on to the heath. As the last pup marched out, the Sheepdog arrived.

At first he thought Pongo had recklessly

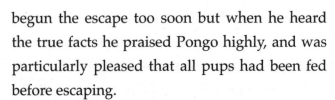 

begun the escape too soon but when he heard the true facts he praised Pongo highly, and was particularly pleased that all pups had been fed before escaping.

'That was Sergeant Lucky's idea,' said Pongo, proudly.

'Good work, Sergeant-Major,' said the Colonel.

'But where are we to go?' asked Missis, anxiously. 'Look, the puppies are shivering.'

They were, indeed, for though it was not freezing it seemed terribly cold to them all after the warm kitchen.

The Sheepdog looked worried – not that anyone could see this as his expressions were always hidden by hair. What was he to do, at a moment's notice, with ninety-seven Dalmatian puppies and two full-grown Dalmatians? At last he said:

'Our big barn for the night, anyway. Pups can keep warm in the straw. It's only half a mile across the heath.'

Half a mile! How little to Pongo and Missis! How much, how terribly much to the tiny

Cadpig! After even a few hundred yards, Pongo was in despair about the long journey to London which lay ahead.

The big pups ran along happily. The medium-sized pups did quite well. Even most of the smaller pups looked as if they were capable of a reasonably long walk. But the smallest pups of all – Pongo's own family – how were they to walk over seventy miles? Lucky, Patch, Roly Poly and the other boys struggled along bravely, but the girls stumbled and panted and had to have many rests. As for the Cadpig, she would never have reached the farm at all if the Sheepdog had not given her a lift. He lay down and she climbed on to his back and held on to his long hair with her teeth. Even so, she nearly slipped off twice.

'She could never stay on our smooth backs,' said Missis to Pongo. 'If only I could wheel her in a doll's perambulator!'

'You couldn't walk to London on your hind legs,' said Pongo, 'even if we had a perambulator.'

At last they reached the big barn at the back of the farm where the Colonel lived. The tired pups snuggled into the hay and straw and instantly fell asleep. Pongo, Missis and the Colonel stood at the door, trying to make plans.

The Colonel said: 'I can't keep you here long. You would be found – besides, I couldn't feed so many. We must get you to London by easy stages, just a few miles a day.'

'But where shall we sleep? Where shall we find food?' said Pongo, anxiously.

'It will need tremendous organisation,' said the Colonel. 'I hope to arrange the first stage at once, by Midnight Barking. I must bark some

distance from the farm or I shall wake my pets.'

Pongo offered to bark with him but the Sheepdog would not hear of it. 'You two must rest. It's now nearly ten o'clock. If my plan goes well I shall wake you at four, when there will still be over three hours of darkness. That will be long enough to get you to the place I have in mind.'

'But my smallest daughter is so weak,' said Missis. 'How can she make any journey?'

The Colonel smiled – not that anyone could see that. 'I have a plan for the little lass,' he said. 'Now, sleep, sleep, both of you.'

So Pongo and Missis went into the dark barn and sniffed out their own family. Only Lucky stirred; he said he was trying to sleep with one eye open, so as to be on guard.

'You close both eyes,' said Missis, firmly.

And Lucky did, quite happy now his parents were there to take charge.

'What would happen if we were found here?' asked Missis. 'Surely the people at the farm are kind? They wouldn't hurt us.'

Pongo had been thinking about this. He guessed that as there had been so much in the papers about himself and Missis and their family, they might all get safely returned to the Dearlys. But the other puppies, what would happen to them? Even the dear, kind Dearlys would not take in eighty-two puppies they did not know. The poor things would be sent to a police station – anything might happen to them. But if once the Dearlys saw them, then all the puppies would suddenly belong to the Dearlys – just as they had suddenly seemed to belong to him, in the dark kitchen. Somehow, somehow he must get them all to London.

Missis felt just the same, but she did not see how the Cadpig and some of her sisters would make the journey.

'Well, sleep, now,' said Pongo, giving her a loving lick. 'Are you glad you didn't, after all, have to bite a human?'

'The Badduns are no more human than Cruella is,' said Missis. 'Still, I'm glad I didn't have to soil my teeth.'

They would not have fallen asleep so easily if they had known what the Sheepdog had just seen. Across the heath, lanterns were moving. The Badduns were out, searching for the missing puppies.

# The Little Blue Cart

PONGO WAS dreaming he was back in Regent's Park running after a stick thrown by Mr Dearly, when a light tap on his shoulder woke him. It was Lieutenant Willow.

'The Colonel's compliments and would you and your lady please come to him?'

Missis was sleeping peacefully. Pongo woke her gently, wondering what dream she would be leaving and if the dark barn would look as strange to her as it had to him a moment earlier. She sprang up at once, dazed and anxious.

'All well,' said the cat, soothingly. 'Food and shelter are arranged for two days ahead. Reception for the Midnight Barking was excellent. Please follow me now.'

She made no mention of the Baddun brothers with their lanterns, searching the heath.

It was still quite dark as they left the barn and

crossed the farmyard. The cat led them to the back door of a large white farm-house.

'Help me to push the door,' she said. 'The Colonel has unbolted it.'

The door opened easily. They went through a kitchen and along a passage, at the end of which was an open door and a glimmer of light. The cat led them through the doorway and they found themselves in a nursery, lit by a night-light. At the far end, the Sheepdog stood beside a little painted bed in which was a very wide-awake two-year-old boy.

'This is my pet, Tommy,' said the Colonel. 'He very much wants to meet you.'

Pongo and Missis went to the little boy and he patted them both. Then he made some odd, chuckling noises. They did not sound like Human nor did they sound like Dog. But the Sheepdog seemed to understand them and Tommy seemed to understand what the Sheepdog answered. Pongo decided this was quite a new language, half-Dog, half-Human.

'Tommy wishes to lend you something,' said

the Colonel. 'He knows how much you need it and is most anxious to help you. See, here it is.'

Pongo and Missis then saw a little wooden cart, painted blue. It was made like a real farm cart, with four high wheels and a wooden railing all round it to keep the hay in – it was full of hay now. At the front was a long piece of wood with a wide cross-bar at the end of it, so that Tommy could drag the cart about.

'You can choose two pups exactly the right size,' said the Colonel, 'and they can use the long piece of wood as a shaft – in between them – and take the cross-bar in their mouths. Then they can pull the cart forward. And, if needed, pups at the back can push with their noses. Your smallest daughter can travel comfortably in the hay, and any puppy who is tired can sit beside her and take a rest.'

Pongo and Missis examined the pretty cart delightedly. They were too big to get between it and the cross-bar themselves but they felt sure plenty of the bigger pups would fit.

'But does he really want us to take it?' asked Missis.

The Sheepdog then spoke to Tommy who nodded his head again and again, while talking his extraordinary language.

'His name and address are painted on the side,' said the Sheepdog, 'and he would be glad if it can be returned one day. But if that isn't possible he will quite understand.'

'If we ever get home, I feel sure Mr Dearly will return it,' said Pongo. 'Please tell Tommy how very grateful we are.'

The Sheepdog translated this to Tommy who smiled more than ever and made more chuckling noises.

'He says he is pleased you are pleased, and would like to see all the puppies. I think it would be safe to march them all past his window when you leave – which should be soon now.'

So they said goodbye to Tommy, and then the Sheepdog, going backwards, pulled the cart along the passage and out through the back door. He had quite a job.

'It's lucky my little pet sleeps on the ground floor,' he said. 'It's because our stairs are so steep.

I could never have got this cart down them.'

They went back to the barn and woke the pups, and all the bigger ones came outside and tried the cart on for size. (The moon was lower now but still gave plenty of light.) One family of eight fitted perfectly, and a dozen other pups could manage quite well, so Pongo arranged that all these should travel close to the cart and take it in turns to pull it, two at a time. The Cadpig was enchanted and settled down in the hay so that pups could practise pulling.

While this was happening, Pongo was told the plans made by Midnight Barking. Only five miles was to be travelled before dawn – which would not be for over three hours – to a village where a friend of the Colonel's lived at a bakery.

'And next door is a butcher's, so food will be all right,' said the Colonel. 'Then you'll do another five miles as soon as it's dark tomorrow – but my friend will tell you all about that. I hope to get you to London in ten or twelve days, billeting you where you can be safely hidden and fed. The last stages of the march will be the most difficult, but there are warehouses, if we can get in touch with their watchdogs. There's a Great Dane somewhere near Hampstead working on that already. Fine fellow. I hear he's a Brigadier-General.'

Ten days or even longer! Missis felt her heart sink.

'Pongo,' she said suddenly, 'when is Christmas Day?'

'The day after tomorrow,' said the Colonel. 'No, bless me, it's tomorrow – because it's Christmas Eve already, even if it isn't light yet. Don't worry, Mrs Pongo. You shall have some Christmas dinner.'

But it was not food Missis was thinking about, but the Dearlys, all alone for Christmas. Sometimes she forgot them for an hour or two, but never for very long. She thought now of that last evening when she had rested her head on Mrs Dearly's knee, trying to make her understand – and of the warm, white drawing-room, where there was to have been a Christmas tree, with presents for the three dogs and the fifteen pups. Missis had heard the Dearlys planning it.

Pongo guessed his wife's thoughts – which was easy to do because his own were much the same. 'Never mind, Missis,' he said. 'We'll be home by next Christmas.'

The pups who were to take turns at pulling the little blue cart were now quite good at it.

'Then off you go,' said the Colonel. 'But first our cows have asked you in to have a drink with them.'

He led Pongo, Missis and all the pups into the dim cow-shed, where the hay still smelt of summer weather. The head cows, Blossom and Clover, were waiting to welcome them and tell them how to drink at the milk-bar. The pups found this easy, especially those who could remember being fed by their mothers – though the smaller pups had to stand on their hind legs and be supported by other pups. The long, warm drink of milk made a splendid breakfast.

At last, after all their kind hostesses had been thanked, it was time to start.

Tommy stood at his window peering into

the moonlight,
watching the march-
past. Pongo and Missis
wrinkled their noses at
him, in their best smile;
every pup turned its head
– except the Cadpig who
lay on her back in the hay-
filled cart and waved all
her four paws.

Pongo said to Missis:
'How different Tommy
is from the bad little boy
who threw a stone at us.'

Missis said: 'The bad
little boy was only bad
because he had never
known dogs.' And she
was probably right.

The Colonel took them
to the crossroads and
started them on their way.

'I wish I could come

with you, but I've a job to do,' he said. Then he and the cat, who was riding on his back, said goodbye hastily and went off so fast that Pongo had to bark his thanks after them. The Colonel barked back that Sergeant-Major Lucky could now be a Lieutenant, then galloped out of sight. Pongo stared in astonishment, wondering what job had to be done in such a hurry. It was a long time before he learned the truth.

The Colonel had just been informed by Lieutenant Willow that the Baddun brothers, having failed to find the puppies on the heath, were now on the outskirts of the village, less than half a mile behind the Dalmatians. He could think of only one thing to do and he set out to do it – with great pleasure.

He galloped until he saw the Badduns' lanterns ahead of him. Then he told the cat to get off his back. The minute she was off, he hurled himself at the Badduns and bit both brothers in both legs. Seldom can four legs have been bitten so fast by one dog. The Badduns howled with rage, fear and pain, dropped their lanterns and limped back to Hell Hall as quickly as possible. (It is difficult to limp well when you are lame in both legs.) They never knew what bit them. They only knew it bit hard.

'Good work, Colonel,' said Lieutenant Willow.

'I'm promoting you to Captain,' said the Sheepdog. Then he gave a modest little cough and added: 'Oh, by the way! I've just made myself a Brigadier-General.'

## Christmas Eve

MEANWHILE, the Dalmatian army was swinging along the road in fine style. Though cold, the night was very still. The pups were rested and hopeful. And the fact that a tired little dog could take a rest with the Cadpig in her cart made tired little dogs feel less tired. Indeed, Missis at first had to insist on the smaller pups taking turns to rest. But progress was not really fast. There were so many pauses while the pups who pulled the cart were changed, pauses while pups got in and out of the cart; and every half-mile, the whole army had a rest. Still, all went wonderfully well until they were within half a mile of the village where they were to spend the day.

There was a hint of dawn in the sky now, but Pongo felt sure they could reach the village before it was dangerously light. He quickened the pace slightly and told the pups to think of breakfast ahead of them at the bakery.

It was soon after this that the Cadpig called out: 'Look! Little painted houses on wheels!'

Pongo saw them at the same moment and he knew they were not houses. They were caravans.

He had seen them once when out with Mr Dearly and had heard Mr Dearly say that gipsies lived in caravans and gipsies sometimes stole valuable dogs.

'Halt!' said Pongo, instantly.

Could they get past the caravans without being seen? He wasn't going to risk it. Between them and the nearest caravan was an open gate. He would lead the puppies through it and take them through the fields until they were well past the caravans. Swiftly he gave his instructions, which were handed on from pup to pup: 'We are to keep dead quiet and follow Pongo through the gate.'

And thus did the owner of one of the keenest brains in Dogdom make one of his few mistakes. For in the caravan nearest to them, an old gipsy woman was awake and looking out of the little back window. She saw the approaching Dalmatians and at once woke her husband. He was beside her at the window just as Pongo led the way into the field.

The old gipsy woman never read newspapers so she knew nothing about the stolen puppies. But she knew that here were many valuable dogs. And she knew something else, which Pongo did not know. There is a connection between Dalmatians and gipsies. Many people believe that it was the gipsies who first brought Dalmatians to England, long, long ago. And nothing like as long ago as that, there were gipsies who travelled round England with Dalmatians trained to do tricks. And these performing dogs earned money for the gipsies. The old woman could remember such dogs and she thought how splendid it would be if all these Dalmatians could be trained as money earners.

'Quick! Close the gate!' she said to her husband. She spoke in the strange gipsy language, which is called Romany. 'The only other way out of that field is through a break in the hedge. I will rouse the camp and we will all stop the dogs there and catch them.'

In less than two minutes, the whole gipsy encampment was awake. Children cried, dogs barked, horses neighed. It was still so dark that it took Pongo five minutes to find the break in the hedge. And when he found it he also found the way barred. All the gipsies were there, with sticks and ropes.

'Back to the gate, as fast as you can!' he cried to the pups.

But when they reached the gate it was closed. They were trapped.

Pongo barked loudly, hoping that some gipsy dog might help him. Many gipsy dogs barked in answer, but they had all been shut up in the caravans in case they should fight the Dalmatians. In any case, they only barked in Romany, so they could not understand a word Pongo said.

But someone else did. Suddenly Pongo heard the high neigh of a horse, close at hand – and, oh, most wonderful, the horse could neigh normally, as well as in Romany. It understood

Pongo and he understood it. Horses are nearly always friendly to Dalmatians – perhaps because of those days when Dalmatians were trained to follow carriages. This horse was not old enough to remember such days but he took an instant liking to Pongo, Missis and all the pups. If these pleasant creatures wished to come out of the field, nothing could be easier. He strolled up, opened the gate with his long, strong teeth and swung it back. Out poured the puppies.

'Lead them past the caravans as fast as you can!' Pongo shouted to Missis, and waited to see the last pup out of the field.

'What a very large family you and your wife have,' said the horse. 'My wife and I have never had more than the one. Well, good luck to you.'

He waved aside Pongo's thanks and then, being a very tidy horse, he carefully closed the gate again. So never did the gipsies – all waiting at the break in the hedge – know how their prisoners got away.

Helter-skelter along the road went Missis, the puppies and, finally, Pongo. (The pups who drew

the Cadpig's cart stuck faithfully to their task.)
The shut-in Romany dogs heard them and shook
the caravans in their efforts to get out. Volleys of
furious barking came from the little windows.

'The caravans bark but the dogs move on,'
remarked Pongo, when he felt they were out
of danger.

A few minutes later they reached the village
where they were to sleep. The Sheepdog's friend,
a handsome Collie, was waiting to welcome them.

'No talk until you're safely hidden,' he said.
'It's almost light.'

Quickly they followed him across the village
green to three old, gabled houses. The baker's
was in the middle, between the butcher's and
the chimney-sweep's. The baker and the butcher
and the sweep were all widowers and, as it was
Sunday, had already gone to spend Christmas
with their married daughters, which was just
as well.

The baker's shop would not have been
nearly big enough to house all the pups but
luckily there was a large bakehouse at the back.

And soon every pup was safely in and enjoying a splendid sausage roll. Pongo and Missis chatted to the Collie while they ate. He shook his head worriedly when he heard about the gipsies.

'A narrow escape,' he said. 'The trouble is that Dalmatians are such noticeable dogs. Ninety-nine of you together are spectacular – though I mean it as a compliment. You'd be so much safer if you were black.'

'Like that nice little pup over there,' said Missis.

'What pup?' The Collie looked across the bakehouse, then said sharply: 'That pup doesn't belong in this village. Who are you, my lad? Where have you come from?'

The black pup did not answer. Instead, he came running to Missis and butted her in the stomach.

'Here, hold hard, young man!' said Missis. Then she gasped: 'Goodness, it is! It isn't! It is Roly Poly!'

The fat puppy who was always getting into mischief had found his way into a shed at the back of the sweep's house and had a fight with a bag of soot.

'Mercy, you'll need some washing!' said his mother.

Then it was that one of the keenest brains in Dogdom had one of its brainiest waves.

'Roly Poly,' said Pongo, 'was there a lot of soot at the sweep's?'

'Bags and bags,' said Roly Poly.

'Then we are all going to be black dogs,' said Pongo.

'Your husband is a genius,' said the Collie to Missis, as he showed them all into the sweep's shed.

There was any amount of soot – waiting to have done with it whatever sweeps do do with soot.

'Ten dogs forward at a time!' commanded Pongo. 'Pups roll! Pups rub noses!'

In a very short time there were ninety-seven pitch-black pups.

'And now, my love,' said Pongo to Missis. 'Let us take a roll in the soot.'

Frankly, Missis did not fancy it. She hated

soiling her gleaming white hair and losing its smart contrast with her beautiful black spots. But when Pongo had helped her with the final touches he said: 'Why, Missis, as a black dog, you're slimmer than ever. You're positively svelte!' And then she felt much better.

Then Pongo said: 'How does soot suit me?'

'Suit soots you beautifully,' said Missis, and all the pups roared with laughter at her mistake.

Then they all went back to the bakehouse and settled down to sleep. The Collie said he would call them as soon as it was dark. They would only have five miles to go – to another bakery – but he felt they should get the journey over early as he had heard there might be snow.

'But there may be cars on the road until late, as it is Christmas Eve – and Sunday,' he told them.

'So you must go by the fields. I shall escort you. Rest well now.'

Poor Missis! When she awoke in the late afternoon and looked around her, she dissolved into sooty tears.

'I can't tell one pup from the other now they're black,' she moaned. But she soon found she could, though she could never have explained how she managed it.

Another meal had been organised but it was not all that could have been wished, because the butcher had meanly locked up his shop.

'This clears the bakery out,' said the Collie, carrying in the last stale loaf. 'But there will be a good supper waiting for you. And the journey oughtn't to take more than three or four hours.' He then went off to see if there was any news coming in by the Twilight Barking.

After half an hour or so, Pongo began to feel anxious. It was quite dark now; they ought to be off. What was delaying the Collie?

'Listen!' said Missis, suddenly.

Very, very faintly, they could hear the Collie barking. He was calling Pongo's name, again and again.

Pongo and Missis ran out of the bakehouse to the little yard at the back. Now they could hear the Collie more clearly. But he was obviously some way off. Pongo barked in answer to him. Then swiftly the Collie told them what had happened.

He was locked in a house across the green, with no hope of getting out. The postmistress had promised to look after him while the baker was away for Christmas. She had decided it was too cold a night for a dog to be out, hauled him in and gone out for the evening. He had tried every door and every window but could undo none of them. It was impossible for him to escort the Dalmatians, as he had promised.

'But you can't miss your way, Pongo,' he

barked. 'Out over the field at the back of the bakehouse and straight on for five miles.'

Pongo told him not to worry. But the poor Collie was most unhappy. 'Here I am, locked in with a warm fire and a good supper – and powerless to help you.'

Both Pongo and Missis told him to eat the supper and enjoy the fire, and thanked him for all he had done.

'And, now, off we go,' said Pongo, bringing the pups out of the bakehouse. 'And no straggling! Because it would be very easy to lose a black pup on a dark night.'

But it was not really a very dark night for already the moon was rising and the stars were out. There was one specially large, bright star.

'The Collie said straight ahead and that star is straight ahead,' said Pongo. 'So we'll steer by it.' He was thankful they were going by way of the fields and not by the road – for he remembered that Cruella had told the Baddun brothers she would come down 'tomorrow night' to count the bodies. Now it was 'tomorrow night' and the great, zebra-striped car would be somewhere on the road from London to Suffolk. How terrible it would be to meet it! He imagined the glare from the headlights, imagined Cruella driving straight at the army of panic-stricken puppies. Yes, he would certainly avoid the roads! But, even so, it was frightening to know that Cruella might be quite near. He put the thought from his mind, as he and Missis got the pups into marching order.

Their way lay through grassy meadows over which the Cadpig's cart trundled smoothly. At every hedge and ditch, Pongo paused and counted the pups to see none had strayed, and Missis changed the pups who drew the cart and the pups who rested in it. Already even the smallest puppies were getting hardier – even the Cadpig got out of the cart and walked three fields before getting in again.

'Soon we shall be able to do ten miles a day,' said Pongo.

They had travelled about three miles when the first disaster of the night happened. There was a sudden bump, and a wild squeal from the

Cadpig. A wheel had come off the little blue cart.

Pongo saw at once that the cart could be mended. A wooden peg which fixed the hub of the wheel to the axle had come out. But could he ever, using his teeth, put this peg back? He tried – and failed.

'Could the Cadpig manage without the cart?' he whispered to Missis.

Missis shook her head. Walking three fields had been enough for her smallest daughter. And her other daughters could not walk more than a mile without a rest.

'Then mend the cart I must,' said Pongo. 'And you must help me, by holding the wheel in position.'

They tried and tried, without success. Then, while they were resting for a moment, Missis noticed that many of the pups were shivering.

'They'd better keep warm by running races,' said Pongo.

'But that would tire them,' said Missis. 'Couldn't they all go to that barn over there?'

They could just see a big, tiled roof, two short

fields away – not very clearly, because the moon was behind clouds; it was this lack of light which made it so hard to mend the cart.

'That's a good idea,' said Pongo. 'And when the cart's mended we can bring it along and call for them all.'

Missis said the Cadpig had better stay in the cart and keep warm in the hay, but the Cadpig wanted to go with the others and see the barn – she felt sure she could walk two short fields. So Missis let her go. Two strong pups the right size to draw the cart stayed behind. They said they did not mind the cold.

So ninety-five pups, led by Lieutenant Lucky, set off briskly for the barn. But when they got there it did not look at all like the barn at the Sheepdog's farm. It was built of grey stone and had long windows, some with coloured glass in them, and at one end was a tower.

'Why, there's a Folly!' said the Cadpig, remembering the tower of the Folly at Hell Hall.

Lucky was looking for a door, but when he found one it was firmly shut. He told the pups to wait for him, while he went round the building looking for some other way in.

The Cadpig did not wait. 'Come on,' she said to her devoted brother, Patch. 'I want to look at that Folly.'

And when they got to the tower they saw a narrow door that was not quite closed. It was too heavy for them to push but they could – just … just – squeeze through.

Inside, this tower was nothing like the one at Hell Hall. And it opened into the grey stone building.

'No hay in this barn,' said the Cadpig.

She had counted on the hay for warmth, but she soon found she was warm enough without it, for there was a big stove alight. It had a long iron pipe for a chimney which went right up through the raftered ceiling. The moon was out again now and its light was streaming in through the tall windows, so that the clear glass made silver patterns on the stone floor and the coloured glass made blue, gold and rose patterns. The Cadpig patted one of the

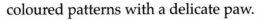 

coloured patterns with a delicate paw.

'I love this barn,' she said.

Patch said: 'I don't think it is a barn.' But he liked it as much as the Cadpig did.

They wandered around – and suddenly they made a discovery. Whatever this mysterious place was, it was certainly intended for puppies. For in front of every seat – and there were many seats – was a puppy-sized dog-bed, padded and most comfortable.

'Why, it's just meant for us all to sleep in!' said the Cadpig.

'I'll tell the other pups,' said Patch, starting for the door. A glad cry from the Cadpig called him back.

'Look, look! Television!'

But it was not like the television at Hell Hall. It was much larger. And the figures on the screen did not move or speak. Indeed, it was not a screen. The figures were really there, on a low platform, humans and animals, most life-like, though smaller than in real life. They were in a stable, above which was one bright star.

'Look at the little humans, kneeling,' said Patch.

'And there's a kind of a cow,' said the Cadpig, remembering the cows at the farm, who had given all the pups milk.

'And a kind of a horse,' said Patch, remembering the helpful horse who had let them all out of the field.

'No dogs,' said the Cadpig. 'What a pity! But I like it much better than ordinary television. Only I don't know why.'

Then they heard Lucky and the others, who had found their way in. Soon every pup was curled up on a comfortable dog-bed and fast asleep – except the Cadpig. She had dragged along one of the dog-beds by its most convenient little carpet ear, and was sitting on it, wide awake, gazing and gazing at this new and far more beautiful television.

Once the moon came out from behind the clouds Pongo managed to mend the wheel – oh, the feeling of satisfaction when the peg slipped into place! Missis, too, felt proud. Had she not held the wheel? She, a dog who had never understood machinery! Quickly the two waiting pups seized the cross-bar in their mouths. Then off they all went to the barn.

But, as they drew nearer, Pongo saw this was no barn.

'Surely they can't have gone in there?' he said to Missis.

'Why not, if they were cold?' said Missis. 'And they are far too young to know they would not be welcome.'

Pongo and Missis both knew that humans did not like dogs to go into buildings which had towers and tall, narrow windows. They had no idea why, and had at first been a little hurt when told firmly to wait outside. But Mrs Dearly had once said: 'We would love you to come in if it was allowed. And I would go in far oftener if you could.' So it was obviously one of those mysterious things such as no one – not even humans – ever being allowed to walk on certain parts of the grass in Regent's Park.

'We must get them out quickly,' said Pongo, 'and go on with our journey.'

They soon found the door in the tower – which the biggest pups had pushed wide open. Because Missis had always been left outside, she disliked these curious buildings with towers and high windows, but the minute she got inside she changed her mind. This was a wonderful place – so peaceful and, somehow, so welcoming.

'But where are the pups?' she said, peering all around.

She saw lots of black patches on the moonlit floor but had quite forgotten that all the pups were now black. Then she remembered and as she drew nearer to the sleeping pups, tears sprang to her eyes.

'Look, look at all the puppybeds!' she cried. 'What good people must live here!'

'It can't be the kind of place I thought it was,' said Pongo.

He was about to wake the puppies when Missis stopped him.

'Let me sit by the stove for a little while,' she said.

'Not too long, my dear,' said Pongo.

He need not have worried. Missis only sat still for a few minutes. Then she got up, shook herself and said brightly: 'Let us start now. Things are going to be all right.'

An hour or so later, just before the evening service, the Verger said to the Vicar:

'I think there must be something wrong with the stove, sir.'

On every hassock he had found a small, circular patch of soot.

## Miracle Needed

'LAST LAP before supper,' said Pongo, as they started off again across the moonlit fields.

It was the most cheering thing he could have said, for the ninety-seven puppies were now extremely hungry. He had guessed this because he was hungry himself. And so was Missis. But she was feeling too peaceful to mind.

They went on for nearly two miles, then Pongo saw a long row of cottage roofs ahead across the fields.

'This should be it,' he said.

'What is that glow in the sky beyond the roof-tops?' asked Missis.

Pongo was puzzled. He had seen such a glow in the sky over towns which had many lights, but never over a village. And this was a very bright glow. 'Perhaps it's a larger place than we expected it to be,' he said, and did not feel it would be safe to go any nearer until some dog came to meet them. He called a halt and barked news of their arrival.

He was answered at once, by a bark that said: 'Wait where you are. I am coming.' And, though he did not tell Missis, Pongo felt there was something odd about this bark that answered his. For one thing, there were no cheerful words of welcome.

Soon a graceful red Setter came dashing towards them. They guessed, even before she spoke, that something was very wrong.

'The bakery's on fire!' she gasped.

The blaze, due to a faulty chimney, had begun only a few minutes before – the fire engine had not yet arrived. No one had been hurt, but the bakehouse was full of flames and smoke – all the food spread out for the Dalmatians was burned.

'There's nothing for you to eat and nowhere for you to sleep,' moaned the poor Setter – she was hysterical. 'And the village street's full of people.' She looked pitifully at Missis. 'All your poor hungry puppies!'

The strange thing was that Missis felt quite calm. She tried to comfort the Setter, saying they would go to some barn.

'But no arrangements are made,' wailed the Setter. 'And there's no spare food anywhere. All the village dogs brought what they could to the bakery.'

Just then came a shrill whistle.

'My pet is calling me,' said the Setter. 'He's the doctor here. There's no dog at the bakery, so I was chosen to arrange everything – because I took first prize in a Dog Show. And now I've failed you.'

'You have not failed,' said Missis. 'No one could say the fire was an act of dog. Go back to your pet and don't worry. We shall simply go on to the next village.'

'Really?' said the Setter, gasping again – but with relief.

Missis kissed her on the nose. 'Off with you, my dear, and don't give the matter another thought. And thank you for all you did.'

The whistle came again and the Setter ran off,

wildly waving her feathered tail.

'Feather-brained as well as feather-tailed,' said Pongo.

'Just very young,' said Missis, gently. 'I doubt if she's had a family yet. Well, on to the next village.'

'Thank you for being so brave, dear Missis,' said Pongo. 'But where is the next village?'

'In the country, there are villages in every direction,' said Missis, brightly.

Desperately worried though he was, Pongo smiled lovingly at her. Then he said: 'We will go to the road now.'

'But what about traffic, Pongo?'

'We shall not be very long on the road,' said Pongo.

Then he told her what he had decided. Even if the next village should only be a few miles away, many of the pups were too tired and too hungry to get there – some of them were already asleep on the frozen ground. And every minute it got colder.

'And, even if we could get to the next village,

where should we sleep, Missis, what should we eat, with no plans made ahead? We must give in, my dear. Come, wake the pups! Quick march, everyone!'

The waking pups whimpered and shivered, and Missis saw that even the strongest pups were now wretchedly cold. So she helped Pongo to make them all march briskly. Then she whispered: 'But how do we give in, Pongo?'

Pongo said: 'We must go into the village and find the police station.'

Missis stared at him in horror. 'No, Pongo, no! The police will take the puppies from us!'

'But they will feed them, Missis. And perhaps we shall be kept together until Mr Dearly has been told about us. They will have read the papers. They will know we are the Missing Dalmatians.'

'But we are not Dalmatians any more, Pongo,' cried Missis. 'We are black. They will think we are ordinary stray dogs. And we are illegal – ninety-nine dogs without collars. We shall be put in prison.'

'No, Missis!' But Pongo was shaken. He had

forgotten they were now black dogs. Suppose the police did not recognise them? Suppose the Dearlys were never told about them? What happened to stray dogs that no one claimed?

'Please, Pongo, I beg you!' cried Missis. 'Let us go on with our journey! I know it will be all right.'

They had now reached the road and were on the edge of the village. Pongo was faced with a terrible choice. But it still seemed to him wiser to trust the police than to lead the hungry, exhausted puppies into the bitter winter night.

'Missis, dear Missis, we must go to the police station,' he said, and turned towards the village. They could now see the burning bakery and at that moment a huge flame leapt up through the roof. By its light Pongo saw the whole village street, with the villagers making a human chain to hand along buckets of water. And he also saw something else – something which made him stop dead, shouting 'Halt!' at the top of his bark.

In front of the burning bakery was a great striped black-and-white car. And with it was

Cruella de Vil – standing right up on the roof of the car, where she had climbed so as to get a good view of the fire. Her white face and absolutely simple white mink cloak no longer looked white. From head to foot she was bathed in the red-gold flicker of the flames. And as they leapt higher and higher she clapped her hands in delight.

The next instant there was a wild clamour of bells as the fire engine arrived at last. The noise, the flames and, above all, the sight of Cruella were too much for many of the puppies. Squealing in terror, they turned and fled, with Pongo, Missis and Lucky desperately trying to call them to order.

Fortunately, the clamour from the fire engine prevented anyone in the village hearing the barking and yapping. And after a little while, the terrified pups obeyed Pongo's orders and stopped their headlong flight. They were very shame-faced as Pongo told them that, though he quite understood how they had felt, they must never, never behave in such a panic-stricken way and must always, always obey orders instantly.

Then he praised the pups who had stuck to the
Cadpig's cart, praised Patch for staying close to
the Cadpig, rescued Roly Poly from a ditch and
counted the pups carefully. He did all this as
hurriedly as possible for he knew now that they
must press on with their journey. There was no
way they could get to the police station without
passing Cruella de Vil.

Their plight was now worse than ever. They
not only had to face the dangers of hunger and
cold; there was the added danger of Cruella.
They knew from the direction her car was facing
that their enemy must have already been to Hell
Hall, learned that they had escaped and now be
on her way back to London. At any moment, she
might leave the fire and overtake them.

If only they could have left the road and
travelled by the fields again! But there were now
woods on either side of the road, woods so thick
that the army could not have kept together.

'But we can hide in there, if we see the car's
headlights,' said Pongo, and explained this to the
puppies. Then the army was on the march again.

'At least the pups are warm now,' said Missis. 'And they have forgotten how tired and hungry they are. It will be all right, Pongo.'

The pace was certainly good for a couple of miles, then it got slower and slower.

'The puppies will have to rest,' said Missis. 'And this is a good place for it.'

There was now a wide, grassy verge to the road. The moment Pongo called a halt the pups sank down on the frosty grass. Many of them at once fell asleep.

'They ought not to sleep,' said Pongo, anxiously.

'Let them, for a little while,' said Missis.

The Cadpig was not asleep. She sat up in her cart and said: 'Will there be a barn soon, with kind cows and warm milk?'

'I'm sure there will be something nice,' said Missis. 'Snuggle down in your hay, my darling. Pongo, how strangely quiet it is.'

They could no longer hear any sounds from the village. No breath of wind rustled the grass or stirred the trees. The world seemed frozen into a silvery, silent stillness.

Something soft and fluffy touched Pongo's head, something that puzzled him. Then, as he realised what it was, Missis whispered: 'Look, Pongo! Look at the puppies!'

Tiny white dots were appearing on the sooty black coats. Snow had begun to fall.

Missis said, smiling: 'Instead of being white pups with black spots they are turning into black pups with white spots – only soon, they will be all white. How soft and gentle the snow is!'

Pongo was not smiling. He cried: 'If they sleep on until it has covered them, they will never wake – they will freeze to death beneath that soft, gentle snow! Wake up, pups! Wake up!'

By now, every pup but Lucky and the Cadpig had fallen into a deep, exhausted sleep. Lucky helped his parents to rouse them, and the Cadpig helped, too, sitting up in her cart and yapping piercingly. The poor pups begged to be left to sleep, and those who tottered on to their feet soon tottered off them again.

'We shall never get them going,' said Pongo, despairingly.

For a moment, the Cadpig stopped yapping and there was a sudden silence. Then, from the village behind them, came the strident blare of the loudest motor-horn in England.

The pups sprang up, their exhaustion driven away by terror.

'To the woods!' cried Pongo. Then he saw that the woods were now protected by wire netting, through which not even the smallest pup could squeeze. And there was no ditch to hide in. But he could see that the woods ended, not very far ahead. 'We must go on,' he cried. 'There may be fields, there may be a ditch.'

The horn sounded again, repeatedly. Pongo guessed that the fire engine had put out the fire and now Cruella was scattering the villagers as she drove on her way. Already she would be less than two miles behind them – and the great striped car could travel two miles in less than two minutes. But the woods were ending, there were fields ahead!

'To the fields!' cried Pongo. 'Faster, faster!'

The pups made a great spurt forward, then

fell back in dismay. For though the woods ended, the wire netting still continued, on both sides of them. There was still no way off the road. And the horn sounded again – louder and nearer.

'Nothing but a miracle can save us now,' said Pongo.

'Then we must find a miracle,' said Missis, firmly. 'Pongo, what is a miracle?'

It was at that moment that they suddenly saw, through the swirling snow, a very large van drawn up on the road ahead of them. The tailboard was down and the inside of the van was lit by electric light. And sitting there, on a newspaper, was a Staffordshire Terrier with a short clay pipe in his mouth. That is, it looked like a clay pipe. It was really made of sugar and had once had a fine long stem. Now the Staffordshire drew the bowl of the pipe into his mouth and ate it. Then he looked up from the newspaper – which he was reading as well as sitting on – and stared in astonishment at the army of pups rushing helter-skelter towards him.

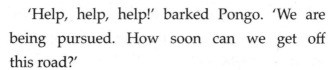 

'Help, help, help!' barked Pongo. 'We are being pursued. How soon can we get off this road?'

'I don't know, mate,' barked back the Staffordshire. 'You'd better hide in my van.'

'The miracle, the miracle!' gasped Pongo to Missis.

'Quickly, pups! Jump into the nice miracle,' said Missis, who now thought 'miracle' was another name for a removal van.

A swarm of pups surged up the tailboard. Up went the Cadpig's cart, pulled from the front and pushed from behind. Then more and more pups jumped or scrambled up until the entire army was in.

'Golly, there are a lot of you,' said the Staffordshire, who had flattened himself against the side of the van. 'Lucky the van was empty. Who's after you, mates? Old Nick?'

'Some relation of his, I think,' said Pongo. The strident horn sounded again and now two strong headlights could be seen in the distance. 'And she's in that car.'

of soot-hounds?' Then he suddenly stared very hard at Pongo's nose. 'Well, swelp me if it isn't soot! And it doesn't fool me. You're the Missing Dalmatians. Want a lift back to London?'

A lift! A lift all the way in this wonderful van! Pongo and Missis could hardly believe it. Swiftly the pups settled to sleep on the rugs and blankets used for wrapping round furniture.

'But why are there so many pups?' said the Staffordshire. 'The newspapers don't know the half of it, nor the quarter, neither. They think there are only fifteen missing.'

Pongo started to explain but the Staffordshire said they would talk during the drive to London. 'My pets will be out of that house there any minute. Fancy us doing a removal on a Sunday – and Christmas Eve. But the van broke down yesterday and we had to finish the job.'

'How many days will the journey to London take?' asked Missis.

'Days?' said the Staffordshire. 'It won't take much more than a couple of hours, if I know my pets. They want to get home to finish decorating their kids' Christmas trees. Shhh, now! Pipe down, both of you.'

A large man in a rough apron was coming out of a nearby house. Missis thought: 'As soon as one danger is past, another threatens.' Would they all be turned out of the miracle?

The Staffordshire, wagging his tail enthusiastically, hurled himself at the man's chest, nearly knocking him down.

'Look out, Bill!' said the man, over his shoulder. 'The Canine Cannon Ball's feeling frisky.'

Bill was an even larger man, but even he was shaken by the Staffordshire's loving welcome.

'Get down, you Self-launched Bomb,' he shouted, with great affection.

The two men and the Staffordshire came back to the van and the Staffordshire jumped inside. The sooty Dalmatians, huddled together, were invisible in the darkness.

'Want to ride inside, do you?' said Bill. 'Well, it is cold.' He put the tailboard up and shouted: 'Next stop, St John's Wood.' A moment later, the huge van took the road.

St John's Wood! Surely, that was where the Splendid Vet lived – quite close to Regent's Park! What wonderful, wonderful luck, thought Pongo. Just then he heard a clock strike. It was still only eight o'clock.

'Missis!' he cried. 'We shall get home tonight! We shall be home for Christmas!'

'Yes, Pongo,' said Missis, gaily. But she did not feel as gay as she sounded. For Missis, who had been so brave, so confident up to the moment they had found the miracle, had suddenly been smitten by a great fear. Suppose the Dearlys did not recognise them now they were black dogs? Suppose the dear, dear Dearlys turned them away?

She kept her fears to herself. Why should she frighten Pongo with them! How fast the miracle was travelling! She thought of the days it had taken her and Pongo to reach Suffolk on foot. Why, it seemed like weeks since they had left London! Yet it was only – how long? Could it be only four days? They'd slept one day in the stable at the inn, one day at the dear Spaniel's, one day in the Folly, part of a night in the barn after the escape from Hell Hall, then a day at the bakery. So much had happened in so short a time. And now, would it be all right when they got home? Would it? Would it?

Meanwhile, Pongo had his own worries. He had been telling the Staffordshire all about Cruella and had remembered what she had said, that night at Hell Hall – how she intended to wait until people had forgotten about the stolen puppies, and then start her Dalmatian fur farm again. Surely he and Missis would get this lot of puppies safely home (it had never occurred to him that the Dearlys might not let them in) but what of the future? How could he make sure that other puppies did not end up as fur coats later on? He asked the Staffordshire's advice.

'Why not kill this Cruella?' said the Staffordshire. 'And I'll help you. Let's make a date for it now.'

Pongo shook his head. He had come to believe that Cruella was not an ordinary human but some kind of devil. If so, could one kill her?

In any case, he didn't want his pups to have a killer-dog for a father. He would have sprung at Cruella if she had attacked any pup, but he didn't fancy cold-blooded murder. He told the Staffordshire so.

'Your blood would soon warm up once you started the job,' said the Staffordshire. 'Well, let me know if you change your mind. And now you take a nap, mate. You've still got quite a job ahead of you.'

The Staffordshire, like Missis, wondered if the Dearlys would recognise these black Dalmatians – and if even the kindest pets would take in so many pups. But he said nothing of this to Pongo.

Missis, lulled by the movement of the van, had fallen asleep. Soon Pongo slept, too. But their dreams were haunted by their separate anxieties.

On and on through the dark went the mile-eating miracle.

## The White Cat's Revenge

THE STAFFORDSHIRE woke them in good time – every pup must be ready to leap out of the van the minute the tailboard was put down.

'Not that my dear pets would hurt you if they saw you,' said the Staffordshire. 'But it might cause delay. The van will stop in a big, dark garage. Streak out, turn sharp left, and you will be in a dimly lit mews – and on your way. We'll say goodbye now.'

'Can we send you news on the Twilight Barking?' asked Pongo.

'Hardly ever get the chance to listen to it,' said the Staffordshire. 'But I shall get news of you all right. I'm a great one for newspapers – they pass the time on the road. Always plenty of them in the van; we use them for packing. Well, here we are.'

The van stopped. The Staffordshire started to bark loudly.

'Let him out, Jim,' said Bill. 'Before he breaks the Sound Barrier.'

Down came the tailboard. Out shot the Staffordshire. This time he managed to knock Jim right down, before turning to Bill, whom he tackled low.

'Just about winded me, he has,' said Bill, proudly. 'Grrh, you Flying Saucer, you!'

Jim got to his feet and spoke lovingly to the Staffordshire. 'If England had six of you, we shouldn't need no army,' he said. 'Come home and get your supper, you Misguided Missile.'

Bill and Jim had been much too occupied to notice the black dogs streaming out of the van, and out of the dark garage into the mews. Snow had been falling for hours, so that London was all white. The pups had scarcely noticed the snow while they were running away from Cruella's car. Now they at once fell in love with this beautiful, feathery stuff – it raised their spirits wonderfully. And they felt well-rested, after their sleep in the van. They were still hungry but they didn't mind that much because they were expecting a wonderful supper. Hearing them counting on this, poor Missis felt more anxious than ever.

Bill, Jim and the Staffordshire had gone out of the garage by another way, so Pongo let the pups play in the snowy mews for a few minutes. Then Missis persuaded the Cadpig to get back into her cart, and off they went. Because of the snow there were very few people about – which was just as well, as the army of black dogs was now very noticeable against the white streets. The only person who saw them was an elderly gentleman on his way to a late party. He rubbed his eyes, then shook his head and murmured: 'And I haven't even begun Christmas yet.'

It took only a few minutes to reach the Outer Circle. How beautiful Regent's Park looked, snowy under the stars!

Pongo said: 'Missis, do you remember what I told you when we said goodbye to the Park?'

Missis answered: 'You told me to think of the day when we would come back with fifteen puppies running behind us. And now we have ninety-seven.'

They had not come back to the Outer Circle by the way they had left it but were at the other side of the Park, close to Cruella de Vil's house. As they drew near to it, Pongo saw that every window was dark, so he thought it would be safe to call a moment's halt.

'Look, pups,' he told them. 'That is our enemy's house.'

Lucky said: 'May we scratch it and bite it?'

'You would only hurt your nails and your teeth,' said Pongo, looking up at the huge house.

Missis was looking down into the area. Something moved there – something only a little less white than the snow. It was Cruella's Persian cat.

Her back was arched and she was spitting angrily. Pongo said quickly: 'Madam, none of us would ever dream of hurting you.'

The white cat said: 'That's the civilest speech I ever had from a dog. Who are you? There are no black dogs round here.'

'We are not usually black except for our spots,' said Pongo. 'We once visited your house –'

He got no further because the white cat guessed everything – as well she might, after all the talk she had heard between Mr and Mrs de Vil.

'And you've rescued all the pups from Hell Hall! Well, bravo, bravo! I couldn't be more pleased.'

Then Missis remembered what Cruella de Vil had said on the night when the puppies were born, and she spoke to the white cat very kindly, saying: 'I might have known you would sympathise – for I once heard you lost many kittens in early infancy.'

'Forty-four, to the present date,' said the white cat. 'All drowned by the fiend I live with.'

'Why don't you leave her?' asked Pongo.

'I bide my time,' said the white cat. 'I wait for my full revenge. I can't do much on my own – I've only two pairs of paws. But I scare the servants away – any cat can make a house seem haunted. I let the place become over-run with mice. And, oh, how I scratch the furniture! Though it's heartbreaking how little she notices it – she's such a rotten housewife. Why not let your pups come in and do some damage now?'

'Oh, please, please let us!' clamoured all the pups.

Pongo shook his head. 'Cruella will be back. I'm surprised she's not home already.'

'Oh, she's been back,' said the white cat, 'and gone out to dinner. She had to, because I scared another batch of servants away this morning – as a little Christmas present for her. Do come in!'

'No, no, Pongo!' cried Missis. 'This is no moment for revenge. We should get the pups home. They are hungry.'

But the pups clamoured louder than ever. 'Please, please, please let us damage Cruella's house!' They made so much noise that Missis could not hear what the white cat was now saying to Pongo. At last he turned, quietened the pups, and said: 'Missis, I now feel that we should do as our friend here suggests. It would take me a long time to explain why, so will you trust me, please?'

'Of course, Pongo,' said Missis, loyally. 'And if you're sure we really ought to be revenged on Cruella – well, naturally, I shall enjoy it.'

'Then follow me,' said the white cat. 'There's a way in at the back.'

Lucky and two big, loud-barked pups were left on guard – they were sorry to miss the fun, but duty was duty.

'Three barks if you sight the striped car or hear its horn,' Pongo told them, then marched all the other pups after the white cat. The little blue cart was left in the mews at the back of the house – the Cadpig insisted on going into the house and getting her fair share of the revenge.

The white cat took them in through the coal cellar.

'Nothing down here worth wrecking,' she said, making for the stairs. Up through the dark house they went, until she paused outside a bolted door.

'Now, if you really can undo that bolt!' she said to Pongo. 'Goodness knows, I've tried often enough.'

'Oh, he's splendid at bolts,' said Missis, proudly.

It was a nice, chromium bolt, well-oiled. It gave Pongo no trouble at all.

There was enough light from the lamps on the Outer Circle to show them a big room in which were many racks of fur coats.

'Why, Cruella must own dozens of them!' thought Missis. And there were many fur stoles, muffs, etc., too.

Pongo barked his orders:

'Four pups to a coat, two pups to a stole, one pup to a muff. Present teeth! Tear-r-r!!!'

There was not space enough in one room to finish the whole job, so the pups spread themselves throughout the house. After that, the fur flew with a vengeance – in every direction. Chinchilla, Sable, Mink and Beaver, Nutria, Fox, Kolinsky and many humbler skins – from kitchen to attic the house was filled with a fog of fur. And the white cat did not forget the ermine sheets. She did good work on those herself, moving so fast that it was hard to see which was clawed white ermine and which was clawing white cat.

'I've been slack,' she said. 'I could have got at these years ago.'

'One needs company for a job like this,' said Pongo.

'No more furs to tear, now,' said the Cadpig, sadly. She had just shredded a little sable tippet, all by herself.

'Quiet!' barked Pongo, suddenly. Had his ears deceived him? No, there it was again – a distant blast from the loudest motor-horn in England! The next instant, the pups outside barked the alarm.

'Down, down to the coal cellar!' barked Pongo.

There was a wild scurry of pups down the dark stairs. The white cat sprang to a window. 'You'll have time,' she cried. 'The car's only just turned into the Outer Circle.'

But Pongo knew how fast that car could come. And pups were falling over each other in the darkness, there were bumps and yelps. Roly Poly fell through the banisters – it was amazing that he was not hurt. But at last they were all streaming out of the coal cellar into the mews.

'In your places for counting!' barked Pongo. He had long ago invented a quick way of counting the army. Pups formed nine rows of ten, and one row of seven which included the Cadpig in her cart. Swiftly, he counted now. Ninety-three, ninety-four – there were three pups missing!

'They must be somewhere in the house,' cried Missis.

'We must rescue them!' Pongo dashed towards the coal cellar – then stopped, gasping with relief. Lucky and the two loud-barked pups were just coming from the front of the house. Pongo had forgotten them in his counting. The army was complete!

'Cruella's nearly here,' said Lucky.

'We must make sure she's gone indoors before we march on,' said Pongo, and he ran into the narrow passage that led to the Outer Circle.

Missis ran after him. 'Be careful, Pongo! She'll see you!'

'Not in this dark passage,' said Pongo.

The striped car went by the end of the passage. A light was on inside and they could see Cruella clearly.

'Oh, Pongo!' wailed Missis. 'She's still got her

absolutely simple white mink cloak!'

Pongo ran on towards the Outer Circle and Missis ran after him. Cautiously they peered out of the passage and saw the striped car stop in front of the de Vils' house. Mr de Vil, who had been driving, helped Cruella out and then went up the front-door steps. He started to search for his latchkey. Cruella stood waiting, with the cloak hanging loosely round her shoulders.

'I shan't sleep if she keeps that cloak,' said Missis.

'And you need your sleep, Missis,' said Pongo.

The same idea had come to both of them. The cloak hung so loosely, so temptingly! And the relief of getting the pups safely out of the house had made them feel daring. Pongo was happy to see his dear wife looking as mischievous as a puppy.

'She'll never recognise us now we're black,' he said. 'Let's risk it! Now!'

They dashed towards Cruella and seized the hem of the cloak. It slipped from her shoulders quite easily – and fell on top of Pongo and Missis.

Blindly they hurled themselves along the
Outer Circle, with the cloak spread out
over them and looking as if it was
running by itself. Cruella screamed.
'It's bewitched! Go after it – quick!'

'No fear!' said Mr de Vil.

'I think an ancestor of yours
is running away with it.
You'd better come indoors.'

The next moment, he
and Cruella started to
cough violently. For
as they opened the
front door they
were met by a
choking cloud
of fur.

Somehow Pongo and Missis found their way to the passage, where they came from under the cloak and dragged it to the mews. Here the pups fell on it. And that was the end of the absolutely simple white mink cloak.

Lights were now flashing on all over the de Vils' house and Cruella could be heard shrieking with rage.

'This is where we march home quickly,' said Pongo.

Suddenly all her high spirits deserted Missis. Home! But would they be allowed into their home? All her fears came back.

Now they were marching along the Outer Circle again. And now they could see the Dearlys' house ahead of them.

There were lights in the drawing-room window.

'Mr and Mrs Dearly haven't gone to bed yet,' said Pongo.

Lights were shining up from the kitchen.

'The Nannies are still awake,' said Missis. She said it brightly; no one could have guessed how frightened she was, though her heart was thumping so hard that she was afraid Pongo would hear it. Why should the Dearlys let a mob of strange black dogs into the house? And unless they did get in, how could they show the Dearlys they were not strange black dogs? Barking would not help. She and Pongo would need to get close to their pets, close enough to put their sooty heads against the Dearlys' knees, or their sooty paws around the Dearlys' necks.

Suppose they were all turned away – ninety-nine hungry Dalmatians, outcasts in the night?

At that moment, snow began to fall again, very, very thickly.

## Who are These Strange Black Dogs?

THE DEARLYS, the Nannies and Perdita had spent a sad Christmas Eve. They had all been very kind to each other. Perdita had washed the humans so much that they all had chapped hands and had to use gallons of hand-lotion. Fortunately, Perdita quite liked the taste of this.

(She had received no news by way of the Twilight Barking. Reception was bad in that part of Regent's Park – which was why Pongo had done his barking, and listening, from Primrose Hill.)

In the afternoon the Nannies trimmed the Christmas tree. They said it was for Perdita but they really hoped to cheer the Dearlys up. The Dearlys put Perdita's presents on it but they had not the heart to get out the presents which they had bought for Pongo, Missis and fifteen puppies just in case they all came home.

Mr Dearly had guessed that Pongo and Missis were searching for their family, but he now feared that family might be scattered all over England, and the best he really hoped for was that Pongo and Missis might return.

When snow first began to fall, everyone felt worse than ever. 'And Missis didn't even take her coat,' said Mrs Dearly. She pictured Pongo and Missis lost, shivering and starving. So did Mr Dearly. But they kept the horrid thought to themselves.

In the evening, the Dearlys invited the Nannies to come up to the drawing-room and they all played nursery card games: Snap, Beggar-my-Neighbour and Animal Grab. They all pretended to enjoy themselves which was very hard work. At last Mr Dearly said he would put some Christmas carols on the gramophone.

Now carols are always beautiful but if you are sad they can make you feel sadder. (There are some people who always find beauty makes them feel sadder, which is a very mysterious thing.) Soon the Dearlys and the Nannies could hardly keep the tears out of their eyes. When Mr Dearly realised this, he thought: 'This must be the last carol we play.' It was 'Silent Night'. Mrs Dearly put out the lights and drew back the curtains at the tall windows, so that they could see the stars while they listened. And she saw it was snowing again.

She went back to the sofa and stroked Perdita who, for once, did no washing but just gazed at the falling snowflakes. The voices singing 'Silent Night' were high and clear and peaceful, and not very loud.

Suddenly, everyone in the room heard a dog bark.

'That's Pongo,' cried Mr Dearly, and dashed to a window.

'That's Missis,' cried Mrs Dearly, hearing a different bark as she, too, dashed to the window.

They flung the window open wide and stared down through the swirling snow. And then their hearts seemed turned to lead by disappointment.

Down below were two black dogs.

Mrs Dearly said gently: 'You shouldn't be out

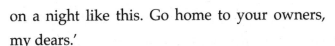

on a night like this. Go home to your owners, my dears.'

(She used the word 'owners' when she should have said 'pets' – that mistake humans so often make.)

The dogs barked again but Mr Dearly said 'Home!' very firmly, for he felt sure the dogs lived somewhere near and had been let out for a last run before going to bed. He shut the window, saying to Mrs Dearly: 'Odd-looking dogs. I can't quite recognise the breed.'

He did not hear the despairing howl that came from Missis. It had happened, just as she had feared! They were turned away, outcasts in the night.

Pongo had a moment of panic. This was something he had not foreseen. But quickly he pulled himself together. 'We must bark again,' he said, 'and much louder.'

'Shall the puppies bark, too?' suggested Missis.

The puppies were all lined up out of sight from the window, because Pongo felt that so many dogs at once might come as a bit of a shock. He now said: 'No. Only you and I must bark, Missis. And one at a time. Then they will recognise our voices sooner or later. We would recognise theirs whatever clothes they wore, whatever colour their faces and hands were.'

So he barked again, and then Missis barked. They went on and on, taking it in turns.

Up in the drawing-room Mrs Dearly said: 'I can't believe that's not Pongo and Missis. And look how excited Perdita is!'

'It's because we are all so longing to hear them,' said Mr Dearly. 'We imagine we do. But there must be something wrong with those black dogs – just listen to them! Perhaps they're lost.' And again he opened the window.

Pongo and Missis barked louder than ever and wagged their tails wildly.

'Anyone would think they knew us,' said Mr Dearly. 'I shall go down and see if they have collars on. Perhaps I can take them to their homes.'

Pongo heard this and said to Missis quickly:

'The moment the door opens, dash in and lead the way up to the drawing-room. Pups, you follow Missis, noses to tails. I will bring up the rear. And never let there be one moment when Mr Dearly can close the front door. Once we are in, we can make them understand.'

The front door opened and out came Mr Dearly. In shot Missis, closely followed by the Cadpig – now out of her cart – and all her brothers and sisters except Lucky, who insisted on waiting with Pongo. What with the darkness and the whirling snow, Mr Dearly did not see what was happening until a pup bumped into him in passing (it was Roly Poly – of course). Then he looked down to see what had bumped him and saw a steady stream of black pups going through the front door and the white hall and up the white stairs.

'I'm dreaming this,' thought Mr Dearly, and pinched himself, hard. But the stream of pups went on and on.

Suddenly there was a hitch. The two pups faithfully dragging the Cadpig's little blue

cart, now empty, could not get it up the steps. Mr Dearly, who could never see a dog in difficulty without helping, at once picked the cart up himself. After seeing the cart, he no longer felt he was dreaming. 'These dogs are a troop from a circus,' he thought. 'But why have they come to us?'

A moment later, Pongo and Lucky went past and the stream of dogs stopped. Mr Dearly called into the night: 'Any more out there?' To his relief, no dog answered, so he went in and closed the door. Pongo's sooty hindquarters were just rounding the bend of the stairs. Mr Dearly followed four steps at a time, still carrying the little blue cart.

The scene in the front drawing-room was rather confused. Large as the room was, there was not floor space for all the puppies, so they were jumping on to tables and chairs and piling up on top of each other. There was rather a lot of noise. Mrs Dearly was just managing to keep on her feet. She had never been frightened of any dog in her life, but she did feel a trifle startled.

The Nannies had taken refuge on top of the grand piano.

Mr Dearly took one look through the door, then dashed into the back drawing-room and flung open the double doors. A sea of pups surged in. And now that there was a little spare floor space, Pongo barked a command: 'All pups who can find space: Roll! Roll, Missis!' And he, himself, rolled with a will.

The Dearlys stared in utter bewilderment – and then both of them shouted: 'Look!'

The white carpet was becoming blacker, the black dogs were becoming whiter –

'It's Pongo!' cried Mr Dearly.

'It's Missis!' cried Mrs Dearly.

'It's Pongo, Missis and all their puppies!' cried the Nannies, from the top of the piano.

'It's considerably more than all their puppies,' said Mr Dearly – just before Pongo forcibly embraced him.

Missis was embracing Mrs Dearly. And in a corner of the room there was a great deal more embracing. Perdita was going absolutely wild, trying to embrace eight puppies at once. They were her own long lost family! It had never struck Pongo that they might be among the rescued pups. He had not even noticed their brown spots, because he had scarcely seen any of the pups by daylight before they all rolled in the soot. It turned out that Perdita's family was the one that fitted the Cadpig's little blue cart so well and had pulled it so faithfully.

Mr Dearly had put the cart down in the back drawing-room and the Nannies had now got off the piano and gone to look at it.

'That's a child's toy,' said Nanny Cook.

'And it's got a name and address on it,' said Nanny Butler. And she read out 'Master Tommy Tompkins, Farmer. Dympling, Suffolk.'

'Dympling?' said Mrs Dearly. 'That's where Cruella de Vil has a country house. She told us about it when we had dinner with her and asked if we'd like to buy it.'

And then Mr Dearly Saw It All. He remembered Cruella's desire for a Dalmatian fur coat, guessed

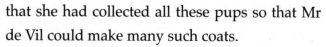
that she had collected all these pups so that Mr de Vil could make many such coats.

'You must have the law on her,' cried both the Nannies together.

Mr Dearly said he would think about that after Christmas, but now he must think about feeding the pups – when all the shops were closed. He hurriedly telephoned the Ritz, the Savoy, Claridges and other rather good hotels and asked them to send page boys along with steaks. The hotels were most anxious to help when they heard that the Missing Dalmatians had come home. 'And at least six dozen more than I ever hoped for,' said Mr Dearly – not that he had had time to count the pups.

Nanny Butler said: 'They must be bathed before they eat.'

'Bathed?' gasped Mrs Dearly. 'All of them?'

'They can't sleep in their soot,' said Nanny Cook, firmly. 'Nanny Butler and I will work in our bathroom and you two can work in yours. And how about asking that Splendid Vet and his wife to pop round and bath pups in the laundry?'

So Mr Dearly rang up the Splendid Vet, who was delighted to be woken up and called out at nearly midnight on Christmas Eve. He and his wife arrived in a few minutes.

Mrs Dearly got out all her best bath salts and bath oils and all the lovely coloured bath-towels given to her as wedding presents. The Nannies lit fires in every room. Then the three bathing teams got to work. Soon the house was filled with steam and the scent of lilac, roses and jasmine, mixed with the delightful smell of wet dogs. It took less time than you would believe, because five pups were put in a bath at a time. They were then wrapped in pink, blue, yellow and green towels and carried to blazing fires to dry. Mr Dearly thoughtfully turned the drawing-room carpet over so that the soot on it would not come off on the clean pups.

By the time the last pup was washed, the steaks were arriving. There were enough for everyone, even the humans – who were by this time pretty hungry. (They had theirs cooked.)

At last the Splendid Vet and his wife went

home and the house settled for the night. Pongo and Missis showed plainly that they wanted to sleep in their own baskets, with their puppies round them on the hearthrug and in arm-chairs. Perdita took her little lot into the laundry, on a rather good satin eiderdown. The other pups slept all over the house, on beds, sofas and chairs. The Dearlys and the Nannies managed to keep chairs for themselves – rather hard ones, but they did not mind because they didn't expect to sleep much. They wanted to be on hand in case any pup needed anything in the night.

When all was quiet in the firelit kitchen and their fifteen pups were asleep, Pongo said to Missis: 'Do you remember that night we left – how we looked back at this kitchen? Look, now, at your legal collar on its peg, ready for you to wear tomorrow – and your beautiful blue coat.'

Missis said: 'I am so hardy now that I shall not need the coat. But I shall wear it from vanity.'

At that moment, they heard a little noise at the window, a little scratching noise. Outside, in the midst of a white blur, were two green eyes. It was Cruella's white cat.

Swiftly Pongo let her in.

'Such goings on at the de Vils!' she said.

Quickly Pongo turned to his wife. 'I haven't explained to you yet, Missis. Our friend here told me that if we could get into that bolted room we could destroy Mr de Vil's whole stock of furs. Cruella made him keep them all there, so that she could wear any she fancied. I hoped we might put an end to his furrier's business. That was why I took the risk of going into the de Vils' house – not to be revenged, but to make England Safe for Dalmatians.'

'And it's even better than I hoped,' said the white cat. 'Because it turns out most of the furs weren't paid for. So Mr de Vil's ruined.'

'The poor little man!' said Missis. 'I feel quite sorry for him.'

'No need to,' said the white cat. 'He's as bad as Cruella. The only difference is she's strong and bad and he's weak and bad. Anyway, they're going to leave England

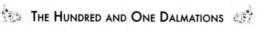 

tomorrow, to get away from their debts.'

'Cruella still has her jewels,' said Missis, regretfully.

'Mostly sham,' said the white cat. 'And those that aren't will be needed by Mr de Vil, to start another business abroad. He says he's going to make plastic raincoats.'

'Cruella won't look very well in those,' said Missis, cheerfully.

'She won't look very well in anything,' said the cat. 'You've heard of people's hair going white in a single night, from shock? That's happened to the black side of her hair. And the white side's gone green – a horrid shade. People are going to think it's dyed. Well, I'm glad to have finished with the de Vils.'

'But where will you go?' asked Pongo.

The white cat looked surprised. 'Go? I shan't go anywhere. I've just come – here. I'd have come long ago if you dogs hadn't barked – that night your pets gave me a kind sardine. They won't turn me out. I'll pop up and find them, now.'

Then Pongo and Missis sank into a blissful

sleep without a care in the world – except that they did want to know what the Dearlys were going to do with so very many puppies . . .

And so did the Dearlys!

•

Those readers who also want to know should read on. Besides, there is a mystery to be cleared up. Most people who are good at arithmetic are likely to think there is a mistake in this book. It is called *The Hundred and One Dalmatians*. Well, Pongo and Missis and Perdita make three. There were ninety-seven Dalmatian pups at Hell Hall including those belonging to Pongo, Missis and Perdita. Three and ninety-seven make one hundred. Where, then, is the hundred and oneth Dalmatian?

He has been mentioned but many readers may not remember him. Those who do not shall soon be reminded of him. And those who do shall soon learn more about him. On to the last chapter, if you please!

# The Hundred and Oneth Dalmatian

Christmas Day at the house in Regent's Park was absolutely wonderful. The rather good hotels sent plenty more steaks, and though there were not, of course, enough presents to go round, the pups were able to play with lots of things in the house which were not intended to be played with (but were played with ever afterwards). The Dearlys took all the pups into the snowy Park; Pongo, Missis and Perdita circling round to make sure none got lost. And, at twilight, Pongo and Missis firmly led the Dearlys up to the top of Primrose Hill and barked over a Dogdom-wide network. They even managed to get a message through to the gallant old Spaniel, for two dogs from a village five miles from him made a special trip in order to bark to him. (He sent back a message that he and his dear old pet were very well.)

Of course, the Dogdom-wide barking was relayed. The furthest-away dog Pongo and Missis spoke to direct was the Brigadier-General Great Dane over towards Hampstead, who was in great barking form.

'There is something very mysterious about this barking at twilight,' said Mrs Dearly. 'Do you think they are sending messages?'

Mr Dearly said it was a charming idea but – And then he stopped. Was anything beyond dogs? Not when he thought of all Pongo and Missis had done. How had they got ninety-seven pups back from Suffolk? Pongo and Missis longed to tell him, but they never could.

As soon as Christmas was over, Mr Dearly decided to act quickly, for he realised that one hundred Dalmatians was too much for one house in Regent's Park. It was even a bit much for Regent's Park.

First he advertised – in case any of the rightful owners of pups wanted to claim them. But none did – for this reason: Cruella had bought all the pups except those stolen from the Dearlys, because it costs a lot to get any expert stealing done these days. (Cruella had paid more to the dog-thieves who stole from the Dearlys than for any litter she had bought.) And, naturally, people who had sold puppies never thought of them as lost, or did anything more about them. Only one owner turned up, the farmer who had owned Perdita. And he was quite happy to sell her to the Dearlys.

So there was Mr Dearly, lucky man, with one hundred delightful Dalmatians. He decided he must take a large country house. Happily, he could afford this as the Government had again got itself into debt and he had again got it out. And this time he had been rewarded by an income to save his income tax on. So he had retired from business – except for being always ready to help the Government with its sums.

One fine day in January, when the snow was all gone, he said to Mrs Dearly: 'Let's drive out to Suffolk and return the little blue cart to Master Tommy Tompkins, and also hunt for a country house. And we'll have a look at the house where the puppies were imprisoned – not that we'll take that one.'

Mrs Dearly laughed at such an idea.

They took Pongo and Missis with them, and Lucky came as a stowaway, under a seat – because he wanted to see the Sheepdog again and be made a Captain. (He didn't stay under the seat long and everyone was delighted to see him when he came out.) When they reached Dympling, they went for a walk round the village and met Tommy Tompkins out with the Sheepdog. So the little blue cart was returned then and there – rather a relief to the Dearlys, who wouldn't quite have known what to say to Tommy's parents. They didn't have to say anything to Tommy as he still wasn't quite talking (though his chuckling noises were at last beginning to sound more like Human than like Dog). The Dearlys saw at once that Pongo, Missis and Lucky knew the Sheepdog – and the tabby cat that came hurrying up.

'And now we'll find Cruella's house,' said Mr Dearly. When they got to Hell Hall there was a large notice outside saying: 'For Sale – CHEAP. Owner gone to warm climate.' And the gates stood wide open. The house was empty.

(The Baddun brothers were now in jail for assaulting the man who came to take away the television, which had never been paid for. They weren't minding jail much because meeting so many criminals was almost better than television; and they now had high hopes of one day appearing on *What's My Crime?*)

'What a hideous house!' said Mrs Dearly.

'What a lovely wall!' said Mr Dearly. One thing had been worrying him. If he took a hundred Dalmatians into the country, how was he to prevent them from running wild? This magnificent wall was just the thing. If only the house were not so hideous!

'Suppose it was painted white,' he said, 'and the blocked-up windows were put back? There's a lovely pond in front – almost a lake.'

Mrs Dearly shook her head. But when they got into the house and saw the fine, large rooms and imagined them all white instead of red, she began to feel differently.

Pongo, Missis and Lucky raced through the kitchen and larder, remembering all that had happened there. The Dearlys followed them and saw the furnace for the central heating. Then they all went out to the stables.

'These would make fine kennels if they were heated,' said Mr Dearly.

Then he looked up and saw the Folly, and both he and Mrs Dearly took a fancy to it. And they decided then and there to buy Hell Hall and make it into a beautiful house.

'Here we will found a Dynasty of Dalmatians,' said Mr Dearly.

Missis was insulted. She thought the word meant a nasty din. But Pongo explained that it meant a family that goes on and on.

Mr Dearly added: 'And we'd better start a Dynasty of Dearlys, to look after the Dynasty of Dalmatians.' And Mrs Dearly quite agreed.

The alterations to Hell Hall were quickly made, and one sunny day in early spring a removal van and an extra large double-decker motor-coach stood outside the house in Regent's Park. The van was for the furniture. The coach was for the Dearlys and the Dalmatians. The Nannies had already gone down by car, to open Hell Hall, Nanny Butler driving. She had added a smart chauffeur's cap to her butler's outfit.

Mr Dearly came out of the house with Pongo and Missis. Mrs Dearly followed with Perdita, and with the white cat on her shoulder. (The white cat, too, was to start a Dynasty at Hell Hall. The Dearlys had promised her a white Persian husband.)

Within the next few minutes, two surprising things had happened. First, just as Missis saw the removal van and said: 'Oh, there's a miracle,' a Staffordshire Terrier flung itself from the van, said 'Here we are again', to Pongo and Missis, and hurled itself at Mr Dearly's chest.

'That's a compliment, if you only knew it,' said Jim, who was standing by the van.

'That's right,' said Bill. 'Old Battering Ram's fallen for you.'

'And I for him,' said Mr Dearly, politely, rising from a sitting position.

Pongo and Missis managed to quieten the Staffordshire before he paid any compliments to Mrs Dearly. And then the second surprising thing happened. A large car had drawn up and the people in it were looking at Pongo, Missis and Perdita with interest. Suddenly there was a wild commotion in the car, and then the door burst open and out sprang a superb liver-spotted Dalmatian. He dashed up to Perdita. It was her long-lost husband.

His name was Prince. The people in the big car were much touched by his faithfulness to Perdita and at once offered him to the Dearlys, saying they would be glad of a good home for him as they were always going abroad and having to leave him in kennels. Prince was delighted. Apart from wanting to be with Perdita, he knew good pets when he saw them.

So the Dalmatians started for Suffolk, one hundred and one strong. They all sat up on the motor-coach seats, looking out of the window, and many people who saw them pass, cheered – for there had been so much about them in the papers that they were now quite famous. And many, many dogs lined the route, as word of the journey had gone out by Twilight Barking. The waiting dogs barked their good wishes and the Dalmatians barked their thanks, so it was rather noisy in the motor-coach. The Dearlys didn't mind. They thought happy barking was a pleasant noise.

Prince was rather shy at first, so Mr Dearly sat beside him and punched him, in a way some big dogs like to be punched. (The punching needs to be hard enough but not too hard; it must, please, not hurt. Mr Dearly was a highly-skilled dog-puncher.) Prince thumped his tail, then suddenly gave Mr Dearly's ear a playful nip, which was much appreciated. After that, Perdita's handsome husband felt he was completely one of the family.

When the Dalmatians reached the village of Dympling, all the villagers were out to receive them, with the Sheepdog, the tabby cat and

Tommy Tompkins well to the fore. (The cows were lowing a loving welcome from the farm.) Tommy had his little blue cart with him and the Cadpig felt just a bit envious – but she was happy to know she had grown too strong to need any cart.

The white Persian Cat, who was now a charming creature (kindness makes kind cats) was extremely gracious to the farmyard tabby. It was the beginning of a firm friendship.

At last the motor-coach drove in through the wide open gates of Hell Hall. The pond now reflected a snow-white house with muslin curtains at all the windows. The front of the house still seemed like a face and had an expression – but now it was a pleasant expression.

The Nannies were waiting at the open front door. As they came to meet the Dearlys, Nanny Butler said: 'Do you know there is a television aerial on the roof of this house?'

And Nanny Cook said: 'Seems wasteful not to make use of it.'

Then Mr Dearly knew that the Nannies wished

for a television in the kitchen and he at once suggested it. Pongo and Missis were delighted, for they knew how very much their smallest daughter had missed it.

But during the many happy hours the Cadpig was to sit watching it in the warm kitchen, she never liked it quite so much as that other television – that still, silent television she had seen on Christmas Eve, when the puppies had rested so peacefully in the strange, lofty building. She often remembered that building, and wondered who owned it – someone very kind, she was sure. For in front of every one of the many seats there had been a little carpet-eared, puppy-sized dog-bed.

# The
# STARLIGHT
# BARKING

# Contents

# The Mysterious Sleeping

NOT LONG AGO there lived in Suffolk a hundred and one Dalmatians whose adventures had once thrilled all the dogs of England. This was when a wicked woman, Cruella de Vil, started a Dalmatian Fur Farm. She imprisoned ninety-seven puppies in a lonely country house named Hell Hall and planned to have their skins turned into fur coats.

Fifteen of the puppies belonged to Pongo and Missis, a young married couple of Dalmatians, who lived in London with a young married couple of humans, Mr. and Mrs. Dearly. Pongo and Missis rescued *all* the puppies and brought them home to the Dearlys who, eventually, took them back to that same Hell Hall where they had been imprisoned – it was for sale cheap as Cruella de Vil had fled from England. Hell Hall then became such a happy home that there was talk of changing its name to Heaven Hall. But the Dearlys thought it was just a bit too noisy for heaven.

Of course there were problems to face, the main one being that the hundred and one Dalmatians did not remain only a hundred and one for long. Many of the pups married early and had delightful families. And Mr. Dearly (who was extremely good at arithmetic) foresaw a time when he and Mrs. Dearly would belong to a thousand and one Dalmatians – and more. Large as Hell Hall and its grounds were, they weren't large enough for that, but the Dearlys could not bear the thought of sending so much as one pup away.

And then a splendid thing happened. Some of the dogs made it clear that they actually wanted to go out into the world. They were always trying to climb the high walls or squeeze through the bars of the tall gates. And they showed great affection for visiting tradesmen. The Dearlys realised that these dogs not only wished for adventure; they wished for their own special humans. (Try as they might, the Dearlys could not be the special humans of so very many Dalmatians.) So Mr. Dearly advertised that a few dogs might consider adopting humans, if exactly the right humans could be found.

Naturally he received dozens of replies – the Dalmatians had become so famous at the time of the Great Dog Robbery. So he opened a hostel, in the near-by village, where applicants could stay until they were fully trained and, eventually, chosen by a dog. Dozens of Dearly Dalmatians were now happily settled all over England and the supply never equalled the demand, as the Dearlys liked to keep at least a hundred and one Dalmatians at Hell Hall. Of course nothing would have tempted Pongo and Missis to leave home. And of their fifteen puppies only one had gone out into the world. She was now the best known of all the Dalmatians. More will be told about her soon.

Also settled with the Dearlys for life were the liver-spotted Dalmatians, Prince and Perdita, and two white Persian cats. One of these cats had rescued herself from Cruella de Vil and, since then, been married. She and her husband frequently had charming kittens who all went to

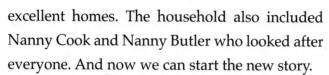

excellent homes. The household also included Nanny Cook and Nanny Butler who looked after everyone. And now we can start the new story.

One brilliant morning in high summer Pongo woke up with the guilty feeling that he had overslept. But if he had, everyone else in the large, airy bedroom had overslept too. Close beside him his dear wife, Missis, was asleep in her basket, one elegant, black-spotted paw twitching as she raced through a dream. Across the room Prince and Perdita were asleep in their baskets. The white cats were asleep in theirs. Mr. and Mrs. Dearly were asleep in their twin beds. And not one bark, yap or whimper came from below, where the old stables had been made into comfortable kennels. If it had been as late as it felt, an uproar would have broken out by now.

Pongo relaxed, stretched and, as he had no wish to sleep any more, decided to count his blessings. The idea came to him because of something he had thought about the night before. He and all the other dogs had gone for a late walk with the Dearlys and then, after the dogs who slept in the kennels and in the kitchen had been put to bed, each with a good-night biscuit, Pongo, Missis, Prince and Perdita had taken the Dearlys for a last stroll under the stars. Pongo had been delighted to hear that one of these was called the Dog Star.

'It's always particularly bright at this time of the year,' said Mr. Dearly. 'In fact, these are called the Dog Days.'

'Because of the star?' asked Mrs. Dearly.

'I suppose so. All I know is that the Ancient Romans believed that the Dog Star, Sirius, rising with the sun – though one can't see the star in the daylight – adds to the sun's heat and makes the weather specially warm.'

'Well, it certainly is, this year,' said Mrs. Dearly. 'And the star's wonderfully bright.'

Pongo then remembered another wonderfully bright star, which had guided him when the weather was very far from warm. He thought of that cold, cold Christmas Eve when he and Missis had rescued all the puppies and were leading them back to London. How terrible it had been when they were pursued by Cruella de Vil in her huge black and white car! But everything had come right and since then there had never been any kind of danger to face. Pongo, strolling, under the stars, told himself he must count his blessings oftener. So now, lying awake in the bright morning, he counted them.

He could always be certain of food, warmth, safety and – most important of all – love (not that a hungry dog can live on love alone). Surely he had everything he wanted? Why, then, was he sometimes just a little bit discontented? What about? It wasn't as if life at Hell Hall was dull; the dogs had plenty of amusements. There were see-saws, swings, a charming little merry-go-round, a small water-shoot into the pond. And often they all went for outings, in two hired motor buses. All the same, whenever he saw a young, adventurous dog proudly leading his newly trained pet out of the tall gates of Hell Hall, while all the resident dogs lined up and barked their good wishes, did he not feel, well, a fraction wistful? He did. And, remembering this now, he found he still felt wistful, and more than a fraction.

Good gracious! What a thing to feel bang in the middle of his blessing counting! And it simply wasn't true. Not for anything in the world would he have left the dear Dearlys. He was *not* wistful. He was a hundred per cent happy dog looking forward to another hundred per cent happy day – and why didn't the day start? Wasn't anyone but himself going to wake up?

At that moment he heard the stable clock strike the quarter. The Dearlys always got up at seven-thirty so Pongo reckoned it would now be a quarter past seven. But it couldn't, it couldn't be as early as that, not with the sun so high – he could see it through one of the wide open windows. The night had been so warm that the Dearlys had drawn all the curtains back.

He sprang up, ran to a window, and looked at the clock. Then, scarcely believing his eyes, he hurriedly awoke Missis, with a kiss that was really more of a bump on the nose. She instantly said, 'Oh dear, have I overslept?'

'Yes, you have and so has everyone else,' said Pongo. 'Will you kindly tell me what time you make it by the stable clock?'

'Oh, *yes*,' said Missis, enthusiastically. She was very proud of being able to tell the time and wished dogs who couldn't would ask her to do so oftener. The reason why they didn't was that she could never remember which hand stood for the hours and which for the minutes. Now, after a long, careful stare, she said, 'It's either a quarter past ten or ten to three.'

'It's a quarter past ten,' said Pongo, 'and goodness knows that's late enough. Why haven't Mr. and Mrs. Dearly wakened?'

Missis looked anxiously at the Dearlys. 'Do you think they're ill?'

'They look particularly well.'

'And they're breathing beautifully,' said Missis. 'In, out, in, out, nice regular breathing. And Mrs. Dearly's smiling.'

'And Mr. Dearly looks as if he might smile at any minute. Yes! He's smiling now.'

'They must be having lovely dreams,' said

Missis. 'It seems a shame to wake them. But I think we should.'

Just then Prince and Perdita woke up and quickly got the hang of the situation. They, too, thought the Dearlys should be wakened.

'Though they never really like it if we disturb them,' said Prince, who was a most considerate dog.

'But this morning it is *necessary*,' said Missis, firmly. 'Because there are two nursing mothers in the kennels who need good drinks of milk.'

'Yes, indeed,' said Perdita. 'And I promised to help them wash their puppies.' Perdita had always been a great puppy-washer.

'Besides, there are young dogs who need their first meal of the day,' said Pongo. 'I can't think why they're not yapping. Oh, we must certainly disturb the Dearlys. But we'll do it kindly.'

Pongo and Prince went to Mr. Dearly. Missis and Perdita went to Mrs. Dearly. All four dogs gave some little *whispered* barks and did some gentle shoulder-patting.

Nothing happened.

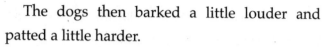 

The dogs then barked a little louder and patted a little harder.

Still nothing happened.

The dogs then barked much louder and patted much harder.

But still nothing happened.

'We'd better lick their faces,' said Pongo. He knew that the Dearlys, much as they loved their dogs, were not fully appreciative of face-licking, and such an attention was likely to make them sit up briskly. But not today. They just went on sleeping – and also, Pongo was pleased to see, smiling. As he couldn't wake them he was glad not to have spoilt their happy dreams.

Just then Missis accidentally kicked the cats' basket and moved away hastily. Delightful creatures though the cats were, they were always *ready* to be defensive – and who can blame them, when they lived with so very many dogs? Missis, expecting them to spring up, got ready to apologise. But the cats did not stir.

'How very strange,' said Missis. And then, greatly daring, she gave both of them a little prod with her paw. The cats, very slightly, flexed their claws; but they did not wake up.

'Perhaps Nanny Cook and Nanny Butler are awake,' said Perdita. 'Shall Prince and I go and see?'

'Yes, if you can get out of the room' said Pongo. He was clever at lifting latches and drawing back bolts, but the bedroom door had an ordinary handle, and not even the cleverest dog can turn a door handle. He was afraid they were shut up in the room until some human let them out. But as he looked towards the door, it swung open – he could only think that the Dearlys had not quite closed it, the night before. Prince and Perdita ran out.

Pongo and Missis made another effort to wake the Dearlys, even biting their ears – tenderly, but quite, quite noticeably; but the Dearlys did *not* notice. They didn't even stop smiling.

Missis then went to an open window and looked out at the sunny morning. After a moment she said, 'Pongo, please come here and listen.'

Pongo joined her and listened but couldn't hear anything. He told her so.

Missis said, 'I meant, listen to the silence. I've never heard it so loud.'

'I don't think you can have a loud silence,' said Pongo, 'but I know what you mean.' He listened again, then said, 'Missis! There are no birds singing.'

'So there aren't,' said Missis. 'You know, I hardly ever notice them when they *are* singing, but now —! It's queer that an un-noise can make so much more noise than a noise.'

Then Prince and Perdita came back and said they hadn't been able to wake the Nannies.

'Though we tried really hard,' said Perdita. 'We sat on them and bounced.'

'Well, what do we do now?' said Prince, looking eagerly at Pongo. Prince was a brave, intelligent dog but he had never had any adventures such as Pongo had once had, and he was fully prepared to accept Pongo as a leader.

Pongo suddenly felt doubtful of himself. It was so long since he had needed to make important decisions. Was he still capable of doing so? For a moment he felt, well, *almost* stupid – he who was known to own one of the keenest brains in Dogdom!

He shook himself – and then felt dazed as well as stupid. But he was determined not to give himself away. He said, trying to sound confident, 'We must find out how far this mysterious sleeping stretches. Missis and I will run to the farm.' The truth was that he wanted to consult his good friend, the Old English Sheepdog, the wisest dog he knew.

'Couldn't we save time by just barking to the farm?' said Missis.

'No,' said Pongo. 'For if we bark loudly we shall wake every dog in Hell Hall and they will all want their breakfasts.'

Some people believe that dogs need only one meal a day, and they can manage with this provided the meal is a large one. But the Dearlys thought two meals a day made a dog's life more interesting, and all the Dalmatians were offered a good, light breakfast, and a good, weighty dinner in the late afternoon. Puppies, of course, needed as many as five little meals a day, and Missis now became very anxious about this. She suggested they should be wakened and fed, the small ones by their mothers and the larger ones on bread and milk.

'But we can't get at the milk,' said Pongo. 'I can't open the refrigerator door. Later, Prince and I can lift the lids of the biscuit bins, so all the grown-up dogs can have something. But we shall need help with the puppies and nursing mothers.'

'Then we'd better set about getting it,' said Missis.

Pongo gave Prince instructions. 'If any dogs wake up, you and Perdita must explain and keep them as calm as possible. Say we shall soon be back. In case of any emergency, just bark for advice. Take good care of Mr. and Mrs. Dearly. I have complete confidence in you.'

Prince looked, and felt, extremely proud. He – the hundred and oneth Dalmatian – had so often wished he had been a member of the household in those dangerous days when the missing puppies had to be found and rescued. And he was always anxious to show how grateful he was to Pongo and Missis for sharing the Dearlys with him and Perdita. 'Count on me,' he said sturdily.

'And of course we count on Perdita, too,' said Missis, kindly. She sometimes thought Perdita's mania for washing puppies – and people – a bit silly, but was very fond of her.

'Then off we go,' said Pongo.

As he and Missis ran downstairs, he wondered how they would get out of the house. It was a long time since he had opened a window and he hoped he still had the knack of it. But as they reached the hall he saw that the front door was a little bit open.

'What wonderful luck,' he said, as he and Missis ran out into the garden. He now planned to get out by way of the old stone Folly – the Sheepdog had shown him how to do this, in the days when Hell Hall was the enemy's camp. But as he looked across the pond at the front of the house he saw that the tall iron gates were not

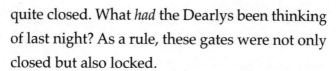 

quite closed. What *had* the Dearlys been thinking of last night? As a rule, these gates were not only closed but also locked.

Now they were only just open and Missis was afraid they might be too heavy to be pushed open wide enough. But as the dogs approached the gates swung inwards.

'How nice of the wind to help us,' said Missis, as they ran through the gates – which instantly closed behind them. 'Oh, how peculiar! The wind must be blowing both ways.'

'But there *isn't* any wind,' said Pongo.

# News From Downing Street

IT WAS TRUE. There wasn't a breath of wind. And the stillness, combined with the silence, made the sunny morning feel very strange indeed.

'Of course the stillness makes the silence louder,' said Missis, 'because as well as there being no birds singing – and no insects buzzing or whirring their wings, I've just noticed – there's no rustling, no leaves or grasses stirring. But somehow I quite like the feel of it, and I like the way *I* feel, most unusually light.'

'Perhaps that's because you haven't had any breakfast,' said Pongo. 'I should have found you some biscuits.'

'I couldn't have eaten a mouthful. Oh, that doesn't mean that I'm ill. I'm just unhungry.'

'Dear Missis, that's a world's record,' said Pongo.

Missis smiled. Her good appetite was a family joke.

'What's more I can't imagine being hungry. And I suddenly know something. When all the dogs at Hell Hall wake up, *they* won't be hungry, either.'

'You can't be sure of that just because *you're* not hungry.'

'Well, if I can't imagine myself being hungry, I can't imagine their being hungry, can I? Anyway, they won't be. Are *you* hungry, Pongo?'

'Well, no. But that may be because I'm anxious.'

'I'm not. I'm puzzled, of course, but that's interesting. And I suppose I'm excited. *I* know how I feel. Do you remember when you persuaded me to try the watershoot? There I was, at the top of the shoot, looking down at the pond. I wasn't exactly frightened, because you were there and the Dearlys were standing by and, anyway, I can swim. But I did feel, well, just as I feel now and it's really quite pleasant. And talking of swimming, how easy it is to run this morning, more like swimming through air.'

'Now that you mention it —' Pongo realised that he was, indeed, moving with great ease but he had too much on his mind to enjoy it. For as well as being anxious about the mysterious sleeping, he was so afraid he might not be equal to – well, whatever he had to be equal to.

Just then, Missis saw two horses asleep in a field and said cheerfully, 'Breathing nicely, aren't they?' Then she suddenly stopped running. 'Oh, Pongo, look'

Curled up in a grassy nest was a sleeping mouse.

Pongo said hastily, 'Missis, dear, I wouldn't.' For Missis was a famous mouse-chaser.

She looked at him haughtily. 'I wouldn't dream of pouncing on the poor little creature. It's only when they run that they're so tempting. Mice shouldn't imitate toys.'

The farm was now in sight and, as Pongo and Missis drew near to it, they at last saw someone who wasn't asleep. The Old English Sheepdog came running to meet them, at a surprising speed for such a large, elderly dog (large even under his enormously thick, woolly coat) who was often a little short of breath.

In the days when he had helped to rescue the Dalmatian puppies he had been a Colonel. Afterwards, with every justification, he had made himself a General. He had always remained on the friendliest terms with Pongo and Missis and often visited Hell Hall. Now he said, 'I was coming to see you. Oh, my dear young friends, I'm afraid the fact that you're here means that you, also, are faced with a dangerous situation.'

'Then your humans are unwakeable, too?' said Pongo.

'All of them, including my dear young Tommy who's usually so very wide-awake. But it isn't only the humans who are asleep. Come and see for yourselves.'

The General led the way. They saw sleeping ducks around the pond, sleeping hens in their pen, sleeping pigeons in their dovecote up in the gable of the barn. A gentle snoring came from the pig-sty and no sound whatever from the cow-shed. Missis at once went to make sure that all cows were breathing satisfactorily; she had loved them ever since that night when they had given drinks of warm milk to the hungry, rescued puppies.

'And I've been to my sheep in the meadow,' said the General. 'I couldn't make the slightest impression on them. Now come and look at my poor Mrs. Willow.'

Pongo and Missis followed him into the kitchen. The tabby cat lay in her basket, utterly asleep.

'Never before has she let me down,' said the General. 'As you know, I think of her more as a dog than a cat. I still can't quite believe...' He kicked the basket and said in a very military voice, 'Wake up, Major!' Then he added tenderly, 'Puss, *please!*'

But the tabby cat went on sleeping.

Pongo said, 'It's been worse for you than for Missis and me, General. We had Prince and Perdita to talk to. You've had no one.' For the Sheepdog was the only dog at the farm.

'Well, I'll admit I was pretty thankful to see you two. Not that I allowed myself to get *too* alarmed, once I saw that all humans and all creatures look perfectly healthy.' The General then turned to Missis. 'Still, I'd like a female opinion on young Tommy.'

They went along to Tommy's room. Though he was still young enough to sleep in his small painted bed, he now thought himself too old to play with the little blue cart he had once lent to help the Dalmatian puppies get back to London. But it was there, on top of the toy cupboard, and Missis gave it a grateful look. Then she assured the Sheepdog that Tommy seemed particularly well. 'Beautifully rosy cheeks, and magnificent breathing.'

'Such an intelligent boy,' said the General, glancing proudly at the books on the bedside table.

'Can he read already?' asked Pongo.

'Well, not the words, but he reads the pictures splendidly. He's particularly fond of something he calls Science Fiction. Don't understand it myself, of course. It seems very mysterious.'

'So I've gathered from television,' said Pongo. 'I'm sure Tommy would be extremely interested in this mysterious sleeping if he wasn't a mysterious sleeper himself. Hello, what's that?'

They all heard a high, shrill barking.

'Bless me, that's Cadpig,' said Missis.

'No, Missis,' said Pongo. 'Her bark couldn't carry all the way from London.'

'Well, it's certainly some dog wanting something,' said the Sheepdog. 'Let's go outside.'

They ran out into the farmyard. The shrill barking continued and now they could make out what was being barked. 'Calling Pongo, Missis or the General!'

'Good gracious, it *is* Cadpig!' said Pongo, and he answered at the top of his bark, 'Hearing you loud and clear! Where are you, my dear?'

'At home, of course,' barked Cadpig.

'At home? Do you mean you're back at Hell Hall?'

'Certainly not,' replied Cadpig, sounding a little bit grand. '*My* home is at Number Ten, Downing Street.'

And now we must learn what had been happening to the smallest, prettiest and bossiest of the fifteen puppies born to Pongo and Missis when they, like the Dearlys, had been 'young marrieds'. A year or so before this story begins, Mr. Dearly – not for the first time – had been asked by the Government to help it get out of debt. He had driven to London and with him, under the seat, went Cadpig, who had heard him say where he was going. When he got out of the car at No. 10 Downing Street, out shot Cadpig so fast that she got through the front door before he did. As the Government was now so worried, the Prime Minister was waiting in the hall to receive Mr. Dearly. Cadpig, who had seen the P.M. on television, recognised him instantly, flung herself at him, and treated him with such slavish affection that he was extremely flattered. A policeman who attempted to remove Cadpig was waved aside and she was allowed (looking both smug and winsome) to attend the financial discussion.

The Government had now got itself into such trouble that even Mr. Dearly didn't know how to get it out. He had at one time been called a wizard of finance but he now felt that a real wizard of magic (plus some kindly gnomes) was needed. Still, he did his best and also said he must put his thinking cap on. (Cadpig thought this an insincere remark, as she knew he didn't own any kind of hat.) He then got up to go and called Cadpig to follow him. She had been lying at the Prime Minister's feet. Now she sprang up, pushed the P.M. back into his armchair, jumped on to his knee and hid her head inside his jasket.

Mr. Dearly apologised for her and said – quite sternly – 'Come on, Cadpig!' She then tried to burrow into the Prime Minister's chest. Mr. Dearly took hold of her collar – and she then flung her paws round the Prime Minister's neck, kissing him and whimpering between kisses. Mr. Dearly, who knew that Cadpig was not a sentimental dog, was astonished at this quite mawkish behaviour. But the Prime Minister was now much more than flattered. He was deeply touched. Tears sprang to his eyes – nowadays he was so often criticised, and even bullied, so seldom treated kindly. He begged to be allowed to keep Cadpig. And Mr. Dearly, seeing that nothing but brute force would dislodge her, felt he must agree.

Not long after this, the Prime Minister spoke on television. Cadpig had loved television since she was a tiny puppy and longed to appear on it. Indeed, that was her main reason for coming to Downing Street. She had a little plan. Just before the Prime Minister finished his speech she came out from behind a curtain, climbed up him, and showed him so much love that his popularity was enormously increased – the British Nation said 'Dogs always *know*'. Since then she had been with him for all his television speeches and she had taken to wrinkling her nose at the Nation in a very fetching smile. She only did this at the end of his speech, so no one ever turned him off half way through. She also eased the tension when very cross people came to see him; and one way and another, she was a terrific success. Most members of the Government hastily bought dogs, but none of these were as important as she was.

And now it was this brilliant daughter who was calling her parents and the General. And it was her own bark they were hearing. Pongo was amazed. As a rule, conversation to London – over sixty miles away – had to be relayed by nearly five hundred dogs. (How well Pongo remembered this, from the time when the Twilight Barking chain had brought news of his stolen puppies!) He said, 'How on earth are you managing it, Cadpig? Is it some new invention?'

'Never mind that now,' said Cadpig. 'Just tell me if things are the same with you as they are here. Everyone asleep but dogs?'

'Every living creature,' said Pongo.

'It's happened all over England – I've had dozens of reports. And I think it may be world-wide – not that I've been able to get in touch with dogs out of England yet, but I hope to soon.'

'How?' said Pongo. 'You can't bark across the sea.'

'Not bark, exactly but – well, I'm barking to you and you're barking to me but I'm almost

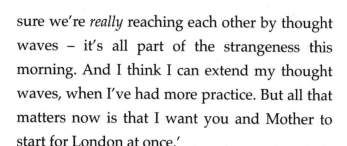 

sure we're *really* reaching each other by thought waves – it's all part of the strangeness this morning. And I think I can extend my thought waves, when I've had more practice. But all that matters now is that I want you and Mother to start for London at once.'

'My dear child!' said Pongo, much honoured. 'Of course we'll come. Unless – just a minute, Cadpig.' He turned to Missis and began to relay what Cadpig had said.

Missis interrupted him. As a rule she had difficulty in catching everything said on long-distance barking but today she had heard every word. 'I'm willing, Pongo,' she said eagerly.

'You don't think we ought to keep guard over the Dearlys?'

'Prince and Perdita can do that.'

'Of course they can,' said Cadpig. She had heard what they said although they had used low tones of bark. 'And I *must* have you here. Delegations of dogs are coming from all over England. I need Mother to help me on the social side and you, Father, must advise me politically.'

'You know as much about politics as I do,' said Pongo.

'Probably much more, by now,' said Cadpig, who had never been famous for modesty. 'I really meant *strategically*. You were splendid at strategy when you saved us all from Cruella de Vil.'

'I was helped by the General,' said Pongo, sounding more modest than he felt. He was really puffed up with pride at his famous daughter's praise.

'Well, the General had better come to London too.'

But the General barked loudly, 'Sorry, but I can't leave Tommy and Mrs. Willow.'

'Oh, bother,' said Cadpig. 'This is no time for personal loyalties. The fate of Dogdom may be at stake. Still, you can advise me by thought waves, can't you?'

'I doubt it,' said the Sheepdog. 'I'm much too bewildered.'

'Well, who isn't?' said Cadpig. 'We've just got to be prepared for *anything*. Now, Father, I

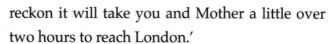 

reckon it will take you and Mother a little over two hours to reach London.'

'Two hours!' gasped Pongo. 'It took us over two *days* when we ran here from London to rescue you all. And we were younger then.'

'But things are different now,' said Cadpig. 'Now listen carefully. This morning, when I couldn't wake the Prime Minister, I was in a great hurry to get help. I dashed down the stairs at full speed and wished I could go faster – and then I found I was going faster. I was skimming over the stairs without touching them, like flying but my feet were only just off the ground. At first I thought I'd merely done a wonderful jump, but I've discovered that I can do it all the time, and so can all the dogs who've come to ask my advice. We've been practising it up and down Downing Street. It's a sort of *swoosh*; you float on the air and you can regulate your speed just by thinking about it. Do you understand?'

'I understand what you're saying,' said Pongo. 'But I can't imagine myself —'

'But that's what you *must* do, Father. You must *imagine* yourself swooshing and then you *will* swoosh.'

'But I'm a very solid dog. Oh, good gracious!' Pongo broke off, staring in astonishment.

Missis was swooshing round the farmyard.

'I can do it, I can do it!' she cried triumphantly.

And now the Sheepdog was swooshing, too.

'Try it, Father,' commanded Cadpig.

Well, if the burly General could swoosh! Pongo launched himself forward – and only managed a jump.

'You're over-anxious,' said the General. 'Take it calmly.'

Pongo took it calmly, but only managed a calm jump.

Missis, swooshing past him gracefully, called, 'Remember that Hovercraft we saw on television. Imagine yourself a Hovercraft, Pongo.'

Pongo vividly remembered the Hovercraft. He thought of it skimming over the waves, just above the waves. And then … He found himself skimming over the land.

It felt delightful, no effort at all. He increased his speed and soon outdistanced Missis and the General.

Missis barked to Cadpig, 'Your father's a magnificent swoosher now.'

'Nothing to it, really,' said Pongo. 'What do you reckon our top speed is, Cadpig?'

'The Minister of Transport's dog has been timing us. She thinks we can do about thirty miles an hour. And she says that should be our speed limit. I've agreed – it's best to humour her; she's doing a very good job – but we've really no way of judging our speed limit, so just come as fast as you can.'

Pongo, after one last burst of speed, pulled up, saying, 'Amazing. I just don't understand it.'

'There are plenty of things I don't understand this morning,' said Cadpig. 'What about the extraordinary behaviour of doors? They open when one wants them to, otherwise I should still be shut up in the Prime Minister's bedroom.'

So that was it. The Dearlys had *not* left the doors open last night.

Missis, still swooshing, said, 'The strangest thing of all is that I'm not hungry.'

'No dogs are,' said Cadpig. 'Which is a blessing, as I couldn't arrange food for all the dogs who are coming to London – though I suppose I could if I needed to, if I really set my *mind* on it. I'm pretty sure this whole business is metaphysical. Don't you agree, Father?'

'Well, yes and no,' said Pongo, deciding that before he met Cadpig he somehow had to find out what 'metaphysical' meant.

'Now I must go,' said Cadpig. 'I've dozens of things to do. Oh, I almost forgot. Please bring a strong force of Dalmatians with you. I may form a private army – which you will command, Father – and we shall need plenty of our own breed.'

Missis stopped swooshing. 'Why do we have to have an army? Must we fight someone?'

'I hope not, Mother. But we must be prepared.'

'But if everyone but us is asleep, who is there to fight?'

'I don't know, Mother. And the enemy you

don't know is worse than the enemy you do know.'

'Nonsense,' said Missis. 'The enemy you don't know isn't there.'

'Anyway, please get to me quickly.'

Pongo and Missis promised they would. Then the barking ended and the sunny morning was silent and still again.

Pongo said, 'How strange that we actually heard her voice across more than sixty miles!'

'No stranger than hearing voices on the telephone,' said Missis.

'But a telephone has wires. Cadpig's thoughts were travelling direct from her mind to ours.'

'Well, no stranger than television, anyway. *That* doesn't have wires.'

'But there are lots of complicated things inside a television set,' said Pongo.

'And there are lots of complicated things inside our minds,' said Missis.

The General then urged them to hurry back to Hell Hall and collect their army. 'And mind you choose good soldiers,' he told them.

Missis said, 'None of them are *any* kind of soldiers. They're just dogs. And do let's go on thinking of them as dogs – for as long as we can.'

# The Meaning of Metaphysical

NOW THAT THEY could swoosh, Pongo and Missis got back to Hell Hall in a couple of minutes. Remembering how light they had felt, when running to the farm, Pongo guessed they had almost swooshed by instinct and he was annoyed with himself for needing to be taught by Cadpig. He must be more alert. And he must certainly find Mr. Dearly's dictionary and learn what 'metaphysical' meant.

Missis was happy to discover that she could swoosh sitting, as well as on four legs. It would make a restful change on the long journey to London. She then became worried because they wouldn't have their collars on as they couldn't put them on for themselves. 'Suppose we meet a policeman?'

'All the policemen will be asleep,' Pongo reminded her.

'Well, that's something to be thankful for.'

As the gates of Hell Hall swung open to let

them in they saw that the front lawn was packed with Dalmatians.

Prince hurried forward to say, 'They all woke up soon after you left. I explained, and there was no panic whatsoever. None of them are hungry but they seem perfectly well, and more peaceful than usual.'

'So I see,' said Pongo, astonished.

At this time of the morning the Dearly Dalmatians were usually at their most boisterous and there was keen competition for the water-shoot, see-saw and swings. Today only the younger dogs were playing. The elder dogs sat still, looking expectant but calm.

Pongo congratulated Prince on the way he had handled things.

'Perdita helped, of course,' said Prince. 'The nursing mothers were a little worried because their puppies had no appetite. But Perdita soothed them. And every pup will start the Emergency spotlessly clean.'

Under a shady tree, Perdita could be seen puppy-washing.

'Naturally, everyone's eager for news,' Prince went on, 'but I've asked them not to rush you.'

Pongo, gazing at the sunny, dog-filled lawn, disliked disturbing so much peace but it had to be done. He stepped forward between Misses and Prince, called all dogs to attention and told them what he had learned from Cadpig. When he described swooshing there was a ripple of movement – many dogs wanted to try it. But Pongo restrained them.

'A swooshing class will be held later,' he said firmly. '*Now* we have to decide who's coming to London. Mothers with puppies must, of course, stay here, and fathers of puppies must stay and guard their families. All other dogs are free to volunteer. I'd like a show of tails.'

Instantly the whole lawn seethed with wildly wagging tails.

'Thank you, thank you,' said Pongo. 'But I mustn't take so many.' He turned to Prince. 'I think we'd better discuss it, while Missis holds a swooshing class – in the yew walk, I suggest. That's long enough for them to practise speed.'

The yew walk was a stretch of grass between two tall yew hedges. Missis, feeling important, led the way there. Every dog except Pongo and Prince went with her. Even the nursing mothers took their puppies to watch.

Pongo then asked Prince if he would stay and guard the Dearlys. 'I shan't feel at ease unless you do. And of course Perdita must stay with you and as many dogs as you think are needed here.'

Prince would have liked to go to London, but he knew where his duty lay as he and Perdita were half-owners of the Dearlys. He also knew that Perdita was a home-loving dog – having been, during a tragic period of her youth, homeless. So he agreed to stay and said Pongo must take all the dogs he wished. 'All my own family will want to come,' said Pongo. 'What a blessing that Lucky's chosen a wife as bright as he is. They'll be a great help. So will Patch. And he's longing to see Cadpig.'

Patch had never married. He had found out that, for the good of the Dalmatian breed, he ought not to hand on his patched ear. But he had not been unhappy. He had become a sort of uncle dog and was tremendously popular with puppies. He was always ready to play with them and he loved them all. But the great love of his life was his sister, Cadpig, of whom he had taken such care when she was a tiny, weak puppy. He was proud of her fame, but he had never ceased to miss her.

Pongo went on, 'I wonder if I can risk taking Roly Poly.'

The fat pup who had had so many accidents was now a fat dog who still had accidents – and as he was larger, *they* were larger. At that very moment there was a roar of laughter from the dogs in the yew walk and Missis was heard saying, 'Oh dear, have you hurt yourself, Roly? You're not supposed to swoosh *through* things.'

'We'd better see what's happening,' said Pongo.

They found that Roly Poly hadn't done himself any harm, though he hadn't done a yew hedge any good. Pongo whispered to Missis, 'I hardly feel it will be safe to take Roly with us.'

'Neither will it be safe to leave him behind,' said Missis. 'And I'd rather know the worst about him than just imagine the worst.'

'And his feelings would be terribly hurt if we didn't take him. I'm afraid some dogs are bound to have their feelings hurt.'

But things didn't turn out that way. It was taken for granted that Pongo would want his own family. And when he and Prince divided the remainder up, like choosing sides in a game (no married couples were separated), the ones who were to remain behind at once took to the idea of guarding the Dearlys and defending Hell Hall, though no one knew what from. It was all part of the perfect behaviour of all dogs on that remarkable morning.

None of the dogs had any difficulty in learning to swoosh, but Pongo wanted to be sure that all the dogs coming to London were strong swooshers, so he left them to practise while he and Missis took a last look at their pets.

First they ran up to the big, comfortable attic which was shared by the Nannies. Nanny Cook, in a frilly nightgown, slept with her mouth open. Nanny Butler, in pyjamas, slept with her mouth firmly shut. They both looked comfortable and splendidly healthy.

'How kind they've always been to us,' said Missis. 'Do you remember that night when they helped to wash the soot off us and all the puppies?'

Pongo said, 'That was when we were at the end of an adventure. Now we're at the beginning of one.'

'Well, thank goodness this one can't have anything to do with Cruella de Vil,' said Missis, 'as we know she had to leave England.'

'But —' Pongo broke off in time. Some months earlier he had heard the Dearlys saying that Cruella had come back. He had kept this from Missis at the time and he would go on keeping it from her. And, anyway, how could Cruella have anything to do with this mysterious sleeping?

They ran down to the Dearlys' bedroom. Nothing had changed. The Dearlys still smiled in their sleep. The white cats, if not actually smiling, were looking as blissful as sleeping cats can.

Missis gave her basket a loving look, then suddenly cried, 'Pongo, I've just remembered! Last night I had an important dream.' As a rule, Missis dreamt about food. In good dreams, jam-tarts grew on trees and chocolate drops came down like rain, and so on. In bad dreams food was often behind glass or in tins that couldn't be opened. But this latest dream was different from any dream she had ever had before and she wasn't sure if it was good or bad. She only knew it was important. 'There was a dazzling bright light,' she told Pongo. 'And – oh dear, I can't remember any more.'

'Perhaps it will come back to you,' said Pongo, though he rather hoped it wouldn't. He enjoyed telling his own dreams, but wasn't fond of listening to other people's. 'I think we should start now, my dear.'

So they kissed the Dearlys and looked very kindly at the cats. And Missis told her basket she

would soon be home (she did this silently because Pongo would have laughed at her for talking to her basket). And then they ran downstairs.

When they reached the hall Pongo said, 'Let's go into Mr. Dearly's study. I want to find out the meaning of that strange word Cadpig used, 'metaphysical'. It'll be in the dictionary.'

Pongo was a splendid reader – how often had he blessed those Alphabet Blocks he had played with as a pup! But he had never looked up a word in the dictionary and he wasn't sure on which shelf the dictionary was kept. Also, the room was only dimly lit because the curtains were still drawn. But as he peered around, a shaft of sunlight came between the curtains (did they draw aside just a little to let it in?) and it shone full on a dark blue book which had 'Dictionary' in gold letters on its back. He nosed it from the shelf and it slid gently to the floor, where it fell open. The bright shaft of sunlight shone on it.

'Bless me, it's opened at the very word I want,' said Pongo.

'I do call that civil,' said Missis.

Pongo found the words which explained 'metaphysical' as puzzling as the word itself. But when he read them aloud to Missis she understood two of them, 'visionary' and 'supernatural'. She said 'visionary' was when you imagined things, and 'supernatural' must mean extra specially natural.

'Or perhaps more than natural,' said Pongo. 'And I see that metaphysics has something to do with the mind.'

Missis said, '*I* think metaphysical means magic – a kind of magic that comes from our own minds. That's why we're able to open doors today, and talk direct to Cadpig – and swoosh. Oh, Pongo, I *like* metaphysical!'

'I don't think I do,' said Pongo. 'I don't think I like things I don't understand.'

'That's because you have such a splendid brain. *My* brain understands so little that it loves things it's not *supposed* to understand. Anyway, I've taken to metaphysical.'

Pongo never thought Missis as silly as she thought herself. And he greatly depended on her instincts. He was a clever dog and he knew it. But he also knew that the cleverer he got, the less help he got from his instincts. So he was happy that he could rely on what his dear wife often called her 'feelings'. And if she was in favour of metaphysical he would do his best to be, too.

He tried to put the dictionary back on its shelf, but could not manage it. Why? When this morning he could do so many things not usually possible?

'It's because you don't need to,' said Missis. 'If you did, I'm sure metaphysical would help. The book will be quite safe on the floor.'

'Not if any puppies get in here.'

So Missis pushed the book under the sofa with her nose and said, 'No puppy will find it there. And when we come back and Mr. Dearly's awake we'll show him where his dictionary is.'

But would they ever come back? Would Mr. Dearly ever wake? Pongo tried to turn these fears out of his mind. Anyway, he must hide them from Missis. He said briskly, 'Now we must hurry.'

They ran out into the sunny garden.

# The Great Swoosh

BY NOW the fifty Dalmatians who were coming to London were accomplished swooshers. Pongo lined them up on the front lawn in rows of four. He and Missis were in the front row with Patch and Roly Poly. Lucky and his wife, Gay, were in the back row to see there were no stragglers. In between, dotted about, were the other members of Pongo's family. They were looking forward to seeing their famous sister, Cadpig, in Downing Street.

When they were ready to start Pongo said to Missis, 'It does seem strange to set out without so much as a drink of water. Shall I ask if any dog is thirsty?'

'Ask if you like but no dog will be – any more than we are.'

Still, Pongo asked. But though the pond was at hand (which the dogs found more tasty than tap water) no dog wanted to drink.

'Very peculiar,' said Pongo.

'Just metaphysical,' said Missis.

Pongo had a few last words with Prince, Missis kissed Perdita affectionately, and all the dogs who were staying behind wished the little army good luck. Then Pongo said, 'Now we'll start very slowly. Then take your pace from Missis and me, and be ready to stop at the farm. I must have a word with the General. Gates, please!'

The tall gates swung open, and out at a slow swoosh went the thirteen rows of four Dalmatians. Then the gates swung together again.

When they were out on the road Pongo increased the pace and they reached the farm quickly – to find that a Beagle, two Spaniels, a very brave Pekinese and four dogs of mixed breed were lined up and ready to join up.

The Sheepdog said, 'I swooshed to the village and recruited them. And I've got myself a bright lad to train as a lieutenant.' He glared down at a small Jack Russell Terrier, 'Not that he'll ever be as good as Mrs. Willow, or as Lucky was at his age.'

'Yes, I will. I'll be better,' said the Jack Russell

Terrier, in a shrill voice, glaring back at the Sheepdog.

'Bless my soul, what impertinence,' said the General. 'Still, I like a bit of spirit.' One reason that the General was so fond of the tabby cat was that she always answered him back and there was no doubt that the Jack Russell was going to be just as good at it.

Lucky had now got the eight dogs from the village into line.

'My guess is that you'll be joined by volunteers all along the route,' said the General, 'which is bound to delay you. So you'd better get a move on.'

'All dogs at the ready,' said Pongo and then, after saying goodbye to the General and the Jack Russell, he commanded, 'Quick swoosh!'

The road from the farm twisted, so the swoosh wasn't really quick at first. But after they were through the village – where all the dogs who were remaining on guard raised a hearty cheer – they were soon on the high road and could go full speed. Pongo found there was no need to bark instructions. Whatever pace he set was instantly followed. He found this puzzling and asked Missis if she could explain it.

Missis at once said, 'It's quite simple. You think a faster thought and we all go faster. You think a slower thought and we all slow down. Indeed, we only move forward at all because you think a forward thought.'

Just then there was a terrific commotion. Roly Poly swooshed backwards and bumped into the dog behind him and that dog bumped into the dog that was behind *him*, and so on right to the back row of the army. Pongo both thought and barked 'Halt!' and was thankful that no one was hurt.

'But whatever happened, Roly?' he asked, while the dogs behind were picking themselves up.

'I was listening to what you and Mother were saying,' said Roly Poly. 'And I accidentally thought a *backward* thought.'

'No one but your Father is to think any thoughts at all,' said Missis. 'And you'd better warn all the other dogs, Pongo.'

But Pongo didn't think this would be wise. 'It might make them nervous. And no dog but Roly Poly would think a backward thought when we're swooshing forward. All will be well if Roly will make his mind a blank.'

'I'll try. I'll try hard,' said Roly Poly.

The swoosh began again but this time Roly didn't budge and was knocked down by the dog behind him. Again the army had to halt. Missis said, 'He made his mind *too* blank – it didn't let your thoughts in, Pongo. Roly, dear, tell your mind that it's to do what your father's mind tells it. Just until we get to London. Then you can think your own thoughts again.'

After that, they swooshed smoothly until they reached the town of Sudbury. Pongo, looking at the closed shops, thought of all the pleasant shopkeepers, now fast asleep. He knew many of them well as the Dearlys often brought him and Missis here on market days. How jolly – and noisy – the market had always been! Now it was deserted except for a group of dogs standing by Gainsborough's statue, waiting to join the army.

Pongo halted so that Lucky could fit them in.

Missis, looking up at the church clock, said, 'Twelve o'clock, my very favourite time ! Both hands are in the same place so I can't get them mixed.' Then, as the clock began to chime, she added, 'Oh, Pongo, do you remember? It was striking twelve the first time we saw this town, when we came to rescue the puppies. But then it was striking midnight, which makes quite a different noise.'

'Not really,' said Pongo.

'Well, it does to me – because the *feel* of midnight is just a little scaring and the feel of midday isn't. Though today even mid day feels a bit peculiar.'

Soon they were on their way again and swooshing through beautiful open country. It was a marvellous high summer day, in fact Missis thought it was the highest summer day she had ever known. The sky seemed farther away than usual and looked more like blue velvet than a normal sky does; Missis felt she would like to stroke it. Tall trees looked particularly tall and their heavy foliage looked particularly soft and furry. Cornfields were turning gold and the very air seemed golden and not just because the sun was shining; the air seemed to have a golden haze of its own. And the whole countryside was utterly still.

Missis said, 'Isn't it strange that, though we're moving so fast, our ears aren't blowing back.'

'And I can't feel any breeze on my nose,' said Pongo.

'All the winds, like all the creatures but dogs, must be asleep. Pongo, I *am* enjoying this peaceful swoosh.'

Pongo felt it wasn't safe to feel peaceful. But he didn't want to worry Missis so he told her to go on enjoying herself.

'You mean, as long as I can,' said Missis, guessing that his sense of responsibility was making him anxious. 'And so I will. But I could enjoy myself much more if *you* were enjoying yourself. Do try. Remember that enjoyment's something you can store up. Once you've had it, no one can take it away.'

'That's a fine maxim, my dear.'

'A what, Pongo?'

'A maxim. It's a word I've heard Mr. Dearly use. I think it means something you specially believe in.'

'Fancy me speaking a maxim !' said Missis, proudly. 'Anyway, try to relax. Perhaps there may be worries ahead of us, but don't let's meet them half way.'

So Pongo relaxed and the whole army of Hover-dogs swooshed peacefully through the still, silent morning, stopping only when dogs were waiting to join the army. But the worries that lay ahead were soon reaching out towards them. While they were waiting for Lucky to fit some dogs in, Pongo felt a sudden stirring in his mind and, a moment later, he heard Cadpig barking. (The thought wave had come just ahead of the bark – like light travelling faster than sound.) He answered at once.

'Thank goodness I've found you,' said Cadpig. 'It isn't easy to get in touch with dogs who are on the move. Where are you and how soon will you be at No. 10?'

Pongo said he thought they were about half way and would be at least another hour.

'You're being terribly slow,' said Cadpig.

Pongo explained that they sometimes had to stop for dogs who wanted to come with them.

Cadpig brushed this aside. 'Let them come on their own.'

'But they don't know the way,' said Pongo. 'I do, because I've often driven to London with Mr. Dearly.'

'They can get to London if they *think* about getting to London,' said Cadpig. 'I've had that information barked all over England. But some dogs just want to be led. Anyway, far too many dogs are coming. There's a seething mass of dogs outside No. 10. Oh Father, do hurry!'

'Anything specially wrong, dear?' asked Missis.

'Nothing I can bark about. But I do have a lot on my mind. I must go, I'm being called – I think we may be getting through to America. Now swoosh your fastest, but look out for traffic when you get near London.'

'Traffic?' said Pongo, astonished.

'I mean dog traffic, of course. There are dog jams all over the place. Get as close to Downing Street as you can and then bark to me. I'll send an escort. Goodbye for now.'

All the dogs had heard Cadpig so Pongo only had to give the order 'Full swoosh ahead' and set the fastest pace he could. Missis didn't care for it at all. She said, 'All the peace is gone. Well, Cadpig never was a peaceful dog. Pongo, did you think she sounded scared?'

Pongo had, indeed, thought so but he didn't want to worry Missis, so he just said, 'Perhaps it was simply that her voice was a little tired. She must have done a powerful lot of barking this morning. Well, we shall soon be there to help her.'

There were now fewer waiting dogs who had to be stopped for, as many of them had started on their own. But when, after a long, fast swoosh, the outskirts of London were reached, traffic problems began and it was no longer possible to swoosh fast. Dogs were coming from all directions, in small groups and long processions, and it was difficult to judge who had the right of way. Pongo wished the traffic lights were working – and suddenly they were! He didn't feel he was a sufficiently powerful wisher to have done this on his own, so he could only think that Cadpig had somehow arranged it.

As they got closer and closer to the heart of London, the streets looked stranger and stranger. There were no humans anywhere, there was no traffic but dogs, all the shops were closed; but wherever there were houses, some front doors were open and dogs were sitting there watching the passing dogs. Nowhere was there any sign of panic. Indeed, the watching dogs looked particularly calm, expectantly calm.

Missis, while they were waiting at traffic lights, said, 'Doesn't it strike you as peculiar that there's so little noise? It isn't normal for dogs to be so silent.'

'I think they're listening,' said Pongo. 'And perhaps they're learning to hear with a sort of inner ear.'

'Well, I don't think it's healthy,' said Missis. 'Sometimes the young dogs at Hell Hall make more noise than I care for, but I'd be glad enough to hear it now. And I don't think I hold with inner ears – or thought waves. How can one be sure one's keeping one's thoughts to oneself? One's entitled to *private* thoughts.'

Pongo was about to say something soothing when he saw a look of horror come into his wife's eyes. He said quickly, 'What is it? What's wrong?' Then he saw what she was looking at.

Partly hidden by some small houses was a factory with a signboard on the top of it on which was painted, in scarlet, CRUELLA DE VIL & CO. Makers of KLOES THAT KLANK.

KLOES THAT KLANK? To Pongo it didn't make sense. But it did to Missis because she was a bad speller. She said at once 'It means Clothes that Clank. But all that matters is that she's back in England – that wicked woman!'

Pongo then confessed that he had known. 'But she's not our enemy now, Missis. She won't want Dalmatian skins any more. Mr. de Vil's no longer a furrier. The Dearlys said he and Cruella are making plastic raincoats.'

'Plastic raincoats don't clank,' said Missis. 'And clanking clothes sound dangerous. Up till now I've quite enjoyed this adventure but if Cruella's back —'

'She can't have anything to do with what's happening today,' said Pongo. 'Just try to keep your mind off her. See, the traffic lights are changing.'

Missis was only too glad to move past the factory but she went on worrying and after a few minutes she said, 'We must warn Cadpig. She must have Cruella locked up.'

'But Cruella will just be asleep, like all humans,' said Pongo.

'You forget. Cruella's *not* human.'

'We were never *sure* of that,' said Pongo. But it was true that they had once believed that Cruella might be some kind of devil. Perhaps the mysterious sleeping wouldn't affect devils I still, he told Missis firmly, 'Anyway, only dogs are awake. And she's certainly not a dog.'

Before long they were in Camden Town, not far from Regent's Park where Pongo and Missis had once lived; then they hurried across Marylebone Road and along Langham Place past Broadcasting House.

Missis said, 'There won't be any broadcasting as there are no humans awake. How Cadpig will miss television!'

Regent Street was very full and not only of swooshing dogs. There were also a great many dogs merely looking in the shop windows. And now there was more noise.

Dogs were chattering quite gaily. Missis heard one say, 'Madam Cadpig's quite right. If we've come to London we might as well enjoy ourselves.' No doubt Cadpig was trying to keep everyone happy.

Piccadilly was even fuller than Regent Street, but Pongo's army managed to get through and then went along Haymarket into Trafalgar Square. 'Nearly there, now,' said Pongo as they swooshed into Whitehall.

Then he wondered if he had spoken too soon,

for the crowd was almost solid – and at the entrance to Downing Street it appeared to be *quite* solid. What was he to do? Cadpig had told him to let her know when they arrived, but there was so much noise that no bark would be heard.

'Well, we must do our very best thought waves,' he said to Missis. And then he asked all the dogs in the army to help. 'Just think, with all your strength, "Cadpig, we're here in Whitehall".'

It worked magnificently. Within a couple of minutes a squad of Police Dogs were forcing their way through to Pongo. The leader said loudly, 'All dogs of Madam Cadpig's own breed are to proceed to Downing Street. All other dogs are to proceed to Horse Guards' Parade.'

Pongo felt responsible for the dogs who had joined him. He said, 'Will they be well looked after on Horse Guards' Parade?'

The leader of the Police Dogs said, 'They don't need looking after. Today no dog wants to eat, drink or even sleep. All they need is a place to sit. And there's no more sitting room in Downing

Street. On your way, boys!'

Half the Police Dogs cleared a way to Horse Guards. Parade. And then the leader said, 'Make way for the Dalmatians!'

Dogs fell back without resentment. Indeed, they were all wagging their tails and there were cries of 'Long live Madam Cadpig and all her Dalmatian relations.'

Missis said, 'I hope I'm not looking smug, Pongo. I hadn't realised how important our daughter has become.'

And so the Dalmatian army entered Downing Street.

# The Cabinet Meeting

CADPIG WAS STANDING at the open door of No. 10. As a pup she had been unusually small and she was still on the small side for a fullgrown Dalmatian. But apart from that, she was an almost perfect specimen of the breed, with beautiful spots, wonderful dark eyes and a most fetching expression. Pongo and Missis had sometimes feared she might have become too grand for them, so they were touched to see how lovingly she greeted them and all her family, giving a specially warm welcome to her devoted brother, Patch. She then spoke most graciously to all the other Dalmatians, remembering many names though it was around a year since she had left Hell Hall.

'Pretty manners,' thought Missis proudly. 'No wonder she's getting on so well.'

Behind Cadpig stood a number of dogs whom she introduced as 'My Cabinet'. These were the dogs who lived with the members of the human

Cabinet and were deputising for them. 'This is the Chancellor of the Exchequer,' said Cadpig presenting a black Labrador. 'He's longing to meet you, Father, because you're so good at figures.'

'It's Mr. Dearly, not me, who's good at figures,' said Pongo. 'I can't do much more than put two and two together. They *usually* make four.'

'With us, they've only been making three,' said the Labrador. 'But things may be better after the Chancellor's had this long restful sleep.'

Cadpig was now presenting the Foreign Secretary, a plump, jovial Boxer. He reminded Missis of someone but she couldn't think who it was.

'And this dear friend is the Minister of Transport,' said Cadpig, smiling at a prettily clipped brown Poodle. 'It was she who got the traffic lights to work. Wasn't that brilliant?'

'I just thought about them,' said the Poodle, 'and, bless me, they happened!'

Other Cabinet Ministers were presented, also some dogs who lived with members of the

Opposition. 'That's the party that didn't win the last Election,' Cadpig explained to her mother. 'But of course we're all on the same side now.'

'Everyone should be on the same side always,' said Missis. 'Think how much time it would save.'

'But I've heard there's a catch in it,' said Cadpig. 'You see, sometimes everyone gets on the *wrong* side.' She then said she wanted a little talk with her parents before the Cabinet Meeting which would shortly start. 'So will the rest of you go out into the garden? The Minister of Transport will act as hostess for me, won't you, Babs dear?'

The brown Poodle said indeed she would and she and all the members of the Dog Cabinet escorted all the Dalmatians except Pongo and Missis, who tried not to look as important as they felt.

As the hall became emptier Missis gave a gasp. She was now able to see that, lying on the black-and-white marble floor, was a policeman. Of course he was asleep but, even so, Missis felt scared. She asked why he was there.

Cadpig said, 'There's always a policeman here, to guard the house, and two policemen outside. The outside ones have been moved by the Police Dogs but I thought this one might as well stay where he is.'

'I can't feel that policemen should be allowed indoors,' said Missis. 'Anyway, he makes the hall look untidy.'

Cadpig said she would get him moved later, if she could think of any place to put him. 'This house is so full of sleepers – secretaries and the like. Now I want you to see the Prime Minister.'

She led the way to the lift, which obligingly opened its doors. Neither Pongo nor Missis had ever been in a lift and Pongo felt sure Missis would be nervous. He said quickly, 'Couldn't we use the stairs?'

'Oh, the lift's perfectly safe,' said Cadpig. 'I know which buttons to press. Though to-day I'm working it by my thoughts.'

'You mean, metaphysically,' said Missis.

Cadpig looked impressed. 'How clever of you to understand that!'

'Your mother has always been very metaphysical,' said Pongo.

The lift took them upstairs; then opened its doors to let them out. Missis thanked it politely.

'This is the flat where we all live,' said Cadpig, 'but there's no one at home but the Prime Minister. His wife's away. Quite a good sort of woman but fussy about dogs getting on beds. This way.'

She took them into a bedroom. A Police Dog, lying by the bed, stood up.

Cadpig said, 'Here are my father and mother, come to help us, Sergeant.'

'And I'm sure they'll be able to, madam,' said the Police Dog. 'There isn't a Police Dog in England who doesn't know how Pongo and Missis rescued the stolen puppies.'

Cadpig was looking anxiously towards the bed. 'Any change, Sergeant?'

'None at all, madam – except that he seems to me to be smiling slightly.'

'You're right,' said Cadpig. 'Oh, *good!* That must mean that he's really relaxing.' She turned to Pongo and Missis. 'How do you think he's looking?'

'Very peaceful,' said Missis. 'And younger than on television.'

'He's an excellent colour,' said Pongo.

'Not too flushed?' Cadpig asked anxiously.

'No, no. Just healthily rosy.'

'He's lost quite a lot of his chubbiness,' said Cadpig. 'That's because he's had so many worries. Well, this is one crisis *he* doesn't have to face.'

Missis said, 'I like him better than I expected to. I think that's because he isn't talking. He talks too much, on television.'

'I agree,' said Pongo. 'He should just sit there with you on his knee, Cadpig, smiling kindly but saying nothing. Could you give him the hint?'

Cadpig shook her head sadly. 'Clever though he is, he can't understand a word I say.'

'That's our trouble at Scotland Yard,' said the Police Dog. 'We dogs learn so quickly, but none of us has ever managed to train a policeman.'

Cadpig gave the Prime Minister a gentle pat

and invited her parents to pat him too, which they respectfully did. Then Cadpig said they must go down to the Cabinet Meeting. 'Much as I hate to leave him.'

'I'll guard him well, madam,' said the Police Dog, standing to attention.

On the way to the life, Cadpig said, 'I want you to take the chair at the Cabinet Meeting, Father.'

'No, no,' said Pongo. 'I shouldn't know what to say.'

'Well, I don't either,' said Cadpig. 'And I'm terribly worried – and I mustn't, I mustn't let anyone but you two know. I'll tell you when we're in the lift.'

The lift doors opened and they all got in. But when the lift had gone down only a little way, it stopped.

'Don't worry,' said Cadpig. 'I *asked* it to stop. This is the only place I can feel sure I shan't be overheard. There are dogs all over the house this morning. Oh, dear!' She suddenly drooped, looking helpless and pitiful, and gave a little moan.

'Now stop being silly, dear,' said Missis briskly, 'and tell us what's wrong.'

Pongo said, 'Has something happened that we don't know about?'

'No, it hasn't,' said Cadpig. 'And *that's* what's wrong. *Nothing's* happened and I can't find out what's *going* to happen. This morning everything was exciting – learning to swoosh, finding I could send my thoughts everywhere and tell dogs what to do. But now I wish I hadn't told them. Thousands and thousands have come to London and I don't know what to do with them.'

'Well, send them home again,' said Missis.

'But if I do that, they'll lose faith in me. And then they won't want to see me on television when things are normal again. And that will be bad for the Prime Minister as well as me.'

Pongo saw that his gifted daughter had bitten off more than she could chew – not a thing that often happens to a dog. He said firmly, 'The dogs might as well be here as anywhere else, provided you avoid panic. You must let them know the situation's under control.'

'How can the situation be under control when I don't know what the situation is?'

'I'll admit that's a bit tricky,' said Pongo. 'But about this Cabinet Meeting —'

'*Please* take the chair, Father!'

'Can't you and your father *both* have chairs?' said Missis.

'Of course there will be chairs for everyone, Mother. Taking the chair means being in charge.'

'And that's what you must be, Cadpig,' said Pongo. 'You must represent the Prime Minister. But you may call on me to speak.'

'What will you say, Pongo?' asked Missis.

'Ah!' said Pongo, in a meaningful tone.

'I don't think "Ah" will be enough,' said Missis.

'I meant that it will come to me, when it needs to. And it will come to you, Cadpig.'

'No, it won't,' said Cadpig miserably. 'I've lost confidence.'

'Then you must get it back at once,' said Missis, who did not fancy being between floors in a lift with a Cadpig who had lost confidence.

'And you can start by making this lift work.'

'Perhaps I can't now,' said Cadpig.

'Well, *I* can,' said Pongo. 'Today we can *all* open doors and make lifts work.' He directed a polite but powerful thought to the lift and it instantly moved downwards.

'Oh, Father, you're splendid,' said Cadpig. 'Though I *think* it would have moved for me.'

The lift stopped suddenly. Missis felt frightened. Then the lift moved downwards again.

'That was just me, testing myself,' said Cadpig. 'Oh, thank you, Father. My confidence is coming back again.'

The lift reached the hall and opened its doors. Missis, having hurried out, remembered to thank them. She thought it wise to keep on their right side – though, as far as Missis was concerned, their best side was the outside.

Cadpig led the way to the back of the house and into a large room which she said was the Cabinet Room. Up till today Missis had thought that a cabinet was a piece of furniture in which ornaments were shut away from puppies. But she had by now gathered that – in Downing Street – a Cabinet was a group of dogs who would help Cadpig to govern England, and this was the room in which they met. She need not have worried about a shortage of chairs. There were more than she could count, placed round a very long table. Tall windows opened on to a terrace which had steps leading down to the garden, where the Dalmatian army was being entertained by Cabinet Ministers. From the terrace, to which Cadpig took them, Missis could see over a wall to Horse Guards' Parade which was packed with dogs.

Pongo said, 'What a magnificent sight! It looks as if every breed of dog is represented.'

'Except Corgis,' said Cadpig. 'They're all sitting outside Buckingham Palace.'

The Boxer who had reminded Missis of someone came bounding up the steps of the terrace. He said, 'Is it all right by you, Cadpig, if I make one of your brothers my Private Secretary? He's a splendid fellow.'

'Good idea,' said Cadpig. 'All Cabinet Ministers had better have Private Secretaries. I'll have Patch for mine. Hi, Patch, where are you?'

Patch came eagerly up the steps – only to be bowled over by the Foreign Secretary, who was swooshing down.

'Sorry, old chap,' said the Boxer, helping Patch up. 'I haven't quite got the hang of this swooshing. The Minister of Transport says swooshers rank as vehicles and keep to the left, but I don't feel like a vehicle. Not hurt, are you? Good. Now where's my new Secretary?'

'Of course he'll have chosen Lucky,' said Missis, proudly thinking how intelligent Lucky was. 'Oh, good gracious! Look!'

The Boxer had joined Roly Poly, who was happily wagging his tail.

Pongo said, 'Cadpig, dear, I'm not sure your Foreign Secretary has made a wise choice.'

Cadpig laughed. 'Oh, George is always putting his paw in his mouth. But he's a dear and so is Roly Poly, so they'll keep each other happy. And perhaps it's safer for them to get into trouble together rather than separately.'

Missis said, 'Bless me, I've just realised who the Foreign Secretary reminds me of. It's Roly Poly – though you wouldn't think a Boxer could look like a Dalmatian, would you?'

'It's something in the expression of their nice round eyes,' said Cadpig. 'I think the Minister of Transport had better have both Lucky and his wife as her Secretaries. She'll need a lot of help, what with the traffic and her topknot. Just arrange for that, will you, Patch? And then come back to me.'

Patch, looking happy and capable, ran back to the garden and found Babs the Poodle, who waved her thanks to Cadpig.

'A pretty creature, isn't she?' said Missis. 'Though I do think that topknot's a bit much.'

'She's been known to have it tied up with a very fancy ribbon,' said Cadpig.

A powerfully-voiced clock began to chime the hour.

'That'll be Big Ben,' said Pongo. 'How close we are to it here.'

Missis carefully counted the strokes and was glad she only had to go as far as three, a nice, easy number.

Cadpig barked down to the garden. 'Time for the Cabinet Meeting.'

Members of the Cabinet, who had been chatting to the Dalmatians, came up the steps to the terrace. Patch came back to Cadpig and Lucky and his wife, Gay, followed Babs the Poodle. Missis expected to see Roly Poly come with George, the Foreign Secretary, but there was no sign of either of them. Missis looked around the garden and saw that they were standing by a door in the wall. The door opened (no doubt it had been asked to) and out they both went.

Missis said to Cadpig, 'I fancy the Foreign Secretary will be late.'

'Well, we can't wait for him,' said Cadpig, taking her parents back into the Cabinet Room. 'Now will every dog take a chair – but not the one with arms. That's the Prime Minister's and I shall represent him. Please sit on my right, Father. And Mother shall be on my left.'

But Missis said she did not want to sit at the table as she didn't know anything about politics. 'When they happen on television I close my eyes and somehow manage to go deaf – unless *you're* appearing, Cadpig. Let me sit by the window here.'

She wanted to watch for Roly Poly. What was he up to? She didn't agree with Cadpig that he and the Foreign Secretary might be safer together than on their own. Together, they might get into twice as much mischief.

'Well, sit where you like, Mother dear,' said Cadpig, climbing up into the Prime Minister's chair. 'Now attention, everyone!'

There was no doubt that Cadpig's confidence had come back. Missis was glad about this and proud of the impressive way her daughter outlined the situation. But it seemed to Missis that all the dogs already knew what the situation was and wanted to know *why* it was and what was going to happen next. Of course Cadpig had nothing to say about this and soon she was calling on Pongo to speak. She introduced him as 'My famous father'.

Missis remembered a speech Pongo had made to her on that could night when he and she were setting out to rescue their puppies. It had helped her and she wished he would say something like it now.

Really, it was strange the way thoughts were dashing about to-day! It seemed that Pongo must know what was in her mind.

'Lady dogs and gentlemen dogs,' he began. 'Long ago when my dear wife and I were setting out on a perilous journey, I told her that dogs who are very well treated sometimes lose their liking for adventure and grow old before their time. Now I feel sure that all the dogs at this table are well treated, and though I don't say any of you are fat, you are all quite well covered. But I won't believe you are stodgy. I think you are all ready for anything. Am I right?'

All the dogs said 'Yes, indeed' or 'Hear, hear' and some of them banged the table with their paws.

Pongo then went on, 'The question is, what are we ready *for*? But if we knew that, wouldn't the adventure be more *ordinary?* Isn't it more exciting not to know what lies ahead? Let us live excitingly from minute to minute and let us count our blessings. Think how much we have learnt since we woke up this morning. We can swoosh, open doors, bark by thought waves. And none of us is hungry, thirsty, too hot or too cold. Perhaps most important of all, we are completely friendly. Close to us here, on Horse Guards' Parade, there are hundreds – no, thousands – of dogs crowded together. But I have not heard one dog-fight. Have there been any?'

A vast number of dogs barked 'No!' and Missis realised that Pongo was sending his thoughts out far beyond the Cabinet Meeting. Perhaps he was sending them all over England – she thought he must be because, from now on, whenever there were cheers they came to her like a great rushing wind. She could not have said if she was hearing with her ears or with her mind. She just *knew* the cheers were happening. And she felt prouder and prouder of Pongo. He went on saying encouraging things and telling all dogs how well

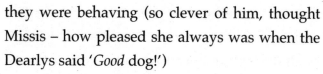 

they were behaving (so clever of him, thought Missis – how pleased she always was when the Dearlys said '*Good* dog!')

Finally he said, 'My dear pet, Mr. Dearly, sometimes reads aloud to Mrs. Dearly, and my wife and I sit and listen. I remember once hearing of a famous Prime Minister who lived in this house who was always telling people to "Wait and See". That is what I say to you, oh dogs of England. Don't worry about what's going to happen. Wait and see!'

This provoked enormous enthusiasm. Missis happened to remember that Mr. Dearly had thought it a very annoying thing to say and many people hadn't liked it. Well, perhaps much depended on how it was said. Pongo said it magnificently and Missis thought it sounded splendid. Like all the other dogs, near and far, she barked delightedly and thumped her tail.

Cadpig sprang up in her chair and said, 'Dogs everywhere! My father has told us what to do. Wait and See! Wait and See!'

WAIT AND SEE! WAIT AND SEE! The rushing

wind of thought grew louder and louder. Missis began to wonder if it was healthy for thought to be so noisy and she was relieved when Pongo barked, 'But let us wait and see *quietly*,' and the cheering died down.

This came as a relief to Pongo too. He was thankful that he could now hear himself think. But he was also worried. How *obedient* the dogs were – and they were obedient to him! What a responsibility! Still, it could hardly be wrong to tell them to wait and see, as there was absolutely nothing else they could do.

At that moment the glass door to the terrace burst open and in came Roly Poly and George, soaking wet. They shook themselves violently, splashing all the dogs near them. One of these was Babs the Poodle, who protested loudly.

Cadpig spoke severely to the Boxer. 'George, keep still! You should have got your shaking over out of doors. And you've missed the Cabinet Meeting. Where have you been?'

The Boxer said, 'I was showing Roly Poly the lake in St. James's Park and he happened to say he could swim and I said I couldn't. He said all dogs can if they try and he'd show me how. So he did and now I can swim like anything.'

'You both ought to be dried,' said Missis. Oh dear, this was a job one needed humans for. Well, rolling on the carpet would help. She soon had George and Roly Poly rolling energetically. They got drier and drier and the carpet got wetter and wetter.

'That's no way to behave at a Cabinet Meeting,' said Cadpig. 'The Prime Minister never lets anyone roll. George, do get back to your office and see if any news has come in.' She explained to Pongo. 'It's the Foreign Secretary's job to deal with foreign countries.'

'Did you get through to America?' Pongo asked.

'Not yet. But we got through to some dogs in Ireland who had managed to, and there seems no doubt that this mysterious sleeping is world-wide. We've talked to lots of European countries. George, do stop rolling.'

'Right you are, Cadpig,' said the Boxer. 'Come

on, Roly Poly, old man. We'll go and have a chat with the Continong.'

But as George and Roly galumphed to the door it was flung open by a Police Dog.

'Pongo and Missis!' he said dramatically. 'You are urgently needed. A Sheepdog is calling you from the country. He says he has astounding news.'

# News From The Country

'FOLLOW ME!' cried Cadpig, dashing out of the room and to the lift, which instantly flung open its doors and took them up so fast that Missis hadn't time to feel nervous. They got out at the top floor and Cadpig led them to a room where the window was wide open. Standing with their feet on the window sill were two Fox Terriers listening intently.

Cadpig joined them at the window and barked down to the crowd of dogs in Downing Street. 'Absolute quiet, please. Important news is coming through.'

Instantly there was silence.

One of the Fox Terriers said to Cadpig, 'This is a Very Important Sheepdog, madam. He's a General.'

'Tell him Pongo and Missis are here,' said Cadpig.

The Fox Terriers barked piercingly; then, as before, listened intently. After only a few seconds one of them said, 'There he is!'

Cadpig beckoned Pongo and Missis to the window. They put their paws on the sill and leaned out as far as they could. At once they heard the General's rumbling bark. They answered him.

'Pongo and Missis?' said the General. 'Yes, I recognise your voices. Amazing, this new invention. I got through to London at once. Well, now, prepare for a shock. The cats are awake.'

'All cats?' said Pongo. There were millions of cats in England, weren't there? And many of them unfriendly to dogs. He foresaw clashes.

'No, no, not all cats. Just Mrs. Willow and your white Persian. They're both with me. And so is someone else who's awake. Young Tommy.'

'Tommy?' gasped Pongo. 'Then the emergency's over. All the humans will be waking.'

'Oh, no, they won't,' said the General. 'All the other humans at the farm are still fast asleep and so are your humans at Hell Hall. I've just been up there, and Prince and I did our very best to

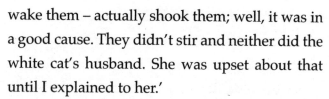 

wake them – actually shook them; well, it was in a good cause. They didn't stir and neither did the white cat's husband. She was upset about that until I explained to her.'

'Please explain to me, too,' said Pongo.

'It came to me in a flash. Well, actually, it came to Mrs. Willow first but I wasn't far behind. Do you remember, soon after you settled in Hell Hall, we made Mrs. Willow and the white cat honorary dogs? And Tommy – he and I could still talk each other's languages then, a kind of Dog-Human – asked if he could be one, too. So he and Mrs. Willow and the white cat are, well, sort of half-dogs.'

'Let me have a word with the white cat,' said Missis, who was longing for news from Hell Hall.

'Can't be done,' said the Sheepdog. 'As they're only half-dogs they can't do everything we do. They can't talk by thought waves and they can't swoosh. But they're fully awake and I'm thankful to say that they don't need food or drink. And it's a great comfort to have them, especially as Tommy's partly got back his knack of being able to talk to me. And he's full of bright ideas and so are the cats. And we simply must join you in London.'

Pongo said, 'But how – if Tommy and the cats can't swoosh? The cats might ride on your back but Tommy couldn't.'

'We've worked out a plan. Tommy will drive the Tractor. He's never *quite* driven it but he's sat with his father and been allowed to put his hand on the steering wheel. And he knows how to turn the engine on. Anyway, we've been practising and it seems that if my Jack Russell and I perch near him, with both the cats, and we all think hard about the Tractor moving forward, well, it does.'

'How fast?' asked Pongo.

'Very, very slowly. In fact, it would take quite a week to reach London. But Mrs. Willow has worked out a scheme. Wonderful brain she has – for a cat. I won't give you the details now, as you'll soon be seeing for yourself. But I'll tell you, that Tractor's never moved so fast in its life. We're starting at once.'

'Well, good luck to you,' said Pongo, wondering what on earth the tabby cat's scheme could be. 'We'll be waiting for you in Downing Street.'

'The white cat insists that we go first to that house where you used to live in Regent's Park. And she wants you to meet us there.'

'But why, General?' asked Pongo.

'Can't tell you now but the white cat says it's *necessary*.'

Then the Jack Russell Terrier was heard barking shrilly. 'We ought to be starting, General. Let's get some action.'

'That'll be enough from you,' said the General ferociously. 'But the cheeky pup's quite right, Pongo. Now you meet us at that house in a couple of hours. Signing off now.'

The barking stopped. Cadpig, who had heard everything, said, 'Well, it's best to humour the dear old gentleman. And you can take a look at the Zoo as you'll be so near.'

'I'd forgotten about the Zoo,' said Pongo. 'Is all well there?'

'It was when I had my last report. All animals asleep except dogs – there are quite a few dogs attached to the Zoo. They're patrolling regularly. Dear me, I wonder if there are any *half*-dogs there? Wolves, for instance.'

'I hope not,' said Missis. She had seen wolves on television and didn't fancy them.

Cadpig said, 'I suppose it's just possible that the General *will* get here in a couple of hours – today, anything's possible. So you might as well get off to the Zoo now, Father. Need Mother come with you? I have to entertain some provincial ladydogs in the drawing room and I thought she might help me.'

'The General asked for me,' said Missis, who very much wanted to see their old home. And there was another reason why she wanted to go to Regent's Park, a worrying reason. She thought she knew why the white cat wished them to meet her there. But she wasn't going to tell Pongo, not until she had talked to the cat.

Cadpig said she could manage on her own and perhaps some of her brothers and sisters would like to see the house where they were born. 'We'll go down and collect them. But I'll keep Patch to help me, if he doesn't mind.'

'Patch would rather help you than see any house in the world,' said Pongo.

They went down to the Cabinet Room and Babs the Poodle said she would willingly spare Lucky and his wife; Gay wanted to see her husband's birthplace. So in the end Pongo and Missis were able to take all their family except Cadpig, Patch and Roly Poly. Cadpig barked to the Foreign Secretary's office, hoping to reach Roly, but the Police Dog on duty there said the Foreign Secretary had taken him out to see London.

'They'll be all right, Mother,' said Cadpig. 'George is quite a dog-about-town.'

Missis was far from sure that made things any safer.

Police Dogs escorted Pongo and Missis and their family until they were through the worst crowds and could swoosh to the Zoo without difficulty.

Missis didn't fancy the Zoo at all, but when she found that all the wild animals were not only asleep but also safely behind bars, she felt less nervous. The dogs attached to the Zoo were most polite and only sorry that Cadpig hadn't come. A keeper's dog said, 'We were hoping to catch a glimpse of her. It's such a pity she can't appear on television as she does when things are normal.'

Pongo wondered why she couldn't. Today, when dogs had such extraordinary powers, why couldn't they make television work? Surely it was just the kind of thing that they could work metaphysically. Indeed television seemed to him quite a bit metaphysical even when things were normal. He must talk to Cadpig about it.

All the Dalmatians were quite used to seeing wild animals, on television, but to see so many sleeping animals was very strange indeed. Elephants, lions, tigers, giraffes, monkeys, polar bears, seals and many, many others lay there utterly still, except for their gentle breathing. Missis need not have worried about the wolves; they slept as deeply as every other animal. Half-

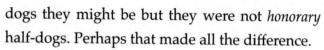 

dogs they might be but they were not *honorary* half-dogs. Perhaps that made all the difference.

Birds in the aviary slept on their perches. And strangest of all were the sleeping fish in the aquarium. They might have been painted fish in painted water.

Long before they had seen everything there was to see, Missis said she thought it was time to leave. She could not really enjoy herself because of her secret thoughts. And she wanted to be at the Regent's Park house when the General and his party arrived, so that no time was wasted before she shared her suspicions with the white cat.

So they said goodbye to the courteous keeper-dogs, who were getting very busy as many sight-seeing dogs were now coming into the Zoo, through the turnstiles which, today, worked without being pushed. And then Pongo and Missis led their family out and along the Outer Circle.

They had not gone far when they heard many dogs barking, and it was a special kind of barking which they recognised as cheering. What could it mean?

The cheering was coming from behind them. Pongo thought a halt, so that he could look back, and a moment later he saw the most astonishing sight. Coming across the bridge over the Regent's Canal, at a tremendous pace, was the Tractor.

At the wheel sat young Tommy, and near him were the General, the Jack Russell Terrier, the white cat and the tabby cat, Mrs. Willow. All of them were gazing straight ahead and none of them noticed the little group of Dalmatians – who saw, as the Tractor swept past, that it was being pushed by a dozen of the Dalmatians who had been left behind at Hell Hall. They were swooshing and so was the Tractor. Its wheels weren't touching the ground.

'It's become a Hover-tractor,' said Missis. 'How very metaphysical.'

'We must follow it,' said Pongo. 'Quick swoosh.'

They caught up with it just as it stopped in front of the house that had once been the

Dearlys'. The Sheepdog, the Jack Russell and the cats got down, but Tommy stayed at the wheel and seemed to be talking to the Tractor.

'He's thanking it,' the General told Pongo. 'It's behaved magnificently. You'd think it was human.'

'You mean canine,' said Pongo. 'Well, between you and it you've been marvellously quick.'

'Prince lent me a dozen strong swooshers,' said the General. 'And we at the front helped by thinking forward thoughts, which is quite hard work.'

Tommy now got down from the Tractor. Pongo and Missis greeted him affectionately and tried to understand what he said. Usually they did understand him, just as they understood most humans, but he was now talking half-Dog and half-Human, as he had when he was very young, and they couldn't get the hang of it.

'Needs practice,' said the Sheepdog. 'I can follow most of it now and he half understands me, which is more than any other human ever did.'

The Dalmatians who had come with the Tractor had joined the ones who had been born in the Regent's Park house and Lucky was pointing out the kitchen window. He said, 'Shall we go inside, Father? I expect the door will open for us if we ask it to.'

Missis at once said, 'The people who live here now might not like us to go in.'

'But they'll all be asleep, Mother,' said Lucky, who wanted to show his wife the broom cupboard where he had been born. He ran up the steps, willed the door to open and pushed it. But nothing happened.

'That's because we don't *need* to go in,' said Missis. 'And anyway, I don't want to see our home now it isn't ours.'

Lucky's wife, who was looking down through the railings, said, 'I can see the kitchen quite nicely, Lucky, and I can *imagine* the broom cupboard, if you describe it.'

As Lucky had only slept in the broom cupboard for the first two weeks of his life he couldn't really remember it, but Pongo helped him out and described the whole house. All the dogs listened – that is, all except Missis. She drew the two cats aside and asked why they'd specially wanted to come here. She said she couldn't believe they'd particularly wanted to see the house.

'Well, I've nothing against seeing it,' said the white cat. 'In fact, I've very friendly feelings towards it as it was the first house I ever lived in where I was treated decently. But the house I really want to see is farther along the Outer Circle. And we must go inside. It's the house where I lived such miserable years with Cruella de Vil. I feel it in my bones that she's back in England.'

'She is!' cried Missis. 'Oh, I guessed you'd suspect her, and so do I. I'm sure she's causing this mysterious sleeping.'

'Then she must be stopped,' said the tabby cat. 'I don't like the world without humans.'

'We must get into her house and, well, *frighten* her,' said the white cat. And she meant much more than she said.

Missis had always thought it wrong for any dog or cat to hurt a human, but she was highly in favour of *frightening* Cruella, so she said at once, 'We must convince Pongo.' Then she stared in astonishment.

Swooshing towards them at a tremendous speed and barking loudly was a Staffordshire Terrier. He pulled up when he reached them but, even so, knocked several dogs down.

'Sorry, mates,' he said. 'Nobody hurt, I hope? (Nobody was.) Well, my old friends Pongo and Missis. Hope you haven't forgotten me.'

'As if we could!' said Pongo. 'You and your miraculous removal van once saved all our lives.'

'Are *your* humans asleep?' said Missis.

'I'll say they are,' said the Staffordshire. 'And not for the want of waking. I was pretty rough with them before I found out that they couldn't help it, poor chaps. Not that I hurt them – I hope.'

'So do I,' said Pongo, knowing just how rough the Staffordshire could be. He lived with two removal men who called him names like 'Canine Cannon Ball' and 'Self-launched Bomb', but they loved him dearly.

'Just dropped in to see a pal at the Zoo,' said the Staffordshire, 'and I heard you were here. Well, perhaps you can tell me what's up with the world today. Think it's got anything to do with that old enemy of yours, the one who stole your pups?'

'*I* do,' said the white cat. 'And we ought to attack her.'

The Staffordshire looked at her in surprise. 'Didn't know there were any cats awake today.'

'Both these ladies are honorary dogs,' said Pongo. 'And good friends of ours.'

'Then they're friends of mine, too,' said the Stafford-shire, giving up the idea of chasing both cats up a tree – only in fun, of course, but cats never understood, they'd no sense of humour. But the white cat was talking sound sense so he said to her, 'Well, if you want to attack the puppy-stealer, count on me. I told Pongo long ago that we ought to do her in.'

'No, no,' said Pongo. 'This strangeness today has nothing to do with Cruella. Let's leave her alone.' But he found everyone was against him.

The General said, 'The woman's a thoroughly bad lot, Pongo. Remember, I saw more of her than you did, in the days when she owned Hell Hall. And the least we can do is to investigate her. Besides, I promised Tommy he should see her.'

Tommy was already up on the Tractor, ready to start. The General, the Jack Russell and the two cats got up, too. Lucky said to Pongo quietly, 'I think you'll have to let them have their heads, Father. But I'll help you to keep order. And all the Dalmatians will do exactly what *you* say.'

But would the Sheepdog, Pongo wondered, and would the Staffordshire? They were both formidable dogs. And the cats were capable of dangerous clawing. As for the Jack Russell, he was barking fiercely, 'Forward to kill Cruella de Vil!'

'Get into position, Tractor-pushers!' ordered the Sheepdog.

Pongo said he and Missis would lead the way. Their family and the Staffordshire helped to push the Tractor so it went at a tremendous pace.

'Faster, faster!' barked the Jack Russell.

'Pipe down, boy,' said the General. 'There's a legal speed limit in London. Better stick to it, Tommy.'

'How?' said Tommy.

'Just think legal thoughts,' said the General.

The Tractor slowed down a little but, even so, Pongo and Missis were rather afraid they might be run over. They were thankful when they reached Cruella's house. How well they remembered it and that snowy Christmas Eve when the white cat had invited them in to destroy Cruella's furs!

'Perhaps she doesn't live here now,' said Pongo.

The white cat had sprung from the Tractor and run down the steps to look through the kitchen window. She called back to Pongo, 'Oh, yes, she does. I can see the giant pepper-grinder she always used at meals.'

Pongo now hoped they wouldn't be able to open the door. He told himself they wouldn't if they didn't need to.

But it seemed they did need to. The door to the kitchen swung open as if to invite them in.

So in they all went.

# The Clothes That Clanked

THE WHITE CAT looked around the kitchen and said, 'Dirty, as ever.'

Several dogs sneezed.

'That's the pepper in the air,' said the white cat. 'She must be using even more than when I lived with her.'

Pongo was reading a recipe which lay on the table. It was headed 'My Favourite Pie'. He said, 'Listen to this. "Line a pie dish thickly with black pepper. Sprinkle with a very little meat. Put a thick layer of white pepper, then a thick layer of horse radish mixed with mustard. Top with red pepper. Serve very hot".'

'You couldn't serve that cold, even if you froze it,' said Missis.

Most of the dogs were sneezing now.

The Sheepdog said, 'We'd better go upstairs. There may be less pepper there – though we may find worse things than pepper. Keep close to me, Tommy. You can't defend yourself as we dogs can.'

Up in the hall, which was painted in violent colours forming angular shapes, Missis said, 'These walls used to be green marble.'

'Fake marble,' said the white cat.

'And the drawing-room walls were red marble,' said Pongo. 'They reminded us of raw meat.'

Missis peered through the open drawing-room door and said, 'Now they're like the hall, only worse.' As well as angular shapes there were angular faces with horrid expressions. And in the dim light that came through the drawn curtains some of the painted faces looked frighteningly real. Missis backed out hastily.

Pongo looked into the dining room and warned Missis not to. 'All the painted faces in there have very long noses. I think they're all portraits of Cruella.'

'I suppose she *is* here?' said the General, doubtfully. 'The house seems deserted.'

'She's probably upstairs,' said the white cat, who had been practising her claws on a purple rug. 'Let's go and see.' She turned to the Staffordshire and asked him to come with her.

'It'll be a pleasure,' said the Staffordshire, looking at the clawed rug. 'I'd say you and I have the same idea, though you favour claws and I favour teeth.'

Pongo said to the Dalmatians, 'You are not to attack Cruella. She *can't* be to blame for what's happening today.'

Missis said earnestly, 'Oh, Pongo, you're wrong!'

*Could* he be wrong? Pongo began to fear he might be. There was something very strange about this silent house with its painted faces, something that felt menacing. And if Cruella *had* bewitched all the humans in the world perhaps they wouldn't wake up until ... well, something was done about her. Anyway, he couldn't stop the white cat and the Staffordshire who were already on their way upstairs. He hurried after them and so did all the others.

The white cat stopped outside a closed door and said 'That's where the de Vils slept.'

The door slowly opened. Beyond it was complete blackness, from which came a mysterious rasping sound. The darkness and the rasping sound were so frightening that the white cat and the Staffordshire drew back, though both of them were brave animals.

The white cat said, 'Often I can see in the dark but not in that kind of darkness. It's blacker than black.'

Pongo, a born leader, said he would go in first.

'I'll come with you,' said the Sheepdog.

'No, General,' said Pongo. 'You must stay with Tommy.'

Missis came and stood shoulder to shoulder with Pongo. She was terrified but determined to act bravely, which is the bravest kind of bravery there is.

The Staffordshire said he was coming too.

'Then get the other side of Missis,' said Pongo, who knew it would be useless to tell Missis not to come. 'And everyone else wait until I give the word to follow us. No, Lucky, you must stay with your wife. Bless me, who have we here?'

The Jack Russell had pushed his way forward, trembling with eagerness. Pongo admired his pluck but told him to take care of the General and Tommy. 'And you two cats hold back. Remember you're only half-dogs.'

The rasping noise had got louder and the room seemed blacker than ever. But slowly, slowly, Pongo, Missis and the Staffordshire moved forwards.

It seemed to Missis that the darkness was thick, as well as black. She felt that, if she opened her mouth, it would choke her.

'If only we could *see!*' thought Pongo.

Then the heavy curtains at the two tall windows parted and slowly drew back just far enough to let two shafts of afternoon light shine in. And what they shone on were two beds. In one bed lay Mr. de Vil, a small, worried-looking man. He was snoring loudly. That was the rasping sound which had been so frightening. It was certainly an odd sort of snoring, but now Pongo knew what it was it seemed to him more funny than frightening.

The Staffordshire said, 'You wouldn't think such a little chap could snore so loud.'

Cruella de Vil lay asleep in the other bed. There was nothing funny about *her*, though she did not, in sleep, look as frightening as when Pongo and Missis had seen her last, that Christmas Eve when she had chased them and all the puppies in her enormous black and white car. But she did not look pleasant and peaceful, as the sleeping Dearlys did. Her mouth was grim, her long nose seemed more pointed than ever, and she was frowning heavily. Perhaps she looked less frightening only because her eyes were closed, those black eyes with a streak of red in them. Even the memory of them made Missis shudder.

'First time I've seen a dame with black and white hair,' said the Staffordshire.

Lucky called, 'Can we come in now, Father?'

'Yes, if you keep quiet and don't crowd round the bed,' said Pongo.

The white cat got there first and said, 'Half her hair turned green with shock, after we destroyed her furs. I suppose she's had it dyed. No ermine sheets now, has she? That was the best night of my life, when I clawed them to bits.'

'Funny kind of sheets she's got now,' said the Staffordshire. 'They look like tin.'

'They'll be plastic,' said the white cat. 'When we drove Mr. de Vil out of business as a furrier he went in for making plastic raincoats. Perhaps there are some of them about.' She flexed her claws hopefully and looked around the dimly lit room.

Some of the dogs were already exploring it and suddenly, mingling with Mr. de Vil's snores, there came a noise like metal hitting metal.

Missis cried, 'Pongo, that factory we saw this morning! Clothes that Clank!'

Pongo then saw that there were racks of plastic coats, just as there had once been racks of furs. But it must be some new kind of plastic. No ordinary plastic raincoat could make the noise these coats made, as the curious dogs examined them. Clank! Clank! The noise got louder and louder. If the de Vils had been wakeable, it would certainly have wakened them.

Young Tommy managed to lift a coat from the rack and held it in the light from a window. It seemed to be made of shining black tin. After a moment he dropped it, murmuring something.

'He says it's too heavy to hold,' the Sheepdog explained. 'The woman must be dressing herself in some kind of armour.'

The white cat went to the fallen coat and put out a paw.

'Don't, dear,' said the tabby. 'You'd only hurt your claws.'

'How right you are,' said the white cat. 'Nothing less than a tin-opener could damage that stuff.'

Missis, who took an interest in clothes because Mrs. Dearly did, looked at the rack of coats – from a safe distance. Some of them were in bright colours, scarlet, emerald, sapphire, flame. Really quite pretty, Missis thought. She went closer, deciding they wouldn't hurt her if she didn't hurt them. At once she scratched her nose on a sharp edge. 'Treacherous,' she thought.

'Well, what else could I expect from Cruella's clothes?'

But she no longer felt that Cruella herself was a menace. And even the white cat seemed to have given up any idea of attacking her old enemy. Only the Staffordshire looked as if he wanted to. He was staring fiercely at Cruella.

Pongo noticed this. He knew that the Staffordshire was a descendant of dogs who'd had to fight for their lives in the days when it was considered sporting to set dogs to fight each other, so he did not blame him for the savagery in his nature. But this was no moment for savagery, so Pongo said firmly, 'Don't touch her, my friend.'

'You Dalmatians are softies,' said the Staffordshire. 'She was your enemy before and she may be again. And if we did her in while she's asleep, she'd never even notice it.'

The Sheepdog said sternly, 'You can't bite a sleeping woman. It would be like shooting a sitting pheasant.'

The Staffordshire felt snubbed. Although he enjoyed his life, travelling around in the removal van, he had sometimes envied country-gentlemen dogs he had seen helping men with guns. He had thought he could get on well with such dogs. Now he knew they would spurn him. He hadn't had the faintest idea you mustn't shoot a sitting pheasant.

Then the General said tactfully, 'Not that I don't admire your fighting spirit. You're a dog I'd have been glad to have with me that night I thought it *necessary* to bite the Baddun brothers who used to work for Cruella. And now, Pongo, we should leave this depressing house. My young friend, Cadpig, may have need of us.'

Then the curtains at the windows drew together again as if they knew that light was no longer needed. Once the room was in darkness it became frightening again. Dogs hurrying to the door bumped into the racks of coats, which clanked more and more. Missis was thankful when everyone was safely out on the landing.

The white cat, looking back, said, 'Perhaps we've been too soft-hearted. We'll never get another chance like that. Still, they say let sleeping devils lie, don't they?'

'They say let sleeping *dogs* lie,' said the Sheepdog. 'And they don't mean it. Every time I take a snooze someone wakes me up. It's usually young Tommy.'

Tommy fully understood that this was a joke. He put his arm round the Sheepdog's neck and they led the way downstairs.

As the front door opened to let them out Missis said to Pongo, 'It turned out that we didn't really need to get into Cruella's house. So why did the kitchen door open to let us in?'

'Because we needed to know that we didn't need to,' said Pongo.

The front door slammed behind them all. Missis looked up at the bedroom window and thought about the black room filled with clanking and snoring, then thankfully took a deep breath of the warm afternoon air.

The Dalmatians who pushed the Tractor were getting into position.

'Pongo and Missis must now come *on* the

Tractor,' said the General. 'We can't have the Prime Minister's parents down on all fours, while we're up there.'

The Staffordshire was standing slightly apart from the other dogs. It would be lonely at home, but he feared he might not be grand enough to come to Downing Street. The General guessed this and said, 'Please come on the Tractor. I'd be glad to have you on my staff during this time of danger.'

'Sit by me,' said the white cat.

'I'll be proud to, ma'am,' said the Staffordshire. Never had he expected to like a cat so much.

Missis was so relieved at knowing she didn't have to be frightened of Cruella that she greatly enjoyed the drive back to Downing Street, through cheering crowds. The streets were as full as ever but the Tractor got through all right.

Dogs were still swooshing in from all over England.

'An impressive sight,' said the General. 'I suppose our clever little Cadpig knows what they're all swooshing here *for*?'

Well, not unless she'd found out since he last saw her, thought Pongo. But he didn't want to give his daughter away so he just said, 'Ah!'

'Top secret, eh?' said the General.

'Oh, I think we shall all know very soon,' said Missis. She was feeling *expectant*. It was a word she had learned before her puppies were born, when the Dearlys had often told people, 'Missis is expectant'. She had liked the word then and she liked it now. To her it meant being excited without being afraid. And how grand she was, sitting up here and being cheered like Royalty. She waved a graceful paw. Really, with their old enemy asleep, there was *nothing* to worry about.

Pongo was glad to see her relief but he didn't share it. He had never really believed that Cruella was now the enemy – and he almost wished she were. For even if she was a devil, she was the devil he knew. As things were, he felt that someone, something, much more powerful than Cruella was in charge today. And that someone, something, was still *absolutely unknown*.

# The Voice

POLICE DOGS cleared a way into Downing Street and said they would take care of the Tractor. And a Police Dog in the hall said Cadpig was upstairs in the drawing-room. Pongo and Missis led the way.

They found their daughter all alone, except for the faithful Patch, and looking very small in the large, beautiful room. She was also looking worried. But at once she smiled brightly and greeted the Sheepdog, the cats, and the Dalmatians who had pushed the Tractor.

'I must have a ride on the Tractor myself,' she said. Then she told Tommy how glad she was to see him, and when the Jack Russell was introduced she said she'd always wanted to meet one. And before anyone could introduce the Staffordshire she ran to him and said, 'But you're our old friend, surely. You saved all our lives long ago.'

'Wonderful memory,' thought Missis.

'Wonderful    pluck,'    thought    Pongo,

remembering how forlorn Cadpig had looked when they entered the room. He told her there was nothing to fear from Cruella.

'Good,' said Cadpig and then asked if everyone would like to see the sleeping Prime Minister.

'We shan't be too many?' asked the General.

'No, no. I've been letting conducted tours go up all afternoon. I feel *be* would like it.' She asked Patch to act as an escort, and then said to Pongo, 'You and Mother won't want to go up again. Please stay with me.'

As soon as the three of them were alone together, Cadpig's bright smile faded. She said she'd had a depressing afternoon, entertaining the provincial lady-dogs. 'Good creatures, of course, but one grows tired of feminine chatter. Oh, dear! This is the time of day the Prime Minister and I used to watch the news on television together. He had a glass of sherry and I had a peppermint cream.'

'I've always been fond of peppermint creams,' said Missis.

'There's a box of them on the table, there – if you *could* fancy one, Mother.'

Missis looked longingly at the box, but what she longed for was the longing for a peppermint cream, not the peppermint cream itself. She was so unhungry that she could not remember what being hungry felt like.

Pongo said, 'At a time like this, one does feel the need for television. It somehow linked us all together. Do you think we could make it work?'

'But there can't be anything on, Father – with all the humans asleep.'

Pongo's idea had been that Cadpig herself should be on television, to please her many admirers. But now he had another idea. He suddenly felt a *need* of television, that it could somehow help him. And today, dogs seemed to get what they *needed*. He looked towards the big television set. It wasn't quite like the one the Dearlys had and he didn't know which knob turned it on and, anyway, he couldn't turn knobs. Well, he couldn't *usually* – but usually he couldn't turn door handles. Perhaps today…

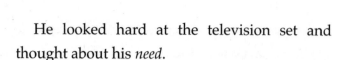 

He looked hard at the television set and thought about his *need*.

Click! One of the knobs turned itself.

Only Pongo noticed this. He would say nothing yet, he would wait until —

A strange sound came from the television, a soft, musical wail, very high and sweet.

'Listen!' cried Missis, quickly looking at the screen, which gradually became luminous.

'How marvellous!' gasped Cadpig.

The three of them stared at the television, hoping for a picture, but the screen remained blank, just an oblong of pale light.

'You see? There's nothing on,' said Cadpig sadly.

But at that moment the screen grew lighter, changing from a greyish white to a silver white, and then it grew so bright that it was as dazzling as powerful headlights of a car on a dark night. And as the screen brightened, the room darkened until the three dogs sat in utter blackness gazing at utter brilliance. Then the edges of the screen darkened a little and the light seemed to be drawing all its radiance into the centre where – brighter than ever and flashing even brighter – it assumed the shape of a star.

Missis cried, 'Pongo! The dream I had last night! I saw a bright light that turned into a star – and it was this star. It was high above the stable roof.'

'Do you mean you woke and saw it through the window?' said Pongo. 'The stars were very bright last night.'

'No, no. Mine was a *dream* star. It was much bigger and brighter than a real star. It was *this* star!'

'Yes, Missis, it was this star,' said a voice from the screen.

It was like no voice the dogs had ever heard before. It was not the voice of a human or of any animal – and yet, strangely, it reminded Pongo of Mr. Dearly's voice, reminded Missis of Mrs. Dearly's voice and reminded Cadpig of the Prime Minister's voice. This made it comforting as well as awe-inspiring.

The Voice went on, 'All dogs saw me in their

dreams last night but few of them remember it as you do, Missis. But they *will* remember it. That is part of the plan.'

'*What* plan?' said Cadpig sharply. 'Tell me at once!' Then she added in her most winning tone, '*Please!* You see, I have so much responsibility.'

'And you are managing very nicely,' said the Voice, sounding amused. 'With the help of your clever parents.'

Missis said, 'Goodness, I'm not clever.'

'There are different ways of being clever,' said the Voice. 'You are intuitive – which means you can often understand things without reasoning them out.'

'Would that be metaphysical?' asked Missis.

'Very metaphysical,' said the Voice, still sounding amused. 'Now Pongo is more *brainy* than you are. Has it not been said that he has one of the keenest brains in Dogdom?'

Pongo was greatly flattered. Many dogs had thought him brainy in the days when he had been cleverer than Scotland Yard at finding his stolen puppies. But he hadn't done anything very dashing just lately. He said, 'I'm afraid my brain has grown rusty.'

'But the rust is wearing off fast,' said the Voice. 'It was clever of you to tell all the dogs to "Wait and See". That's kept them happy. And it was clever of you to turn the television on, even if I did put the idea into your mind.'

'*You* did?' asked Pongo.

'I did indeed,' said the Voice. 'Oh, you and I can work together, brainy Pongo. And I can work with metaphysical Missis. As for Cadpig! Now how shall we describe Cadpig? Clever *and* intuitive. Very, very pretty. And, shall we say, just a trifle bossy?' The Voice was now quite playful.

'Well, don't I need to be?' said Cadpig. 'With thousands of dogs waiting for me to tell them what to do?'

'And you shall tell them,' said the Voice. 'Now listen carefully. You must get my instructions through to every dog in England. Many of them can be reached by your thoughts but there are some dogs, often in lonely places, who have not yet learned to read thoughts. You must talk to them by the old-fashioned Twilight Barking. All dogs must be made to understand. At midnight tonight all dogs in London are to be in Trafalgar Square. All dogs in provincial towns are to be in town-hall squares or public parks. Country-town dogs are to be in market places. And dogs in villages and deep country are to be in open spaces, village greens or on tops of hills – places where they can see the sky. And all, all, are to be in their places by midnight.'

'And then what will happen?' asked Cadpig.

'Oh, you must take your father's advice and "Wait and See",' said the Voice.

And suddenly Missis felt frightened of it – or was it the word 'midnight' that had frightened her? Only that morning she'd told Pongo she found midnight scaring – and now she was being asked to sit in Trafalgar Square at midnight waiting for something to happen. It would be very frightening indeed. But she kept her fears to herself, so she was astonished at what the Voice said next.

'Yes, Missis, it *will* be frightening. But don't you sometimes enjoy being frightened? Don't you find it pleasantly exciting?'

'No,' said Missis.

'*I* do,' said Pongo.

'There speaks my brave Pongo,' said the Voice. 'And how does my little friend Cadpig feel about it? Is *she* frightened?'

'I haven't got time to be,' said Cadpig. 'What's worrying me is all the thought-sending and barking I'll need to do. Have I to send the news over *all* England? And how about Scotland?'

'Scotland, too, and Wales. You needn't reach across the sea.'

'But isn't this thing happening all over the world?' asked Cadpig.

'Certainly it is. But you can leave the rest of the world to me, dear bossy Cadpig. Now each of you may ask one question. But that question mustn't be "What's going to happen?".'

Instantly Pongo, Missis and Cadpig felt that was the one question they wanted to ask.

'Hurry up,' said the Voice.

Pongo said, 'Who are you?'

'Oh, that would be like telling you what's going to happen. Wait and see, Pongo. Wait and see.'

Cadpig said, 'If I need your help, how can I call you?'

'You can't. You must manage on your own. Now your question, Missis, and be quick. In five seconds I shall leave you.'

Missis tried hard to think of some really important question but she couldn't, and already the star was less brilliant. At last she said, 'What's happened to Roly Poly?' As far as she knew, he was still on the loose in London with George, the Foreign Secretary.

'Oh, that fat funny son of yours,' said the Voice. 'I'm afraid I can't see him at the moment and I haven't time to look for him. I have to make appearances all over the world. See you at midnight.'

The star vanished, leaving the screen empty. Then the television turned itself off, with a loud click, and the room, which had grown so dark, was lit by daylight again.

Cadpig said, 'Did you like him?'

'Was it a him?' said Missis. 'I thought it was a her.'

'Oh, no, Missis,' said Pongo. 'But perhaps we'd better call it an it.'

'Isn't that rather rude?' said Missis. 'Suppose he, she or it can hear?'

'Well, a voice on its own is always called "it",' said Pongo.

Cadpig said, 'I hope it *can* hear. I want it to know that I liked it at first, but then I thought it was making fun of us – which wasn't a kind thing to do, when we're all so anxious.' She looked hard at the television and added, 'If you've anything to say about that, click on.'

But nothing happened. And just then the party that had been up to see the Prime Minister came back. Pongo, Missis and Cadpig at once began to tell what had happened, and as the three of them barked at once it was very confusing, but at last they made themselves understood.

'Well, at least we know that there's someone

in charge,' said the General. 'But who?'

Young Tommy, wildly excited, began talking his extraordinary language very fast. The General listened carefully and then said, 'This may be important. Tommy thinks that whatever it was that talked to you must have come from Outer Space.'

Pongo remembered the books of Science Fiction he had seen in Tommy's room. The little boy might well be right. Pongo decided to ask him some questions. But that very instant the television turned itself on again, with a loud click.

This time there was no star. There was just the Voice, saying loudly, 'Pongo, don't pry. Tommy, keep your silly ideas to yourself. Now, Cadpig, get busy or there will be dogs who don't know what they have to do at midnight and that will be *most unfortunate* for them.' Then the television snapped off.

Tommy was looking hurt. The Sheepdog licked him affectionately and they had a few words together. Then the Sheepdog explained.

'Tommy says it's all right. The Voice isn't as cross as it sounds. Tommy says his father has no patience with Science Fiction and is often very nubbing about it. But he's really the kindest of men.'

'What's Tommy's father got to do with it?' asked Cadpig.

'Tommy says the Voice sounded like his father's.'

'I must start work,' said Cadpig. 'It'll take me hours to get my thoughts over the whole country. And the Voice said there must be the old-fashioned Twilight Barking, too. Father, could you and Mother cope with that for me?'

'Willingly,' said Pongo. 'But not from Downing Street. We'll bark from Primrose Hill, as we used to.'

'Splendid,' said Cadpig, then she sent Patch for a Police Dog and gave instructions. 'Clear a way for Pongo and Missis from Downing Street to Primrose Hill. All traffic lights are to remain green until they have passed.'

When this had been arranged, Pongo and

Missis swooshed downstairs, out into Downing Street and then along Whitehall. (All dogs made way for them and there were many barks of 'Bravo, Pongo! Wait and See!') Soon they reached Trafalgar Square.

Pongo said, 'This is where we shall be at midnight.'

'Dogs should be in their baskets at midnight,' said Missis. 'Oh, Pongo, I wish it was last night! Don't you?'

Pongo found he didn't. He said, 'Think of it this way, Missis. We've had many, many peaceful nights in our baskets. It'll be fun to have just one midnight in Trafalgar Square.'

'If it *is* fun,' said Missis. She had felt so happy, driving back to Downing Street on the Tractor, but not since she had heard that Voice. Then she reminded herself it had sounded quite kind … at first, anyway.

The last few minutes of their swoosh were across Regent's Park. That afternoon, Missis hadn't had much chance to look at it. Now she liked remembering how often she and Pongo and the Dearlys had walked here when they were young married couples.

They crossed the Outer Circle and swooshed to the top of Primrose Hill. Pongo said, 'How different everything is now, from when we barked to get news of our puppies. Then it was bitterly cold – you wore your beautiful blue coat. And the trees in the park were bare.'

'It's hard to remember them bare,' said Missis, looking down at all the leafy tree-tops.

By now it was early twilight. The air was still soft and warm and there still wasn't a breath of wind.

'We must start barking,' said Pongo. '*Real* barking, this time.'

It was quite a while since they had joined in the Twilight Barking. Except in emergencies, as when the puppies had been stolen, it was only a gossip chain, a way in which dogs could talk to their friends. There was so much gossip always going on inside the walls of Hell Hall that the dogs there seldom barked to the outside world. If the General wanted a word with the Dalmatians

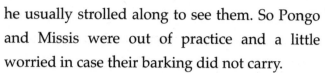 

he usually strolled along to see them. So Pongo and Missis were out of practice and a little worried in case their barking did not carry.

And at first they had reason to worry, for when they gave the three sharp barks which signalled that an important message was coming, no dog answered.

'We must bark louder,' said Pongo.

So they tried again. They barked to the north, they barked to the south, they barked to the east and west. Still no dog answered.

'We simply mustn't fail Cadpig,' said Pongo. 'She's depending on us. Once again, Missis. And this time we'll make a special effort to the north. There was a splendid Great Dane over towards Hampstead who used to be a great help.'

Again they tried – never in her life had Missis barked so loud. Still there was no answer. But they went on and on. And at last, floating through the summer twilight, came a great, booming bark.

'He's still there,' cried Pongo. 'He's still there and he's heard us!'

'Can I believe my ears?' boomed the Great

Dane. 'Is it really my old friends Pongo and Missis, after all this time, and on this most extraordinary day when the barking-chain has been at its worst. All these new-fangled thought waves have been so confusing.'

Pongo said anxiously, 'But you have had the thought waves, sir? You know what's been happening?'

'Well, yes. But thought waves are so vague. And there are no set times for standing by to receive messages. Much as I admire your daughter, I wish she wouldn't toss her thoughts into the air just when the mood strikes her. And I can't make head nor tail of what she's sending out from Downing Street this evening. Why are dogs to go to Trafalgar Square? Why doesn't Cadpig say?'

'Because she doesn't know,' said Pongo, and then told the Great Dane about the Voice, and how it had said that Twilight Barking must be used for dogs who couldn't receive thought waves.

'Well, that's sensible, at least,' said the Great

Dane. 'And you'd better leave the whole job to me. I've had firm promises from friends north, south, east and west, to be standing by for Twilight Barking, thought waves or no thought waves. Now let's get it clear. Cadpig said dogs in large towns are to go to town-hall squares or public parks. Country-town dogs go to market places. Dogs in villages and deep country go to open spaces, village greens or tops of hills. Everyone to be there by midnight. Right?'

'Exactly right,' said Pongo. 'And you, yourself, will join us in Trafalgar Square?'

'Oh, I couldn't come all that way. I'm no longer a chicken.'

'But it's easy if you swoosh, sir. Have you got the knack?'

The Great Dane said he's swooshed round the lawn a bit, but a dog of his weight felt a fool floating on air, and he'd just step out on Hampstead Heath at midnight. 'That's a perfectly good open space. Now clear the line, will you? I've got a big job to do if I'm to get the barking chain started in every direction.'

'Good luck,' barked Pongo; then signed off.

Missis said, 'What did he mean when he said he was no longer a chicken? Was he ever a chicken?'

Pongo laughed. 'It was just an expression, Missis. He meant he was no longer young.'

'But when he was young he was a puppy, not a chicken.'

'He was indeed, Missis, dear,' said Pongo.

Then they heard the Great Dane barking again as he started work. How well Missis remembered that booming bark bringing the first news of their stolen puppies! She was thankful that all those pups were now fully grown, sensible dogs, capable of taking care of themselves – all but Roly Poly; he was more than fully grown but would never be sensible. Where *was* he? She felt anxious about him but didn't mention this to Pongo. There was no point in worrying him.

Pongo had his own worries and he didn't mention these to Missis. The truth was that when he looked up at the darkening sky, already dotted with pale stars, and thought about midnight in Trafalgar Square, he was anxious about *all* dogs. What was going to happen?

# In Trafalgar Square

CADPIG HAD MADE no special arrangements
for them to get back to Downing Street as she
hadn't known when they were coming, and the
main streets were now more crowded than ever.
But in the days when Pongo and Mr. Dearly had
both been young bachelors they had often gone
for walks in the little back streets and Pongo
remembered these well. So he had no difficulty in
getting Missis as far as Whitehall. There – almost
within sight of Downing Street – they got stuck,
for masses of dogs were coming towards them,
eager to reach Trafalgar Square.

Pongo sent thought waves to Cadpig but
could get no answer, and there were no Police
Dogs anywhere near to help. Then Missis
said, 'If we can swoosh just above the ground
by believing we can, couldn't we rise higher
and swoosh *over* the dogs who are coming
towards us?'

'Well, we can *try*,' said Pongo doubtfully.

'Then both together, and we must believe extra hard.'

They rose up in the air like a couple of helicopters. Pongo stopped when he was well above the heads of even the tallest dogs, but Missis believed so hard that she rose up quite twenty feet.

'That's too high,' called Pongo. 'Come down lower.'

'Oh, I like it up here,' said Missis.

'But it's not safe. If you suddenly stop believing, you'll have so far to fall.'

'Let's meet each other half way,' said Missis.

So she came down and Pongo rose up, and they swooshed along about ten feet from the ground, waving to the dogs below and creating a great sensation.

'It was clever of you to invent this High Swoosh,' said Pongo.

'Just metaphysical,' said Missis.

They turned into Downing Street and came down neatly on the doorstep of No. 10.

The Police Dog on duty told them that Cadpig

was holding a Cabinet Meeting, but when they got to the Cabinet Room they found that the meeting was over.

'None of us could think of anything to say,' said Cadpig, 'so we just passed a vote of confidence in ourselves.'

There was no news of Roly Poly or George, the Foreign Secretary.

Cadpig was glad to hear that the Great Dane had taken over the Barking. 'He'll do a splendid job. And I think I've made a good one of sending out thought waves. Dogs are quicker and quicker at picking them up and they're getting the knack of relaying them. What's worrying me now is how we're all going to get to Trafalgar Square. I've got Police Dogs there keeping room for us on the steps and terrace of the National Gallery, but they're finding it harder and harder to control the dog traffic in the streets.'

Missis then explained her discovery of the High Swoosh and many of the Cabinet Ministers went out to the garden to practise it.

'Tommy and the cats won't be able to high-swoosh,' said Cadpig. 'They may have to be left behind.'

'We'd better discuss it with the General,' said Pongo.

They went up to the drawing-room, where the Sheepdog and his party were sitting, and explained the situation. Tommy and the cats were most unwilling to be left behind. They asked why they couldn't come on the Tractor.

'Because we can't possibly get the Tractor along Whitehall', said Cadpig. 'It's packed solid with dogs.'

'Why shouldn't the Tractor high-swoosh?' said Missis.

'I suppose it's just possible,' said Pongo. 'If enough dogs push it and think upward thoughts, as well as forward thoughts.'

So they called all the Dalmatians in from the garden and went out into Downing Street to practise. There was plenty of room there now as all the waiting dogs had gone to Trafalgar Square. And from the very first the Tractor showed willingness to rise up a good six feet.

'Then we'll start soon,' said Cadpig, 'and make sure of our seats.' She sent Lucky and Patch to call all the dogs from the garden and get them into position, while she took a last look at the sleeping Prime Minister.

'Pongo and Missis must come on the Tractor,' said the General, 'and my young friend, Cadpig. It will increase her prestige.'

Cadpig, when she came downstairs, was glad to agree. She had been so upset at leaving the Prime Minister that she hadn't enough spirit to manage a High Swoosh. Also, she felt that if she increased her prestige it would be good for the Prime Minister's prestige, too.

It was certainly a most remarkable procession that at last set out. Tommy was at the wheel of the Tractor, and the General, the Staffordshire, the Jack Russell and the cats sat near him. Cadpig and her parents sat on the Tractor's roof, so that the crowds could get a good view of them. All the other Dalmatians (except the missing Roly Poly) grouped themselves round the Tractor to help it with upward and forward thoughts. And behind, high-swooshing, came all the dogs who had been on duty at No. 10, now acting as an escort to all the Cabinet Ministers (except the missing Foreign Secretary). Babs, the Minister of Transport, high-swooshed most gracefully. Her top-knot was tied up with ribbon, which Lucky's wife had managed to put on for her.

The whole caninecade was wildly cheered as it passed over the heads of the dogs in Whitehall and Trafalgar Square. Police Dogs had managed to keep enough room for the Tractor to come down, and soon all the dogs from Downing Street were settled outside the National Gallery.

Pongo, Missis and Cadpig sat high up between two pillars and could see right across the Square. It was solidly packed with dogs and so were all the streets leading to it. All dogs were well behaved but of course they were talking, so the noise was pretty deafening.

'It's hard to hear oneself think,' said Missis.

'I don't want to hear myself think,' said Cadpig. 'I'm too nervous.'

Missis, too, was nervous. It was night now

and, though the stars were bright, they did not give enough light for her to be sure that those four huge lions in the middle of the Square were not live lions. She had caught a glimpse of them earlier and they hadn't been live then, but today anything was liable to happen. She felt almost sure she saw one of them move.

'I do wish the lights were on,' she said.

'So do I,' said Pongo, guessing Missis was nervous.

And then, as so often today, their wishes *worked*. The street lights lit themselves. Lights flashed on in the buildings around the Square and far beyond. Sky-scrapers, dotted about London, turned themselves into hundreds of brilliant boxes, rising high above the small, old houses that clustered around them. There was enough light now for Missis to see that the lions weren't real, and what moved were the dogs sitting on the lions. She looked up to the top of the tall column in the centre of the Square and saw a glow of light shining up on the figure of a man.

Pongo said, 'Doesn't the statue of Nelson look fine?'

'Splendid,' said Missis. 'Pongo, who *was* Nelson?'

'He was the very great admiral who once said, "England expects that every man will do his duty". Only he didn't say it; he signalled it with flags.'

'Very metaphysical,' said Missis. 'Quite like our thought-waving. Pongo, if you changed what Nelson said a little, it would be a fine thing to say to all the dogs here.'

Pongo thought so, too. And when, soon, he was asked to make a speech, he finished up with 'England expects that every *dog* will do his duty'. This was an even bigger success than 'Wait and See'.

'No dogs seem at all anxious,' said Cadpig, listening to the applause for Pongo's speech. 'They're as cheerful as they have been all day.'

'They're more than cheerful now,' said Missis. 'They're terrifically hopeful. Can't you feel it, Cadpig?'

Cadpig found that she could. Great waves of hopefulness seemed to be washing towards her. Hopefulness must be catching, she thought, suddenly feeling hopeful herself. In fact, she felt much more than hopeful; she felt happy. It was wonderful to be Cadpig, the first dog Prime Minister, who had done such a splendid job all day. All Dogdom loved her and she loved all Dogdom. She felt *marvellous*.

And now Pongo, too, felt marvellous, as gay as when he had been a young bachelor dog courting Missis. As for Missis, she no longer felt anxious about anything. *Of course* Roly Poly would be all right; he always was. And how proud she was of Pongo and of Cadpig – and of herself. Had she not invented the High Swoosh? And here she was, in a position of honour, with her famous husband and her famous daughter.

Everywhere happiness was flowing freely. The General was telling the Staffordshire and the Jack Russell of that excellent night when it had been his duty to bite the Baddun brothers. All the Dalmatians from Hell Hall were wrinkling their noses in enormous smiles. The Minister of Transport, Babs the Poodle, was doing a little dance with the Chancellor of the Exchequer, which was loudly applauded. All the Cabinet Ministers looked as if they had just won a General Election.

And the thousands and thousands of dogs in Trafalgar Square and the streets leading to it were now so happy that they were singing. They made a high, wailing sound which they all thought delightful. (Tommy and the cats weren't quite sure they liked it, and they weren't as deliriously happy as the dogs were; but they were perfectly cheerful.)

How beautiful the lights of London were! And Pongo now found that the brilliantly lit windows of the very tall buildings led his eyes upwards to the stars. Surely they were unusually large? They had been large last night, when he and Missis had walked round the garden with the Dearlys (how long ago that seemed), but they had not been *astonishing*, as these stars were. They were not only large; they were also dazzlingly bright and they seemed much closer than usual. And the more he looked at them, the happier he felt.

He wanted to share that happiness so he barked very loudly, 'Look up, look up! Look up at the marvellous stars!'

All the dogs in Trafalgar Square and the streets leading to it instantly did as he told them. Then the singing died away and from every throat there came a sigh of happiness. It was like the noise dogs make when they relax in comfort after a splendid walk, only it was much, much more happy. Then there was absolute silence and stillness, with every dog gazing upwards as if spellbound.

Pongo had never known such happiness. It was like food to the hungry, warmth to the shivering, love to the lonely. He would have liked to ask Missis if she was as happy as he was but he could not; he could do nothing but look up at the stars. But soon he felt quite sure she did feel happy and all the other dogs did too – because, somehow, there was only happiness to feel.

He never knew how long the happiness lasted. Indeed, he soon barely knew who he was or where he was; it was almost as if he stopped being himself and became the happiness. But not quite. One little bit of his mind was still Pongo. And suddenly that little bit of his mind heard Big Ben striking. He counted the strokes – Boom, Boom, Boom. Was it midnight already? Was this the great moment? Would they soon know – what?

And then the lights of London went out, all together. But the stars were still there, as big and as bright and as close as ever. And one particular star looked even bigger and brighter and – yes, it was coming closer, much closer.

Missis gasped, 'Oh, Pongo, it's going to fall on us!'

But the star did not fall – though what happened was almost more frightening. All the other stars went out, as the lights of London had gone out. Only the huge star remained, coming closer and closer. And then that, too, went out and there was no light at all, not so much as a glimmer. Everywhere there was inky blackness. And out of the blackness came the last boom of Big Ben, striking midnight.

# The Starlight Barking

NEVER IN HIS brave life had Pongo been so frightened. Never before had he *trembled* with terror. He tried hard to be brave, tried to stop trembling. But he could not; he just shook and shook.

Then he found that Missis and Cadpig, between whom he was sitting, had moved closer to him as if for comfort, and they were trembling even more than he was. At once he told himself that he must not let them know he was afraid. They must feel that he was able to protect them, that he was a solid, rock-like dog. No solid, rock-like dog would tremble, so he just *had* to stop. There was nothing else he could do to help. He could not bark anything encouraging because no sound would come out of his mouth.

No sound would come out of any dog's mouth. Not one of the thousands of dogs who were assembled there could so much as whimper, let alone bark. Everywhere there was blackness, silence, terror.

Pretending to be brave helped Pongo to feel brave and gradually his keen brain began to work. Why was there no panic? The huge crowd of dogs might, at first, have been frozen with fear, but that would not last. Why did they go on being silent? There was not even any scuffling. Such absolute stillness was unnatural.

He suddenly knew that they were all being *controlled*, by someone, something, immensely powerful. And just as he realised this he saw a faint, hazy light high up in the air. The light grew strong enough for him to see that it was on the top of Nelson's column. For a moment the figure of Nelson could be seen and then Nelson vanished and there was nothing but the light, which soon became a dazzling blaze. At first it was a shapeless blaze but it gradually shaped itself into a star – like the one that had appeared on the Downing Street television but much, much larger and brighter. It was bright enough to illuminate all Trafalgar Square and the streets leading there. Indeed, Pongo thought it must be bright enough to illuminate all London.

For a few seconds the silence lasted. And then, from the heart of the star, a voice spoke. It was the same voice that had spoken from the television set, but now it was much more powerful and most wonderfully kind.

The Voice said, 'Greetings to all dogs. Forget your fears. It was necessary for you to know darkness and terror, as a contrast to light and joy. But all that is over now. From now on there is nothing ahead of you but bliss.'

A great sigh of relief came from all the assembled dogs.

The Voice went on, 'That is, there will be bliss if you will accept bliss. The choice will be yours.'

Missis whispered to Pongo, 'What *is* bliss, exactly?'

'A special kind of happiness,' Pongo whispered back.

It seemed that the Voice could hear whispers for it at once said, 'Bliss is *perfect* happiness, Missis, which none of you have ever experienced – except for a little while tonight, before the darkness. Do you remember?'

'Oh, was *that* bliss?' said Missis. 'Well, it certainly was marvellous.'

'Yes, Missis, bliss is marvellous,' said the Voice. 'And I am offering it to you all for ever and ever.'

Cadpig suddenly spoke up loudly and clearly. When first she had heard the Voice it had reminded her of the Prime Minister's and it still did. She was never afraid of the Prime Minister and she was always very firm with him. So now she said bravely, 'May I ask, on behalf of all dogs, who you are?'

Many dogs barked, 'Bravo, Cadpig!' And there were barks of, 'Yes, yes! Please say who you are!'

For a moment there was silence.

'Goodness, I've offended it,' Cadpig whispered to Pongo.

The Voice heard the whisper and said kindly, 'No, Cadpig, I am not offended. You have the right to ask that question and it shall be answered.'

Now the star blazed brighter and the Voice spoke louder, in a deep tone that was musical but also a bit like thunder – not frightening thunder, though; just gently powerful thunder, rolling around the midnight sky. The musical thunder said:

'I am Sirius, Lord of the Dog Star. For millions of years I have looked down on the Earth. I remember dogs when they were wild and savage animals. I have seen them change to tamed and often pampered creatures. And wild or tame, I have always loved them and wished they could be with me on my lonely star. But never in the past did I feel I had the right to entice them away from the Earth. Now, at last, I have that right. For soon, through human foolishness, there may *be* no Earth – or no Earth as you know it now. And those few of you who survive will be desperate, starving wretches, fighting each other, eating each other, just in order to go on living a life that isn't worth living. Do you understand? I know one dog who does: your Prime Minister, Cadpig. She could not live at Downing Street without understanding. You know what I mean, don't you, Cadpig? Answer me.'

Cadpig said, 'You mean that humans may some day destroy the Earth with terrible bombs, in a terrible war. I know some humans believe that – but not all humans, and none of them want it to happen. And *I* don't believe it will. Why, the angriest dog in the world would not want to destroy all dogs – and itself – in order to win a fight. It wouldn't make sense.'

'Well, it wouldn't make sense to a dog,' said Sirius. 'But dogs won't have any say in the matter. And neither will most humans. Oh, it may never happen. You're right in saying no one wants it to. But there *is* a risk, which gives me the right to rescue you all. Though perhaps I am only making it an excuse. The real truth is that I want you all so much.'

The musical thunder of the Voice was now gently coaxing. It reminded Cadpig of the way the Prime Minister spoke on television when he specially wanted people to like him. At such times she always tried to help by putting her head on his knee and looking at him lovingly. Remembering this made her think of the poor dear man fast asleep in Downing Street and she said loudly, 'But, Lord Sirius, how could we leave our pets?'

'Your *pets?*' The Voice no longer sounded gently coaxing. 'You have no pets. You have owners. Oh, you pretend they are the pets. And some humans encourage you to pretend this and even say, "Oh, my dog owns me". But they know it isn't true and you know it, too. They put collars and leashes on you. They make you go where *they* wish. They shut doors, to keep you in or out as the fancy strikes them. Which of you, until today, has been able to open a door?'

Missis whispered to Pongo, 'You can open doors that have latches, not handles. You can even draw back bolts with your teeth.'

Sirius said, 'There's no point in whispering, Missis. I can even hear your thoughts. True, Pongo can open some doors, but there aren't many of those doors left. And anyway, he can't – nor can any of you – go just where you like, when humans are awake. Even Cadpig, who thinks she can always get her way with the Prime Minister,

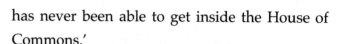 

has never been able to get inside the House of Commons.'

It was true. She had tried, and been carried home – oh, shame – by a policeman. Pongo guessed she was upset and put a steadying paw on hers.

Sirius went on, 'Not that Cadpig isn't a most remarkable dog. And so is that great leader, Pongo, and so is metaphysical Missis who invented the High Swoosh; and that famous General, the Sheepdog, and his brave little friend the Jack Russell, and the gallant Staffordshire Terrier, and every member of Cadpig's Cabinet. In fact, *all* dogs are remarkable. Let us now praise famous dogs.'

Sirius then mentioned every breed of dog. This took a long time as every breed responded with enthusiastic barks. And he did not forget dogs of mixed breed for whom, he said, he had a special admiration. 'Such dogs are often both beautiful and intelligent. But what are they called by humans? They are called mongrels, a most insulting name.'

One dog of mixed breed answered Sirius back. 'Some of us are much loved. I have a good home.'

'But your owners are always apologising for you,' said Sirius. 'Haven't you heard them say, "Oh, he's just a mutt. We call him Heinz or Fifty-seven Varieties."?'

The dog didn't answer. It so happened that his name *was* Heinz. But what was wrong with that?

Sirius continued, 'Anyway, there isn't one dog in the world even though he be the Champion of his breed, even the Best Dog in the Show – who isn't dragged about by his neck, bathed when he doesn't wish to be bathed, shut up, forced to obey. And many unfortunate dogs are beaten, starved, arrested by the police —'

'Oh, please, no!' murmured Missis.

'But it does happen,' said Sirius. Then his tone became kinder. 'Don't worry, Missis. It won't happen any more, to any dog – not if you join me on the Dog Star.'

Cadpig said, 'How could we? How could we ever get there? We should need millions of rockets.'

Sirius laughed. '*Rockets*, Cadpig? Rockets are cumbersome, expensive and highly dangerous – though no doubt they are the best method of travelling into Space that men can think of. But the mind of a star can do better than the minds of men. Remember, we stars *live* in Space. Once you decide to come with me, I shall arrange it quite simply.'

Missis said, 'Should we just have to do an extra-High Swoosh?'

'Exactly, Missis. A very, very High Swoosh – quite easy if you wanted to.'

'But suppose we stopped wanting to, half way?' said Missis.

'You won't be able to. You will be there in the twinkling of a star – once you *decide*.'

Missis looked round Trafalgar Square. Perhaps some dogs would at once decide to go to the Dog Star. If so, would they instantly swoosh upwards?

Sirius knew what she was thinking. He explained, 'It must be a mass decision, Missis – or rather, it must be a majority decision. Nothing will happen until all dogs have made up their minds. Then it will depend on what *most* dogs wish.'

Like the General Election, thought Cadpig, which again reminded her of the Prime Minister. She would never decide to leave him. But suppose most dogs wished to leave the Earth, then she would have to. And then what would happen to him?

Sirius answered her thoughts. 'He, and all other humans – and all sleeping animals – will simply wake to find a dogless world. And they won't remember there were ever such animals as dogs.'

'But there will be our collars and leashes – and kennels and dogbeds and all sorts of things to remind them of us,' said Cadpig.

'I shall work something out about that,' said Sirius, 'though it might be simpler to let them all go on sleeping for ever.'

Cadpig had heard the Prime Minister say he would like to sleep for a week, but she was sure he would not like to sleep for ever. And what a

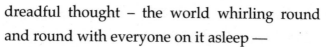 

dreadful thought – the world whirling round and round with everyone on it asleep —

Sirius interrupted her thoughts by saying gently, 'Well, we'll let them wake up, then. And of course I know that many of you love humans. I admire your faithfulness and I *understand* it, because as well as being a star I am also a dog. See!'

Something very strange began happening at the top of Nelson's column. At the heart of the star a shape formed. At first Cadpig thought that Nelson was there again; then she saw that the shape wasn't a man. It was a dog, a white dog with black spots.

'Father! Mother! Look!' cried Cadpig.

Pongo and Missis, staring upwards, instantly realised: Sirius was a Dalmatian! But almost before they had taken this in, the General gasped gruffly, 'Bless my soul, the fellow's a Sheepdog!' Then there were delighted gasps from all the dogs sitting outside the National Gallery and then from all the dogs in and around Trafalgar Square, as each dog saw that a dog of its own particular breed was on the top of Nelson's column.

Cadpig said to Pongo. 'What's the matter with them all? Surely there isn't any doubt that Sirius is a Dalmatian? I don't understand.'

Pongo understood all right. Long ago he had heard Mr. Dearly say something about some saint who had been all things to all men. Well, Sirius was all things to all dogs – or, to be precise, he was all dogs to all dogs. Was that a good thing to be? Pongo supposed it must be, if it was something a saint had been. And it certainly proved how wonderful Sirius was.

The vision of dogs was fading now and the star was back in all its dazzling brilliance, and from it came the voice of Sirius sounding very gentle and very coaxing. 'Well, now you have seen why I understand you all so well. And you can remember the bliss I gave you. Wouldn't you like to feel that bliss again?'

'Oh, yes, please!' barked many dogs.

'But some of you aren't sure,' said Sirius.

Missis said, 'I'm quite sure I'd like some more nice bliss, but not if it would mean coming with

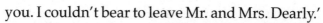 

you. I couldn't bear to leave Mr. and Mrs. Dearly.'

'Neither could I,' said Pongo. But was he sure? He suddenly felt he wasn't sure of anything. He had begun to feel terribly confused and he didn't know why. But he did know this was no way for one of the keenest brains in Dogdom to behave.

The General, who up to now had not spoken directly to Sirius, said, 'Look here, Sir, now that I've seen you, I feel I can speak dog to dog. And you, being the breed of dog you are, will understand my problem. I have obligations to sheep.'

'The sheep will not miss you or need you,' said Sirius. 'And no humans will miss or need any dog. Dogs will simply be forgotten.'

'What would happen to Tommy and our other two honorary dogs?' said the General.

'That depends on what they want,' said Sirius. 'Ask them.'

Tommy and the cats had not been able to understand Sirius so the General had to explain.

Tommy instantly said, 'I'll go with Sirius. I want to explore Space.'

'Well, we don't,' said both the cats, together. And then the tabby told the Sheepdog not to be fooled by such nonsensical ideas; and the white cat said some very rude things about stars that didn't know their places and stay in them.

Possibly Sirius didn't fully understand cat language. Anyway, he merely said, 'Then Tommy shall come and the cats shall stay. Well, that's something decided. And now may I hear from the rest of you?'

Thousands of dogs barked an answer. The noise was deafening – but no one could have said what the general wish was. Some dogs wanted to go with Sirius, some didn't. Many dogs wanted longer to decide and many, many dogs – in fact, most dogs – just said they didn't know. And then, one dog with a very loud bark said, 'Let Pongo, Missis and Cadpig decide. We trust them. All day they have told us what to do. Let them tell us now.'

And then it seemed that every dog for miles barked, 'Yes, yes! Let Pongo, Missis and Cadpig decide!'

Pongo now knew why he was so confused. It was partly because of the noise and the excitement – he had always needed peace and quiet to think in. But most of all it was that he felt his mind was being invaded by the glorious, dazzling presence of Sirius. If only Sirius would let him think his own thoughts for a little while!

And Sirius miraculously understood. He said gently, 'All right, Pongo. Go into the National Gallery and think in peace. Take Missis and Cadpig with you, and any dogs you wish.'

'How long may we have?' asked Pongo.

'One hour. It is now almost one o'clock. When Big Ben strikes two I shall expect your decision. Until then – so that you won't feel influenced by me – I shall leave you.'

The star began to fade. A great sigh rose from thousands of dogs and Pongo knew what it meant. The dogs did not want to lose Sirius. And Pongo now found he didn't, either. He felt as he did when the Dearlys drove away from Hell Hall and didn't take him with them – only now he felt worse. Did that mean he loved Sirius – and loved him even more than he loved the Dearlys?

Now the star had completely vanished and Nelson was back on his column. The lights of London were shining again and so were the distant stars.

Cadpig said, 'Which dogs shall we take into the National Gallery with us, Father? Shall the members of my Cabinet come?'

'Of course,' said Pongo politely, though he did not think the members of Cadpig's Cabinet were particularly bright. 'And all our friends who came from Downing Street with us must come too.' Then he spoke to all the dogs in Trafalgar Square. 'Please keep as quiet as you can so that we can hear ourselves think. But remember we're only trying to decide what's best for you all and if any dog feels he has something terribly important to say, we hope he will come in and say it.'

A dog with a shrill voice barked, 'I think I speak for many of us when I say we miss Sirius. We feel lonely.'

'Yes, yes!' The words seemed to come from

thousands of dogs.

'So do I,' said Pongo.

Surely this loneliness meant that he and all the other dogs wanted to be with Sirius? But Pongo told himself he mustn't decide too quickly, mustn't mind the loneliness. Perhaps it was a trick Sirius was playing on them. He had said he was leaving them so that they would not feel influenced by him, but perhaps he knew how much they would miss him and that leaving them was his most powerful way of influencing them.

The doors of the National Gallery had silently opened. Slowly Pongo, Missis and Cadpig led the way towards them. Big Ben began to strike one o'clock.

Perhaps, thought Pongo, the next hour would be their last on Earth. Perhaps, just in one short hour, all the dogs in the world would be on their way to a star.

# What Answer?

PONGO HAD NEVER been inside the National Gallery. Picture Galleries, he knew, did not admit dogs, which was something he had always regretted as he was fond of pictures. And now, alas, when he could have had the run of the place, it was no moment to look at them. He led his party across the dimly lit entrance hall, up the wide steps and into a long gallery. The light here was almost as dim as in the entrance hall, but across the gallery was an archway beyond which the light was brighter and —

Pongo couldn't believe his eyes. There was a horse there, with a rider on it, an upright horse fully awake, and so was the rider. Then the sleepers were waking up! Humans would soon be in charge again! Dogs need not have this tremendous responsibility of deciding their own fate.

Then he saw the horse and the rider were only painted, in a large picture. They were not real – and yet, somehow, they *were* real, in a way Pongo couldn't understand. He only knew that they made him remember men and horses very vividly and feel very fond of them.

He and all the dogs with him settled down on the polished floor of the gallery. Then Pongo took a vote. He found that only Tommy and the cats had made up their minds. Tommy still wanted to go with Sirius, the cats still wanted to stay on Earth. But after a moment Cadpig said, 'I wish to stay. I can't *believe* the Prime Minister won't miss me.'

This made a great impression on Cadpig's Cabinet, all the members of which now said that, if she stayed, they would.

Then Lucky said, 'Father, I feel sure all the Dalmatians from Hell Hall will want to do what you and Mother decide to do.'

All the Dalmatians from Hell Hall at once said, 'Hear, hear!'

Missis said, 'And of course *I* shall do what *you* wish, Pongo.'

Pongo turned to the General who said he was

an old dog to learn new tricks, but Sirius seemed a decent fellow and if Tommy wanted to go – 'Not that I hold with people coming here from Space. I've always thought Space should keep itself to itself.'

'I shall follow my General,' said the Jack Russell.

'Thanks, lad,' said the General, gruffly.

Pongo looked at the Staffordshire, who said, 'I'm out of my depth, mate. Space sounds very airy-fairy to me, but I must say that bliss stuff was like a good kip by a warm fire after a slap-up meal. And naturally, I liked the look of Sirius.'

Of course you did, thought Pongo – knowing that, to the Staffordshire, Sirius would have looked like a Staffordshire.

Cadpig said, 'Father, there are far more Dalmatians from Hell Hall than there are dogs in my Cabinet. So it's what *you* decide that will count. Unless, of course, a majority of the dogs in the world disagree with you.'

'It's no use thinking about that,' said Pongo. 'All we can do is to make our own choice. How much will you mind if I decide to go?'

'I don't know, Father. In a way, I *want* to go – if I can go with a clear conscience. I only know that *I* can't decide to leave the Prime Minister.'

So that leaves it all to me, thought Pongo – and I just don't know what to do. He was puzzled that he should even consider going off with a star to a star. Even if the Dearlys did not miss him, would not he miss them, most terribly? Of course he would, and yet he still felt drawn to the star. What was this mysterious attraction? He had once heard Mrs. Dearly quoting a poem about 'the desire of the dog for the star' (she had said 'moth', not 'dog', but that must have been a slip). Was it, then, natural for dogs to be drawn towards stars?

Oh, if only someone would explain to him and give him some really good advice! He looked towards the painted horse and wished it could be a real horse who would talk to him. Horses could be very helpful. He remembered the horse that had saved him and Missis and all the puppies they were rescuing, when gipsies had locked them in a field. But the painted horse could do nothing, except look very noble – and somehow that was a little bit of help.

It was at that moment that he heard a dog barking 'Pongo, where are you?' in the entrance hall, below. Surely he knew that booming bark? He barked back, 'Here, sir – up the stairs!' and, a couple of seconds later, into the gallery at full tilt came the Great Dane from over towards Hampstead. And not only the Great Dane. Riding on his back was a tiny creature. A white kitten? No, more like a white puppy. But somehow it looked too grown up to be a puppy. Could it be a miniature dog?

'How splendid that you managed to get here, sir,' said Pongo. And the Sheepdog – a General recognising another General – rose, wagging his tail.

'Talk about swooshing!' said the Great Dane. 'Part of the time I seemed to fly.'

'That's the *High* Swoosh,' said Missis. '*I* discovered it.'

'Well, it took me by surprise and my little

friend nearly fell off. By the way, don't mistake him for a puppy. He's full grown and three years old – a Chihuahua, ridiculous name for a breed but he can't help that, can you, Sam? He's my very good friend, sleeps in my bed and acts as a hot-water bottle. Well, Pongo and Missis, we meet at last face to face. And I know who *you* are.' He wagged his tail at the Sheepdog. 'We've often sent messages to each other over the Twilight Barking, and we will again, when this Emergency comes to an end.'

'But what end will it come to?' Pongo slipped in quickly.

'Do you mean you're in any doubt? Aren't you going to send this star back where it belongs?'

'We're not quite sure yet —'

The Great Dane cut Pongo short. 'I knew it, I knew it! I said to Sam – he came out to Hampstead Heath with me – I said, "They'll be fooled, all those dogs in Trafalgar Square". Crowds are always fooled. They get so worked up that they can't think for themselves. I know about these things because I live with a Professor who often talks about them. All you dogs are the victims of mass hysteria.'

Missis was shocked. Dogs as well as humans suffer from hysteria and she never felt it was safe even to mention the word. She said nervously to the Great Dane, 'Surely that lovely bliss wasn't hysteria?'

'Now I'll tell you about bliss, Missis,' said the Great Dane. 'It was all part of a clever trick. First this Sirius fellow works us up into enjoying ourselves and then he plunges us into total darkness – I'll admit even I was scared when the stars went out – and then he appears and lights things up again. Well, naturally we feel relieved so we're pleased to see him. He'd worked up a marvellous entrance for himself.'

'Bliss was more than just enjoying ourselves,' said Pongo.

'Perhaps it was a bit more,' said the Great Dane, grudgingly. 'The fellow's certainly a very clever trickster.'

'I didn't feel he was a trickster,' said Pongo. 'I felt that he loved us.'

'Well, even Sam and I were fooled at first. But we soon found him out when he started changing himself into dogs. To me, he looked like a Great Dane and to Sam he looked like a Chihuahua. Now, apart from being ridiculous, that's dishonest. I take it that all you dogs saw him as being of your own breed?'

There were excited murmurs from all the dogs in the gallery.

'But I don't think he meant that to be dishonest,' said Pongo. 'It was to make us feel he understood us all.'

'You know what humans feel about people who are two-faced,' said the Great Dane.

'*I* don't,' said Missis. 'I didn't know there *were* any people with two faces.'

Pongo explained hurriedly, 'It just means – well, people who aren't sincere.'

'Exactly,' said the Great Dane. 'And as there are getting on for one hundred breeds of dog, Sirius is one-hundred faced. And if you think that's a sincere thing to be, I don't.'

Cadpig felt the Great Dane was being a bit

bossy. So she said in rather a haughty voice, 'If I might speak a word or two —'

'Who's this?' said the Great Dane, glowering.

'My daughter – at present our Prime Minister,' said Pongo.

The Great Dane's manner became charming. 'What, Cadpig? Honoured to meet you, my dear. You're a very clever dog. Surely *you* don't want to go with Sirius?'

'As a matter of fact, I don't. But I think you're being unfair to him. He said he wanted to save us from The Bomb. Surely that's a real danger? I'm always hearing about it.'

'So am I,' said the Great Dane, 'from my Professor. But Sirius can't possibly know that his star will be a safe refuge. My Professor says the next war's quite likely to be fought in Space – while we sit down here safely watching it on television. Now it's nearly two o'clock. Let's all get ready to say to this fellow, "Sirius, go home". Don't you *want* to, Pongo?'

Pongo had begun to feel he did. The loneliness he had felt when Sirius vanished had grown weaker and his loyalty to the Dearlys had grown stronger. (Surely he had never *quite* felt he could leave them?) He even felt a loyalty to the whole world that he had always known. But he couldn't believe that Sirius was a trickster. And he remembered the great sigh he had heard from thousands of dogs when Sirius disappeared. He said quietly, 'But it isn't only what *I* want, sir. I have to decide on behalf of so many other dogs. And I'm nearly sure that most of them wish to join Sirius.'

'Pongo,' said Missis. 'I think some dogs wish to speak to you.'

Peering into the gallery were three dogs of mixed breed, one large, two small. All of them looked in poor condition and seemed very nervous. Pongo at once invited them in and, as they drew nearer, he saw that they were pitifully thin. This was particularly noticeable with the largest dog, because his bones were so big. He had a fine head and intelligent eyes; and though his dark coat was now matted, it was easy to see that he could be a handsome dog if well fed and well groomed. He came in a little ahead of the other two and was obviously the leader.

Pongo welcomed all three dogs and asked what they wished to say.

The big, bony dog said, 'We speak for all the lost dogs. Some are from Lost Dogs' Homes, some are strays. Some did not come to London because they could not believe they would have the strength. But those of us who are in Trafalgar Square, over a hundred of us, have talked to many dogs who could not be here – as you know, today our thoughts can travel anywhere. And they all feel as we do. You said that any dog who had anything important to say might come and say it. And to us, this is very, very important.'

'Then of course you must tell me,' said Pongo. He spoke in a kind, encouraging tone but his heart sank. He had almost been convinced by the Great Dane that he must refuse to go with Sirius – but surely these pitiful creatures would want to? Surely they would wish to escape from their unhappy lives on Earth?

'Thank you,' said the big, bony dog. 'I should

tell you first that we admire Sirius and believe in him. And we are deeply grateful for this wonderful day. Some of us had forgotten what it was like, not to be hungry. And today we have hardly felt like lost dogs – because, in a way, *all* dogs have been lost. I mean they have all been on their own with no humans to depend on. So we have not felt envious. Oh, none of us will ever forget this day that Sirius has given us!'

'And so you want to go with him?' said Pongo.

'*Oh, no!*' said the big dog. And the two smaller lost dogs also said 'No!' in very shrill voices.

'But why not?' said Pongo, much astonished.

'We are not ready,' said the big lost dog. 'We want our lives here first. Always there is hope for us. Nearly all strays are taken to Lost Dogs' Homes – and then, very often, kind people come and offer them homes. Most of us can remember homes. Many of those homes weren't good ones and many of us were turned out, deliberately lost. But we had loved the people who treated us so unkindly and we want our chance to belong to someone again.'

'You could belong to Sirius,' said Pongo.

'That wouldn't count,' said the big lost dog. '*Everyone* would belong to him. We all want someone of our very own.'

The Great Dane said kindly, 'And I hope you get someone. You all deserve to. And now, Pongo, hasn't that helped you to make up your mind? It's time you did.'

It was, indeed. Big Ben had begun to strike two. And at that moment the room was flooded with light. Pongo knew where the light was coming from. Sirius, the blazing star, was back on top of Nelson's column. And as the great clock finished striking, they heard the musical thunder of his voice.

'I am here, Pongo!'

'Send him away, Pongo!' said the Great Dane.

'Tell him, not yet!' said the big lost dog.

Pongo, Missis and Cadpig led the way to the steps and down them to the entrance hall, with all the other dogs following. But even when Pongo went out through the doors into the dazzling light, he did not know what he was going to say.

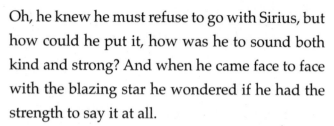 

Oh, he knew he must refuse to go with Sirius, but how could he put it, how was he to sound both kind and strong? And when he came face to face with the blazing star he wondered if he had the strength to say it at all.

He did not have to. For Sirius, who could read the thoughts of all dogs, already knew. From the heart of the star came the great voice saying, 'So the answer is 'No'. And it comes not only from you, all you dogs here in London. I can hear it from all over the world. And I know now that there could not be any other answer. Of all creatures, dogs have lived closest to mankind and they will never desert mankind. And though I do not think such devotion is deserved, I can admire it. And it is something in men's favour that they can inspire it and, in their way, return it. May you never regret your choice, oh Dogs of the World.'

The Great Dane said, 'Sir, I have misjudged you.'

'But you were quite right to call me one-hundred-faced,' said Sirius. 'And when I am back in Space, in all my loneliness, I shall comfort myself by being every breed of dog there is. I shall *imagine* it. And imagination can be more real than reality, though that's something even I can't explain. And now we must be business-like.' The deep, musical voice became brisk. 'All dogs must be home before sunrise, because then you will all be ordinary dogs, without power to swoosh or to open doors.'

'Some of us live farther away than others,' said Pongo.

'That will be allowed for. All dogs will reach home in time, provided they swoosh steadily and on no account turn back. Remember, the special powers given to you will only last just long enough to get you home. But there's no need to panic. All crowds must break up in an orderly way. Those on the outside must leave first. Pongo, you and your party must wait until Trafalgar Square is cleared.'

'But will dogs know their way home in the dark?' asked Missis, anxiously.

'All they will have to do is to think forward

thoughts towards their homes and swoosh steadily. Now I must leave you. I have a longer journey than any of you.'

Pongo saw that the star, though still brilliant, was growing smaller. He called loudly, 'Shall we ever see you again, Sirius?'

'You can always see me in the Dog Days of high summer, when I shine my brightest – if you remember to look.'

'Oh, we will, we will,' barked very many dogs. And then, as the star grew smaller and smaller, every dog in and around Trafalgar Square barked, 'Goodbye, Sirius, goodbye!'

'Goodbye!' The voice that came from the dwindling star was now little more than a murmur. And then every dog heard a strange sound which was like a soft summer breeze stirring the leaves of many trees.

'What was that, Pongo?' asked Missis.

Pongo said, 'Perhaps it was the sigh of a lonely star.'

Now there was only a tiny point of light high on Nelson's column. And in another second even that had vanished. Trafalgar Square was in total darkness. Then the lights of London came back and quite ordinary stars were twinkling in the sky (if any stars are ordinary). And the Great Dane and the Sheepdog, speaking at the same moment, told Pongo it was time for action and all dogs must be hurried on their way.

'Then you two Generals do the hurrying, please,' said Pongo, who was feeling very much upset. And so, he saw, were Missis and Cadpig who kept saying, 'Oh, poor Sirius! Oh, poor lonely Sirius!' So Pongo comforted Missis, and Patch comforted Cadpig, and the two Generals very loudly told dogs how to get out of the Square. And by the time it was cleared Pongo was quite himself again – which he certainly needed to be, if he was to get his large party safely home. He hoped Sirius had made allowance for the extra swooshing power needed for the Tractor, with Tommy and the cats on it.

'We must go as fast as we can,' said Missis. 'It would be dreadful if Tommy didn't get home by sunrise.'

'It would be dreadful if any of us didn't get home by sunrise,' said Pongo. 'But don't worry, Missis, dear. We shall.'

But would they, *all?* Pongo earnestly hoped that Missis would not suddenly remember something which all the excitement had driven out of her mind – for if she did, he would never get her to leave London. *Roly Poly was not with them. Where, oh, where was Roly Poly?*

# A Race with the Sun

NOW THAT THE Square was cleared, Cadpig was in a hurry to get back to Downing Street, as the Prime Minister often woke in the night and would be most upset if she wasn't there. She said a loving good-bye to all her family, especially to Patch, and promised to send messages by the Twilight Barking.

'I hope we shall soon see you on television,' said Patch.

'Oh, I'm sure you will. And I heard the Prime Minister say that the next time he has to be out of England he'll send me to stay at Hell Hall, so we shall meet again very soon. How I wish you could all be with me when the Prime Minister wakes up!'

'*We* want to be with the Dearlys when they wake up,' said Pongo.

'Ah, the dear, dear Dearlys,' said Cadpig, but her thoughts were really with the dear, dear Prime Minister.

The dogs in Cadpig's Cabinet left with her, to return to their own homes. The Staffordshire left for St. John's Wood and the Great Dane, with Sam the Chihuahua on his back, set off for Hampstead, after arranging to keep in touch with the Sheepdog and the Jack Russell. (The Jack Russell had taken a great fancy to the Chihuahua because the tiny creature made him feel such a big, strong dog.) The three lost dogs had already gone, with all the other lost dogs, to the Battersea Lost Dogs' Home. All were taking this chance to get into it, knowing they would be fed and have the chance of being adopted by kind people.

Pongo assembled his party. Tommy, the cats, the Sheepdog and the Jack Russell mounted the Tractor, and the Dalmatians who had brought it to London got into position for the return journey.

'You and I will lead the way, Missis,' said Pongo. He knew that if they lined up in rows of four – as they had, when coming from the country – she would instantly realise that Roly Poly wasn't beside her. Now, perhaps, she wouldn't notice it. Anyway, he gave her no time to think. He told all the Dalmatians who weren't pushing the Tractor to fall in behind him and Missis, and then quickly barked the command, 'Quick swoosh for Suffolk.'

It was surprising how quickly the visiting dogs had got out of London. Already the streets were deserted except for a few dogs standing outside their own front doors.

'Very different from this morning,' said Pongo. 'Are you glad we're on our way home, Missis?'

'Yes, Pongo,' said Missis. 'But something's worrying me. And I can't think what it is.'

'Don't try to,' said Pongo. 'Just keep your mind on swooshing steadily.'

'Yes, Pongo,' said Missis. But she still sounded worried.

Pongo said, 'Missis, dear, if you should suddenly remember what's worrying you, don't let that stop you swooshing – or the dogs behind will stop, too, and the Tractor may bump into them. Now just let's think of getting home to our good beds and the Dearlys.'

'Oh, *yes!*' said Missis happily, and she thought

about this so hard that they had swooshed out to the suburbs before she began worrying again. If only she could find out what she was worrying about! She felt sure it must be important.

Pongo noticed that her pace was slackening. 'Just a little faster, Missis, dear,' he urged. 'Think forward thoughts.'

Forward thoughts! What did that remind Missis of? Who was it that, this morning, had thought a backward thought? It was Roly Poly! Where was he? *That* was what had been worrying her! Oh, how could she have forgotten?

She gave a quick cry and almost stopped swooshing but Pongo urged her on. 'Steadily, steadily, Missis. Just keep up your pace. Now, what is it?'

She told him, finishing by saying, 'We must go back.'

'No, Missis,' said Pongo firmly.

'But we can't leave Roly behind. Pongo, please stop swooshing. Let me talk to you.'

Pongo saw that she couldn't go on, feeling as she did. And the whole army could do with a few minutes' rest. So he barked an order to slow down, making sure that the Tractor-pushers understood, and called a halt.

He then explained to Missis why he had felt they must start without Roly. 'We'd no way of finding him. And I had to do what was best for us all – as I must now. At sunrise we shall lose our power to swoosh. We can't risk being stranded miles and miles from home.'

'But the sun won't rise for hours yet,' said Missis.

'It will. Summer nights are short. And remember, Sirius warned us we must on no account turn back. Roly will be all right, Missis. Sooner or later George the Boxer will bring him back to Downing Street and he'll be kindly treated.'

'But no one will know where he belongs. He isn't wearing his collar – and Cadpig can't *tell* anyone he's her brother.'

'Perhaps she can *hint* it,' said Pongo.

Missis shook her head sadly. 'We may never see him again. But it'd be something if I knew he was safe. Let's see if Cadpig has any news of him.'

Missis at once began barking, calling Cadpig. But the only answers she got were from near-by dogs.

Pongo said, 'I'm afraid we've lost our power to reach Cadpig by thought waves. And we *must* swoosh on.'

Already the night sky was paler. Pongo felt anxious. What *counted* as sunrise? Would they be all right until they actually saw the sun or would they stop being able to swoosh as soon as darkness changed to grey dawn?

'Just one more bark, first!' begged Missis. 'And please help me!'

'We'll *all* help,' said Pongo, and gave the word, 'Every dog is to bark with Missis, calling Cadpig. Three times! Now!'

The noise was tremendous. But after the third bark there was dead silence.

'We've done our best, Missis,' said Pongo gently, and he warned everyone to be ready to start swooshing.

'Listen!' cried Missis.

Pongo listened, then said, 'That's just a faint bark from some dog a mile or so away.'

But Missis was now wildly excited. 'That's not just *some* dog. That's Roly Poly!'

Again Pongo listened. The bark *was* like Roly's. Were they getting through to London?

'Roly, my darling!' barked Missis. 'Where are you?'

And now there was no mistaking the answering bark. 'I'm here, Mother – coming as fast as I can. Please wait for me!'

Then the tabby cat, on the Tractor, miaowed loudly, 'I can see him!' And a moment later Roly Poly, swooshing at full tilt, was knocking dogs over right and left. He just managed to pull up as he reached his parents.

'Where *have* you been?' cried Missis.

But Pongo said, 'You're not to tell us until we're safely home. Just get into line between your mother and me. Now all dogs at the ready! Quick swoosh!'

After a few minutes Missis whispered to Roly.

'Are you tired, Roly? Are we swooshing too fast for you?'

'Oh, this is nothing after what I've done today,' Roly whispered back.

'No whispering!' said Pongo sternly. 'Save all your breath for swooshing.' He was thankful that swooshing needed so little breath, but wanted to be on the safe side in case extra speed was needed.

Soon they were right out of London. They knew this first by the sweet fresh smell that came from the fields. Pongo looked anxiously at the sky. It was still, he told himself, a night sky but only just. He had seen it look like this when there was a moon behind clouds. Tonight there was no moon and he knew that, gradually but certainly, the dawn was coming. He called a halt and asked if every dog felt capable of swooshing faster. All, including the Tractor-pushers, said they did.

'Splendid,' said Pongo. 'Missis and Roly, stop whispering. Now off we go.' And he set a faster pace.

At this speed they simply streaked through

the countryside. Soon they were in North Essex, soon through it and into Suffolk. But the dawn was keeping pace with them. By the time they were through Sudbury the sky was no longer a night sky.

'Faster!' Pongo commanded.

And now they went so fast that Pongo feared it might be too much for Missis. 'Are you all right?' he asked her.

'Yes, Pongo,' said Missis. 'But it isn't my idea of a pleasant swoosh. This morning everything was so peaceful – and so still. Now the wind's awake. I'm just a little afraid my ears may blow off.'

But they were still with her when at last the village nearest to Hell Hall was reached and a halt called, so that the Jack Russell could jump from the Tractor and run to his home. (All the other dogs from the village were already back.) Then it took only a minute to reach the farm.

'Get to bed quickly, Tommy,' said the Sheepdog. 'We must leave the Tractor in the road.' (Tommy's father never could understand how it got there.) 'There isn't a minute to spare. Look at the eastern sky, Pongo.'

Pongo saw with dismay that there was a faint flush of pink. He was about to command, 'Quick swoosh' when he realised that, though the tabby cat was safely home, the white cat wasn't and she couldn't swoosh. 'You must ride on my back,' he told her.

But the white cat refused – though politely. 'I'm quite a weight, these days, with all the good food I get. I'll just walk home. And if the gates won't open for me, I can climb the wall – without any help from Sirius. So off you go.'

'Then *quickest* swoosh,' ordered Pongo.

The pink flush in the sky was growing stronger.

'Faster, faster,' cried Pongo.

Now he could see the walls of Hell Hall, now he could see the gates, firmly closed. Would they open?

The Dalmatians halted outside them.

'Please, please, kind gates!' begged Missis.

The gates swung inwards – and there, waiting on the lawn, were Prince, Perdita and all the

Dalmatians who had remained at Hell Hall.

'Oh, we were so afraid you wouldn't get here in time,' said Perdita.

'Did *you* see Sirius, too?' asked Missis.

'I think all the dogs in the world saw him,' said Prince. 'And if I understood him rightly, we should all get to our beds instantly. At any moment the doors will close – and refuse to open for us.'

Pongo nodded. 'Every dog to his bed,' he commanded.

The dogs who slept in the stables converted into kennels went as fast as they could – and Pongo noticed that they *ran*, now; they didn't swoosh. The magic was fading.

'Now upstairs, quickly,' he told Missis.

'Do just let me hear where Roly's been,' said Missis.

Roly Poly was one of the dogs who slept in the kitchen. He was on his way there now but he turned back.

'Oh, I just went to Paris,' he said, trying to sound casual.

'You didn't, you couldn't have,' said Missis.

Surely Paris was in France, across the sea? 'Oh, Pongo, I *must* hear about this!'

They were in the hall now. Pongo said to Prince. 'You and Perdita run upstairs and *stop* the bedroom door from closing. And bark if it tries to. Now, Roly!'

Roly Poly said, 'It was George. He's always wanted to go abroad. The Foreign Secretary – I mean the human one – is always going, but he can't take George because of the quarantine laws. So after I taught him to swim this morning, he thought we might both risk swooshing across the Channel – and we did it quite easily; we didn't even get our feet wet. And then we swooshed to Paris and it was wonderful. We had lots of fun. Then we were told to look at the sky at midnight, and we saw Sirius – on top of the Eiffel Tower. And he *noticed* us, he knew we were English dogs. And he said we could have a little extra swooshing power, to get us home in time. That's how I managed to catch up with you.'

'Did you like Paris better than London?' asked Missis.

'You can talk about that tomorrow,' said Pongo.

From upstairs Prince called, 'This door is beginning to feel restive.'

'Upstairs instantly!' Pongo told Missis, giving her a push.

She went obediently but called back to Roly. 'Did you get on well with the French dogs?'

'Splendidly,' said Roly. 'And you should have seen George with the French lady-dogs. Ooh, la, la!'

Pongo and Missis hurried into the Dearlys' bedroom.

'Now you can let the door have its way,' said Pongo.

The minute Prince and Perdita left the door, it very firmly closed. And all over Hell Hall doors could be heard closing, the kitchen door, the front door, the doors of all the kennels and – last of all – the tall iron gates clanged together.

'How well and peaceful the dear Dearlys look,' said Missis, getting into her much-loved basket. '*Won't* they be surprised when they wake up and find out they've missed a whole day?'

'I don't think they *will* find out,' said Pongo. 'And I don't think they, or any humans, will ever know about this day we've lived through. And perhaps many dogs will forget it.'

Missis said she never would, and Perdita, now settling in her basket, said she wouldn't either.

'But perhaps we shall think of it as a dream,' said Prince, as he too settled down. 'And in some ways it was like one, with so many things happening at once. Pongo, how was it that Sirius could talk to all the dogs in the world, in so many different places, all at the same time?'

Pongo shook his head. 'I just don't know.'

'Oh, *I* do,' said Missis brightly. 'In Space there probably aren't any clocks. And where there are no clocks there's no such thing as time. But it's simpler to believe it was all done by magic. Magic's so easy to believe in.'

'Yes, indeed,' said Perdita.

'Though there's a new word for magic now. It's "metaphysical". I'll explain that to you, tomorrow, Perdita'. Missis relaxed in her basket, then said in a surprised tone, 'I'm *hungry!* How nice! Now I can look forward to breakfast. Of course I haven't minded going without food today – I haven't missed it. But I do believe I've missed missing it. And I'll tell you something else. I think there would be a catch about that nice bliss. After a while, you wouldn't notice it. Oh, hello!'

The white cat had climbed in through the window. She said, 'It's like that night I climbed through your kitchen window in Regent's Park, after I ran away from Cruella de Vil.'

'Oh, dear,' said Missis. 'How dreadful it is to think that Cruella will soon be waking up.'

Pongo grinned. 'Well, at least we shall always hear her coming, in those clanking clothes. Go to sleep, Missis dear.'

The white cat joined her husband and gave him a fairly hard push. She adored him but that was no reason why he should have more than his fair share of their basket. He did not stir and soon she, too, was asleep. And so were Missis and Prince and Perdita – and, of course, the Dearlys.

Only Pongo was still awake.

He remembered how, only yesterday morning, he had lain here hankering for adventure. Well, he'd had the adventure, and he was very, very glad it was over. He couldn't imagine ever longing for another. How fortunate he was! He looked lovingly at the sleeping Dearlys.

And suddenly he was frightened. Why hadn't they wakened? True, the dogs had talked in whispers, but early morning whispering usually woke the Dearlys who always said, 'Quiet!', very firmly. Why were they so *heavily* asleep? Perhaps they *weren't* going to wake.

Then Pongo noticed a marvellous sound. Outside, birds were twittering, lots of birds. If the birds had woken up in the normal way, then so would the Dearlys. And then a shaft of early sunlight shone full on Mr. Dearly who half opened his eyes, then turned over and slept again.

All was well, Pongo told himself, gazing at the rising sun. Mr. Dearly, when walking round the garden under the stars, had said that Sirius, the

Dog Star, rose with the sun, though one couldn't see stars in the daylight. Was Sirius there now? And could he still read the minds of dogs? Just in case, Pongo sent him a message. 'Perhaps one day, Sirius, we shall be ready to join you and accept bliss. But not yet. You see, we do have quite a lot of bliss already.'

And then Pongo, feeling as young and happy as a puppy, rolled over on his back and went to sleep with his four paws in the air.

THE END

# About the Author

Dodie Smith was born in Manchester in 1896 into a family of theatre lovers and actors. She moved to London aged fourteen and studied at the Royal Academy of Dramatic Art. After graduating, Dodie wrote plays and books while working in a furniture shop.

Dodie's first play, *Autumn Crocus*, was performed in 1931,

under a different name: C. L. Anthony. The play was a roaring success and her real identity was uncovered by the newspapers, with the headline 'Shop Girl Writes Play'.

Alec Beesley, a friend from Dodie's 'shop girl' days, became her trusted business partner and they married in 1939. They moved to America in 1940, and Dodie was very homesick. This inspired her classic novel *I Capture the Castle*, published in 1948.

Dodie and Alec loved dogs. Their first Dalmatian was called Pongo, and soon they had nine spotty canines. Pongo and his friends were so beautiful that a friend commented 'those dogs would make a lovely fur coat!' This in turn inspired Dodie to write *The Hundred and One Dalmatians* and *Starlight Barking*.

# FARSHORE MODERN CLASSICS ARE BOOKS TO TREASURE

## SHOWCASING THE VERY BEST OF CHILDREN'S STORYTELLING

**SPECIAL BONUS MATERIAL INSIDE EACH ONE!**

Available in all good bookshops and online

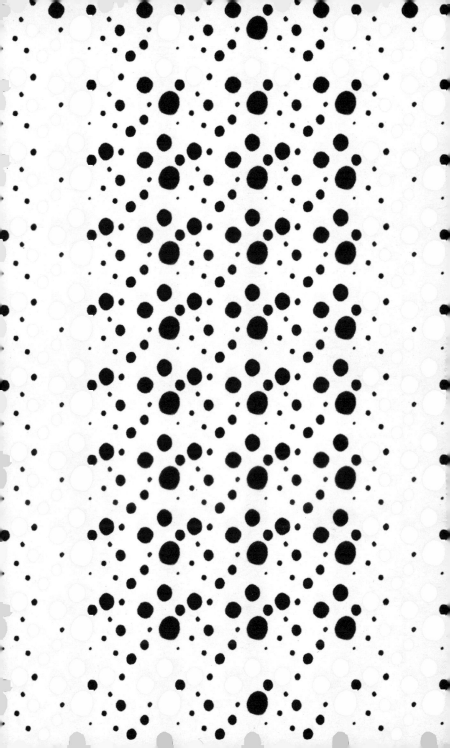